Coming Home
to
Heritage Cove

Helen J Rolfe writes contemporary women's fiction and enjoys weaving stories about family, friendship, love, secrets, and community. Characters often face challenges and must fight to overcome them, but above all, Helen's stories always have a happy ending.

You can visit Helen online at www.helenjrolfe.com, on Facebook @helenjrolfewriter, on Instagram helen_j_rolfe and on Twitter @HjRolfe

Titles by Helen J Rolfe

The Friendship Tree
Handle Me with Care
In a Manhattan Minute
The Summer of New Beginnings
You, Me, and Everything In Between
Christmas at Snowdrop Cottage

Magnolia Creek series:
What Rosie Found Next (book 1)
The Chocolatier's Secret (book 2)
The Magnolia Girls (book 3)

New York Ever After series:
Christmas at the Little Knitting Box (book 1)
Snowflakes and Mistletoe at the Inglenook Inn (book 2)
Wedding Bells on Madison Avenue (book 3)
Christmas Miracles at the Little Log Cabin (book 4)
Christmas Promises at the Garland Street Markets (book 5)
Moonlight and Mistletoe at the Christmas Wedding (book 6)

Heritage Cove series:
Coming Home to Heritage Cove (book 1)

Orion Publishing - Books written as Helen Rolfe:

Valentine's Day at the Café at the End of the Pier (Pier series, free short story)

Spring at the Café at the End of the Pier (Pier series, part 1)

Summer at the Café at the End of the Pier (Pier series, part 2)

Autumn at the Café at the End of the Pier (Pier series, part 3)

Christmas at the Café at the End of the Pier (Pier series, part 4)

The Little Café at the End of the Pier (Pier series, entire collection)

Summer Nights in Lantern Square (Lantern square series, part 1)

Falling Leaves in Lantern Square (Lantern square series, part 2)

Christmas in Lantern Square (Lantern square series, part 3)

Snowfall in Lantern Square (Lantern square series, part 4)

The Little Cottage in Lantern Square (Lantern square series, entire collection)

The Little Village Library

A Summer Surprise (The Kindness Club on Mapleberry Lane, part 1)

An Autumn Promise (The Kindness Club on Mapleberry Lane, part 2)

A Winter Wish (The Kindness Club on Mapleberry Lane, part 3)

A Christmas Gift (The Kindness Club on Mapleberry Lane, part 4)

The Kindness Club on Mapleberry Lane (entire collection)

For my readers...thank you for picking up this book and the others I have written along the way. I hope you enjoy reading the stories as much as I love writing them.

Coming Home
to
Heritage Cove

Helen J Rolfe

Chapter One

Melissa slowed and pulled into the lay-by. The welcome sign for Heritage Cove loomed up ahead and for five long years – unless you counted the time she tried to come back here, lost her nerve and did a one-eighty in her car before driving off again – she'd turned her back on the picturesque village on the east coast of England.

Until now.

She looked at the long, straight stretch of road in front of her, which after the sign would bend and curve around to the left. She shut her eyes and wiped the tear that dared to snake down her cheek. She didn't have to look hard to know that the sign with the village name in loopy writing had at last been replaced. A terrible accident one winter had left the seemingly unbendable metal poles doubled over like trees in the wind, the white steel placard so misshapen that the writing was no longer readable unless you already knew what it should say.

She stared ahead. The sign might have been mended but her personal scars would never fully heal. One split second and her life had changed for good.

Head on the steering wheel, she took deep breaths. She could do this. This was Barney, a man as close to a father figure as she would ever have, and she'd come this far. She had to see him, she had to be here for him, although it had been so long she really wouldn't blame him if he told her to go away.

Fury rose in her that Harvey hadn't elaborated on Barney's condition in his email. Harvey had been a constant in Melissa's life ever since they were kids, they'd fallen in love somewhere along the line, but then it had all gone to pieces. His email had come right out of the blue and its sketchy details had only sent her into a panic. Ever since she'd read it, all kinds of scenarios had been whirling around in her head, everything from Barney having heart failure after an operation following a fall to getting an infection – anything that could take him away from her for good and make her realise she'd left it too late to come. But protecting herself from hurt before it could happen was the only way Melissa knew how to deal with life. She couldn't explain it to anyone else, she didn't always understand it herself.

A knock on the car window made her jump but she didn't recognise the woman on the other side. Thank goodness, she wasn't ready to tackle the inevitable conflict she would surely face from the people she'd left behind in Heritage Cove and completely lost touch with.

'Are you all right?' the woman asked when Melissa opened her window. She had to raise her voice over the din of a combine harvester as it passed, taking up more than its fair share of the road.

'I'm fine, just needed a minute.' In her wing mirror Melissa spotted the jeep the woman was driving. Practical for some of the surrounding farmland, that was for sure.

'It's warmer today than usual, I have some water in my car if you need a drink.' Dead-straight hair the colour of spun gold reached down to her waist and looked at odds with her dungarees, covered in black dirt and dust.

'Thanks, but I have some.' She patted the bottle poking out of her bag. 'And perhaps you're right, the weather may have caught me out. I really should know better.'

'Are you looking for somewhere in particular? Or just visiting?'

'I'm visiting, and I know exactly where I am.'

'You know the village?'

'I do.' At one point she would never have thought she'd leave Heritage Cove, population approximately seven hundred. The village hadn't suffered the curse of being surrounded by new housing estates, it maintained its beautiful fabric of grassland and farmland, country roads weaving in and out of the village, lanes sprouting off at intervals taking you to hidden parts. Heritage Cove had always had a feel of seclusion even though it wasn't all that far from major road links – although a journey could take five times as long as expected if you were unfortunate enough to be stuck behind a farm vehicle. 'Do you live here?' Melissa asked the woman.

'I work in Heritage Cove,' she smiled, 'but I live in Southwold. You know it?'

'Southwold is a lovely place. I spent many summers there as a kid.' Beautiful beach huts, each one unique, were iconic to the area, its pier and tea rooms a childhood memory Melissa had always cherished. Majestic houses looking out across the sea had set her imagination running riot over who lived there, who got to walk on the sands every day. She could remember her mum calling after her as she tore down the planks of the pier to catch the half-hourly pee-show whereby water was pumped from a well to the top of the clock before a pair of iron sculptured boy figures dropped their trousers and peed into the depths below. The fountains had made Melissa and older brother, Billy, laugh every single time and the novelty had never worn off.

3

'What brings you here?' The woman's voice interrupted her special memories rising to the surface.

'I lived here once upon a time.'

'Ah, then you'll know Fred Gilbertson.'

'The blacksmith, of course. He's still around?' From what she remembered he was well into retirement age when she lived here.

'He's been unwell so I've been helping out with his business while he takes time out.'

'I hope he's better soon.'

'I'm sure he will be. I can pass on my regards if you like. Who should I say they're from?'

'Melissa,' she smiled. 'And please do.'

'Nice to meet you, Melissa, I'm Lucy. Where are you staying?'

'At the Heritage Inn.' Relieved it was no longer owned by the Parsons, she could at least retain some anonymity there. She could hide out, commute from here to the hospital, and when Barney was home she'd be on hand to see him properly. She owed him that much after being absent for so long. And who knows, perhaps she'd get by without too many people taking much of an interest in her. After all, her hair had toned down to auburn rather than fiery red now she was in her early thirties and she no longer had the harsh fringe and high ponytail she'd once favoured either. At work she wound it up and out of the way but at home she wore it the same way as now – long, loose and wavy, cascading around her shoulders. Her boyfriend, Jay, often commented on how soft her hair was; she always laughed and told him it was the salon shampoo she spent a small fortune on. She certainly hadn't used that in Heritage Cove. A lot of things, big and small, had changed since then.

4

'Enjoy your visit to the Cove. I'll see you around, I hope.' Lucy smiled and went back to her jeep.

The Cove…Melissa hadn't heard anyone say that in a long while. It was a local nickname for the village and she'd put it out of her mind along with everything else until her sudden return, which had come out of the blue just as she'd always suspected it would.

She sipped her water to make sure she didn't add dehydration to her problems and when Lucy went on her way Melissa tried to psych herself up to drive on too. But a line of four horses leisurely trotting past and towards Heritage Cove kept her in the lay-by a little longer and she turned to thinking about how everything had flipped on its axis over the last thirty-six hours.

Yesterday morning she'd been at the airport having just flown in with the rest of the cabin crew on their flight from Dubai to London Heathrow.

'I'm sorry,' she had apologised to a colleague who almost bumped into her as he tried to pass her in the passenger boarding bridge. Eager to meet up with Jay in the terminal when he came in on a different flight, she'd been wheeling her case with one hand while checking her messages and emails on her phone with the other. And the name in her inbox had stopped her in her tracks. Harvey. It took her a moment to grasp the fact that after five years without a phone call, message or email, the man she'd once considered the love of her life was making contact.

She read Harvey's words a couple of times before she carried on walking. Short and to the point, the email was about Barney, the man who was like another father to the both of them. He'd had a fall, he was in hospital, and that was all it said.

5

Jay was in the waiting area at the gate already. 'Good flight?' she asked as she felt the warmth of his arms around her briefly.

'Shaky landing but touched down an hour ago. I've been reading the paper while waiting for you.' He kissed her fleetingly, enough for a work environment.

How was she supposed to break the news that after finally aligning their schedules so they had a whole week off work together, she had to travel back to the village he'd never once visited? It was the part of her she kept hidden from Jay – not that anything was a secret, more that moving on had meant closing the door on a time in her life that hadn't been easy to bear.

In one of the windows that looked out over the tarmac she caught sight of their reflection as they walked, pilot and flight attendant who'd been together for over four years and would soon announce their engagement. A couple of weeks ago in one of their favourite Italian restaurants Jay had asked her to marry him, she'd agreed without hesitation, and now all they needed was a ring to seal the deal.

'How was your flight?' he asked as they walked their way down the long halls, the familiar route they'd trod hundreds if not thousands of times.

'Straightforward,' she said. 'Always a good thing. Especially after last week.'

The previous week she'd had an irate passenger who'd thrown a drink at the man in the seat next to her, except most of the red wine went over Melissa's uniform as she was walking past. Another flight attendant had cautioned the passenger, who later apologised to Melissa – lover's spat, apparently – but soon after they'd calmed that incident down they'd had a baby with a worryingly high temperature who would need medical attention the second they landed, and shortly after that they'd hit some turbulence that saw a passenger fall and twist his knee.

As she walked next to Jay now, smiling at other cabin crew passing in the opposite direction, Melissa knew she'd done well to keep her pain buried deep all this time and not dwell on Heritage Cove or anyone there. These days she always looked together and unflappable, particularly at work in her charcoal uniform, the tailored dress that had a touch of sophistication added with a turquoise neck scarf to keep away the draught circulating constantly on flights no matter what class you chose to sit in. Looking immaculate, holding things together, was part of the job, what she'd trained for. She wished it was as easy to have that control in your personal life because at work, nothing could get in the way. It didn't matter whether you were tired, or had a headache, or felt anything less than one hundred per cent, flight attendants had an image to portray. It didn't matter if the aircraft was struck with sudden turbulence, you couldn't show your fear – even though she'd had enough moments where she'd been terrified it would be her last flight. Her job was to smile, to comfort, to aid her passengers as though nothing got to her, as though the minutiae of everyday life didn't affect her in the same way as it did them. But nothing could be further from the truth. She was only glad Harvey's email hadn't come when she was in Dubai, before she'd returned on the flight and had to do her job, that she'd read it only after she'd seen passengers safely off the aircraft and had finished up, ready for what Jay still believed was a bit of holiday time together.

A little old lady stopped and asked the way to baggage claim, directing her question to Jay. Melissa was used to it, because Jay did wear a pilot's uniform exceptionally well. The classic, double-breasted dark suit with creases in the fronts of the trousers that daren't steer off course, the four gold stripes on his jacket sleeves and the cap with the airline's emblem covering neatly cropped ebony hair made him appealing to plenty of women.

His polished shoes continued their familiar tapping along the floor until they reached the carpeted sections, then started again when the surface changed. Coordinating time off wasn't an easy thing to do and she was still working up the confidence to tell him their planned staycation in his beautiful classic Windsor townhouse wasn't going to happen, the leisurely strolls and brunches wherever they chose would have to be put on hold.

Cabin-crew life looked glamorous to outsiders with all the jetting off to exotic locations but in reality it was hard work. So was the job of the pilot, but Jay was always happy to drive them back to his place in Windsor and let her kick back in the passenger seat of his BMW.

Out in the car park they climbed into the plush seats and, as they set off, Melissa's eyes shut from exhaustion and the shock of Barney's fall, of Harvey's abrupt contact that he surely must have known would worry her. She waited until Jay had negotiated the car park exit, the roads surrounding the airport, and they were firmly on their way home. And when he groaned as they slowed to millipede pace along the M4, she found her moment. 'I need to go back to Heritage Cove.' She daren't look at him, instead focusing on the bank of cars ahead of them, the rear windscreen of the one in front filthy except for where its wiper blade had shifted grey dirt in an arc and left a clean section in the centre.

When the man in the truck next to them lit up a cigarette and its smoke somehow curled through the vehicle pollution over to their car, Melissa did up her window and faced Jay. 'Did you hear what I said?'

'I did.' He waited until the ten miles per hour reduced once again to a standstill. 'But I didn't think you were serious.'

'Unfortunately I am.' The only thing she'd ever told Jay about Heritage Cove was that she was born there, she'd spent her childhood in a village she'd outgrown since her parents died, and she'd wanted to get away. She hadn't told him anything more, he hadn't asked, and she'd floated along in an existence of denial ever since. It had been the easiest way. Just as she ignored any malaise when she was up in the air with full make-up and a smile on her face, any time the village or her years growing up were mentioned she kept up the pretence that those times were normal, no dramas needed to be discussed or reflected on. It helped too that her brother had left the village years ago, before even she did, and moved to Scotland, where he had a wife and family. It meant that her links to Heritage Cove had reduced and she could talk with Billy on the phone without having to hear about the village and its residents. And if he mentioned them, she quickly found a way to turn the conversation around.

Looking out at the drizzle now, the sort of rain that tricked you into thinking you couldn't possibly get wet, coming down from the greyness blanketed above, she longed for the blue skies of Dubai, the scorching temperatures she'd just left, the feeling of another world that wasn't quite reality.

'It's taken ages to arrange time off with each other,' Jay complained when he realised she was completely

9

serious. 'Why do you need to go now? Why all of a sudden?'

'It's Barney.'

'Who's Barney?'

'The man I still send cards to, I've told you about him before.'

He shook his head but as he negotiated moving to the outside lane in the vague hope of progressing a little further, something seemed to click. 'You're right, sorry, I must've forgotten. I didn't think you were that close.'

'He's in hospital, he had a fall.'

'Is it serious?'

'I've no idea.' Barney had once been everything to her. She'd never forgive herself for abandoning him, for leaving him the way she had, but staying had become too painful. And just because she hadn't seen him and didn't get in touch often, it didn't mean they weren't still close. Harvey's email had proven that. As soon as she'd read his message, her feelings had come right back to her and she knew she had to see Barney.

She wasn't going to mention that it wasn't Barney himself who had contacted her and, thankfully, Jay didn't ask. He was too busy moving back into the middle lane now that the traffic was progressing.

After Melissa left for London all those years ago she stayed in touch with her best friend, Tracy, for a while but, over time, their phone calls had stopped. Melissa's life had moved on, she'd got a job she loved, she was off travelling the world. For a time she'd called Barney to let him know she was safe and well; they'd chatted often, and he'd always told her never to feel guilty for living her life the way she needed to. But because Melissa's job took her out of the country so much, the phone calls gradually stopped happening. Barney wasn't a homebody either so coordinating their times was difficult – or, if Melissa was entirely honest, shutting herself off had been the easiest option. So instead, she'd sent Christmas and birthday cards as well as the odd letter and Barney had done the same in return. She'd sent postcards from exotic locations as a way of telling him that she was living her best life, that leaving hadn't been the wrong decision, that she was seeing the big wide world as she'd always wanted. Neither of them ever mentioned Harvey in any correspondence, but Melissa hoped he'd gone on to find happiness in the same way that she had.

And part of her happiness was Jay. In the car now, she reached a hand up to his face and ran her fingers across his cheek and along his strong jaw. 'I'm sorry, I know how much you were looking forward to our week off.'

With a sigh he shook his head. 'You'll keep, I guess.' And he beamed a smile her way to tell her that it wasn't great, but he understood. 'Hey, I could always come with you.'

'No need, honestly. I'll be at the hospital half the time anyway, at least until Barney gets out, and then I'll be at his place helping as much as I can.' She said it with as much conviction as she could muster, because part of her panicked that Barney wouldn't get home, that this was it. She would've left it too late to say how sorry she was for her absence. How had she left it so long? And how had she not seen how selfish she was being?

Melissa would email her boss the moment she got home and clear an extra week of unpaid leave so she didn't have to rush back to work, because if Barney was really bad, there was no way she'd leave him to fend for himself. He was loved in the community of Heritage

11

Cove, but he had no wife, no children, no siblings, and it was Melissa and Harvey who, despite not being blood-related, were the closest thing he had to family.

Jay put a hand over hers, mistaking her frown of concern for guilt at cancelling their pre-arranged time off together. 'We'll have a staycation together another time, no big deal.' His gaze came her way, his sharp blue eyes that missed nothing at thousands of feet up in the sky. 'If you don't need me with you, at least let me drive you up there.'

'No need. I'll want my car to get to and from the hospital. But thank you.' She put her hand on his knee and gave it a squeeze, maintaining physical contact between them while he handled the gear stick, the wheel, focusing his attention on the road.

'Well don't stay away too long,' he said. 'For selfish reasons, the bed's much better when you're in it.'

'You should be used to it, we're rarely on the same schedule.'

'True, but this is different. I'll know you're not all that far away.'

'I won't be far away, and I'll be back in a few weeks.' Then she'd get back to normal, back to Jay, back to her job and jetting off somewhere far, far away from everything else.

He covered her hand with his, looking at her whenever he could. His attentiveness had been one of the things that attracted Melissa to Jay right from the start. She'd spent some time on her own, determined to prove that she could do it, because if she didn't let anyone get close, she was protecting herself. It was a barrier she put up so she'd never feel so devastated and heartbroken again. But then, one night on a stopover in Singapore, she'd found herself alone in a bar after all the other cabin crew had gone to bed and Jay had asked her to have a drink with him. For the first time in a long while she'd felt like the centre of someone's universe, she felt needed. They'd dated whenever they could, spending any spare minutes they had together. And Melissa had felt that she was finally getting the true fresh start she'd yearned for.

Now, in the lay-by approaching Heritage Cove, the soothing clippety-clop of the horses' hooves faded as they trooped one after the other across the road to presumably head towards the riding school. The cottage Melissa's parents had once owned and that Melissa had lived in until she left the village was down that way, past the paddocks, and had been rented out for the last five years. Jay wanted her to sell it and instead put the money into a bolthole in France, Spain or Portugal but, so far, Melissa hadn't bothered to get in touch with an estate agent. Maybe now she was here it was time to do so, to get rid of the cottage once and for all, another tie she could discard and move away from.

She looked again at the sign saying Heritage Cove, there ahead of her. It was now or never. She put the cap back on her bottle of water and prepared to drive on, check in at the Heritage Inn and then take herself off to the hospital.

But instead of driving on, she made the most of the quiet country road and the lay-by that made it possible to turn around and she headed back the way she'd come. She'd go to the hospital first, see Barney, anything to put off check-in – or, more to the point, anything to avoid Heritage Cove for a little bit longer.

Who knew? Maybe she'd be at the hospital so long that it would at least be dark by the time she came back to the village and she could face it in full sunlight after a good night's sleep.

Maybe by then she wouldn't have such a feeling of dread pooling inside of her.

Chapter Two

'Would you stop fussing?' Barney demanded for the third time in as many minutes. Harvey was at his bedside in the hospital; he'd been here since the early hours, waiting to be allowed inside. If he'd had his way he would've slept in the chair all night to keep an eye on the man who'd always been there for him when his own father had not.

'Don't you have a job to do, lofts to convert and work on?' Barney moaned. He'd just had breakfast but it seemed that hadn't gone any way to improving his mood. 'You've been here every day for the last week.'

'My job doesn't come first, some things are more important.' Harvey stopped smiling when Barney shrugged his hand away from his arm. 'Stop being so grumpy, it doesn't suit you.'

'Of course it does, and if it's the only way I'll be left alone to get some peace and quiet, then I'll be as miserable as I like.' Fair-skinned Barney usually had a bit of colour in his cheeks but not since he'd had the fall. He looked gaunt and his frustration left a scowl that deepened the wrinkles on his forehead.

When the nurse came in to do her checks, Harvey was grateful to take his mind away from Barney's mood and the fact he was somehow viewing this fall, this temporary setback, as the start of his demise. It wasn't like Barney, who only days before had been happily showing off his short back and sides at the local bakery after going to the barber and having his silver, almost white, hair cropped back into the tidy way it should be. Over the last day or so Barney had continually – when he was talking rather than griping – claimed an inability to look after himself properly anymore. He'd talked about the lonely house awaiting his return and although he didn't say he was scared to be alone, Harvey could tell that was what he meant. It was as though the fall and fracture of his hip had snatched the seventy-three-year-old's confidence and therefore independence away from him.

'He's been here since first thing, you know, hanging around well before he was allowed in,' the nurse told Barney, referring to Harvey as she pulled the stethoscope from her ears and loosened the cuff she'd put on Barney's arm to check his blood pressure. 'Same as every day you've been in here, he's been by your side. You're lucky to have him.'

'Stupid boy, he should know I'll tell him if I need anything. I'm hardly likely to get myself into trouble lying in this bed, am I?'

'Family tend to see it a different way and they want to be here for you anyway,' the nurse, Sharon, chirruped on in her overly happy way. She probably saw miserable old buggers like Barney every day of the week. But the chances of him cheering up while he was in here were very slim. Harvey wondered whether she saw beneath the façade like he did, whether she guessed that, deep down, Barney was scared and that usually, instead of being this rude, he'd have nothing but kind words and smiles for people unless they crossed him.

'He's not family,' Barney murmured, looking out the window across grey rooftops, which, mingled with an equally slate-grey sky, didn't help much either.

Sharon held her clipboard against an ample chest. 'Then you must be a very close friend,' she told Harvey before putting a hand on Barney's shoulder. 'Sometimes our friends become our family.'

While the nurse carried on with her checks Harvey went to grab a coffee, not that it tasted much good out of the vending machine, but at least it would give Barney a bit of space.

The nurse was spot on when she said that friends often became family. Barney had been in his life since Harvey was eight years old. Harvey had been hanging around the village one summer, bored as anything, and he'd gone to the old barn via the road that cut behind Barney's house so he wouldn't be seen. As he'd done many a time without being caught, he'd climbed up into one of the trees to pluck a ripe apple but while he was pulling the firm fruit from where it hung, a voice had yelled out to him and scared him half to death; he lost his footing and tumbled out of the tree to the ground. The man who had shouted at him came tearing over but Harvey was lying in a pile of leaves that had cushioned his fall and was already laughing away when another apple, disturbed by the pandemonium, dropped down and clonked him on the head. The man had laughed too, most likely in relief, helped him up, and it had been the start of a very happy friendship that, decades on, was still going strong. The day Harvey tried to steal an apple, Barney had made him help collect more of the fruit and they'd taken it into the barn, where Barney had shown him how to make fresh juice. From that day on he'd been allowed to come over whenever he liked, drink as

17

much of the juice as he wanted, and it became his escape every day after, that first day ending up with him racing home as fast as his skinny little legs would let him so as not to break curfew. Out of the barn he'd gone, across the courtyard, through the gap between the trees, down the path to the pavement and then up and around the bend and into the village itself before heading to his own house. It was a route he'd be wholly familiar with very quickly and still was.

Harvey pressed the button on the vending machine and the coffee groaned its way out as though it couldn't really be bothered to add flavour for anyone, least of all him. Over the years, Harvey had told Barney very little about his home life but he hadn't really needed to. Everyone in the village knew about the Luddington family – the dad who was a bully, the mum who tried to do her best by her two sons, Harvey, whose home was still in Heritage Cove, and his younger brother Daniel, who was no longer interested in being a proper part of their family. Daniel had eventually left the Cove at eighteen after endless run-ins with their dad, Donnie. The pair probably would've killed one another if Daniel hadn't left when he did, their tempers were a match. Harvey was left behind to pick up the pieces for his mum, who was devastated Daniel had left them behind, but at least they had their own lives now, in a beautiful village, minus the aggravation.

He took his coffee back to the ward and the first thing Barney said when Harvey appeared at his bedside was, 'I'm sorry for being an ungrateful grouch.'

'No worries at all.' Harvey tentatively pulled up a chair and sat down.

'What's the coffee like?'

'Iffy, but it might keep me awake a while longer.'

18

'Bad as the food then,' he harrumphed.

'Unfortunately.'

'Nurse is happy with my progress.'

'That's great.' Harvey took another brave sip of coffee. 'We'll soon have you home. They mentioned it would probably happen today.' When Barney nodded he asked, 'What happened when you fell? You still haven't really explained.'

Barney muttered. 'It's no great mystery, I fell off a ladder.'

'But did you lose your balance? Were you dizzy?'

'I've already been through this with the doctors and nurses. Honestly, you'd think you lot were trying to confuse me with all your questions.'

'This is purely for my peace of mind.'

'There's no mysterious tale to tell. I was trying to repair a beam in the barn, that's all. I'm getting too old, I know.'

'That wasn't what I was getting at.'

'Well it's true, it's a fact.' Barney looked up at the ceiling. 'This place needs a fresh lick of paint, the whole hospital does. Do you think it's their mission to make these places as depressing as possible?'

Pleased at least to see the old man's sense of humour trying to escape, Harvey agreed. 'It may well be. I mean, they don't want to encourage patients to hang around too long, do they?'

Barney relaxed into the familiar friendly banter, a father-son-like way of talking to each other that neither of them had ever had before they came into each other's life.

'I can fix the barn up,' Harvey assured him. 'It needs quite a few things doing, but no more climbing up ladders for you, leave it to me.' He pulled a face after a sip of coffee and set the cup on the window sill.

'That bad?'

'Worse…thought I could manage it but I'll pour it away.'

'Listen, don't go fixing up things around the barn or the house, you've got your own job to do. It can wait.'

'I can fit it in, not a problem.'

'Really, there's no need.' He looked away.

'Barney, what are you talking about? You always make sure the barn is in good repair so it's ready for the Wedding Dress Ball every year. You hate things to be left until the last minute.'

Barney shrugged noncommittally. 'Don't worry yourself about it.'

'You're going to pay someone else?'

'No, I'm just going to leave it.'

Harvey ran a hand across his chin. 'Now we both know you're not going to do that. The Wedding Dress Ball is in just over a month. It's a safety issue and you wouldn't want it on your conscience if someone got hurt by the glass breaking in one of the little windows, or if one of those beams came down mid-dance, or if –'

'I'll stop you right there. No, I would never forgive myself, you're right. Which is why it's not happening.'

'What's not happening?'

Again the ceiling held Barney's attention, his eyes fixed on the yellowish surface punctuated only by stark lighting. 'The Wedding Dress Ball isn't going to happen, I'm cancelling the whole thing.'

'You can't be serious.' The Wedding Dress Ball had been running for more than four decades, with Barney at the helm every single time. It was a tradition older than Harvey himself. Everyone in the village looked forward to it and it always raised a great deal of money for Barney's nominated charity. 'You run it every year, without fail.'

'Yes, well not this year.'

'But –'

'I don't want to hear another word about it. The Wedding Dress Ball is off, full stop. I'm past it. I've been kidding myself that I can keep it going. I started the event on a whim, I don't want to do it anymore.'

'Tickets have already been sold.'

'Then I'll give people their money back.'

Harvey had forgotten how rank the coffee was and reached out for his cup, took another sip and grimaced. He looked around for a sink but he'd have to find one out of the ward to get rid of it.

'Can you find out when can I get out of here?' Barney complained again without turning to face Harvey.

'I'll go and see what the hold-up is.'

'If you would.'

Harvey was there and back within minutes, pouring away his coffee before he did anything else. 'They're waiting for the doc to swing by and as soon as he does, any second now, you're out of here.'

Barney managed a small smile and faced Harvey. 'Thanks, son.'

The address always pleased Harvey. No matter whether he was eight years old and waiting to grow taller than the girls in his class at school or thirty-three and six-foot-five, hearing it always told him his place in this man's life. 'They did want my assurance that you have someone at home to help you, so I've told them that'll be me. No arguments.'

'I suppose if I fight you over it I'll have to stay here,' Barney remarked with a trace of the usual humour.

21

'Too right you will.'

'Then I'll take the lesser of two evils.'

'Thought you might.'

Barney turned over properly in bed to face him. 'Was it the blonde or the red-headed nurse you spoke to?'

Harvey laughed. 'Why does it matter?' One strong hand toyed with the palm of the other, which had a small cut from pulling out a big weed from the beds of the elderflower bushes at his property. He'd been inspecting the clusters of elderflowers that would, come August, produce berries ripe for picking. The rush would be on to get every last one, dish them out to whoever wanted any, and freeze or dry some for his own use.

'It matters,' said Barney, 'because the blonde has the hots for you.'

'She does not.'

'She does. You can't see things from my vantage point, put it that way.'

'There's not much wrong with you apart from that hip, is there?' He ran a hand through the dark brown tufts of his hair that could do with a cut.

'I want to see you settled, that's all. Don't be like me, don't end up alone.'

'And you think a fling with a nurse will accomplish that?'

'Wouldn't hurt.'

'Well, I'm settled enough thank you. I have a job I enjoy, I'm not stuck at a desk, I'm out in the fresh air, I have mates to go to the pub for a drink with – you don't need to worry about me.'

'Just looking out for you.'

'And I appreciate it.' He only wished Barney would let him do the same in return. 'While I was talking to the nurse I asked about your recovery. She said it'll be three to six weeks until you're back to normal activities.'

'You know, I've read about this.'

'Recovery after a hip fracture and replacement?' This was looking hopeful.

'No, about people my age going about their business one minute, happy, not a care in the world, and then one fall, one accident, one illness, and it's all downhill.'

It wasn't quite the positive approach Harvey was hoping for. 'I'm going to help you recuperate, I'm there for you. Please don't think this is the end.' Barney didn't say anything. 'And you love putting on the Wedding Dress Ball, to hear you talk of cancelling is a shock. Wait until you're back in Heritage Cove, make a decision then.'

'I've made up my mind. The ball has had its time and if someone else wants to do it then let them be my guest. It's a lot of hassle I don't really need.' Barney had never referred to the ball as a hassle. Even the year he'd had an out-of-the-blue summer cold and felt rotten, Barney had still given the organising his all and the event had gone ahead as planned. 'Best to give everyone their money back.'

Harvey sat, arms outstretched along his thighs. He looked up at the corner of the ceiling in the ward where a cobweb hung, detached at one end and dangling down, perhaps too scared to float to the floor and become a part of the hopelessness surrounding Barney's bed. His gaze flicked over to the window, the dullness of the sky, the scaffolding on a building over the bypass that ran between the hospital on one side and a shopping centre on the other. He watched Barney turn his head away from him yet again, this time to look at the pale blue curtain that separated his own section of the ward from

23

the rest, where in one bed there was an old lady who'd been in here a fortnight, in another a cantankerous old man who moaned at everyone who set foot in the ward day and night, visitors and staff.

Perhaps what he was about to say could shock Barney into the present moment. 'I got in touch with Melissa.'

It worked, Barney finally met his gaze. 'Now there's something I thought I'd never hear from you.'

'I haven't heard back from her yet, but she knows about the fall, she knows you're in hospital.'

They hadn't spoken about Melissa in a long time. Barney tried now and then but knew what response he'd get. Harvey didn't much enjoy talking about the woman who'd broken his heart. She'd moved on, left him behind, and there wasn't a lot he could do to change it. Perhaps it was his own fault – he hadn't stopped her; in fact, as far as she knew, he'd just changed his mind and hadn't wanted to go to London with her. He'd never told her the real reasons why because he didn't want her to feel guilty, to stay in Heritage Cove just because he couldn't leave. Any fool could see she needed to get away, but it was her never looking back that had hurt him so deeply.

Melissa hadn't come back to the Cove after she left. She hadn't even come to see Barney in all this time, and for that Harvey wasn't sure he could ever forgive her. But he'd had to let her know about the fall. As Barney lay there on the floor that day, Harvey's heart was squeezed with a ten-tonne weight and it was a moment of clarity. Nothing in life was for certain. Barney had always been there for them both, but he was getting older, he wouldn't be around forever, and the thought terrified Harvey. Waiting for the ambulance to turn up, Harvey had thought about Melissa and how she'd feel if

Barney didn't pull through. It had been enough to tell him he had to get in touch with her. Part of him didn't want to, part of him wanted to punish her for her lack of interest, but he didn't have it in him to do it. And so once he was at the hospital he'd got in touch with her best friend Tracy, who still lived in Heritage Cove and had Melissa's email address – he'd deleted it a long time ago - and he'd sent the brief message to tell her about the accident.

'I guess I need to thank you for telling her.' Barney brightened for a moment. 'Maybe she'll call. I hope you didn't worry her too much.'

Harvey hoped he had. 'I just told her the facts.'

'We haven't talked about her in a while.'

'No, we haven't.' Because she hadn't looked back, so why should he?

Daniel had done the same thing – upped and left, just like Melissa. You'd think he would be used to it somehow.

Barney winced, trying to lever himself up in the bed, and Harvey went to him. 'Let me help you.' He adjusted the pillow so Barney could settle himself back down again. 'Any better?'

'A bit…where's that doctor? He should be here by now, letting me go home.'

'I'm sure he'll be here as soon as he can.'

'I know I'm not the best patient,' said Barney.

'Really?' Harvey laughed. 'Never would've known.'

Barney managed a smile but tiredness was sweeping over him like the winds that came off the sea in Heritage Cove on a blustery day, the gusts that stopped you from making your way down to the beautiful spot where the wine-glass-shaped cove spread out before your eyes. It was inaccessible except to pedestrians, something

25

Harvey appreciated because it kept it quiet, a local hideout more or less. Tourists still came to the village, but plenty couldn't be bothered to make the trip down to the water's edge on foot and heeded the warning signs about exercising caution on the climb down to the golden sands below. Instead, they drove on further, to just outside Heritage Cove, where there was a far more accessible beach with a car park and an easy trip down to the sea.

'I'll let you rest,' Harvey told Barney. 'I'll go for a wander and hopefully by the time I get back the doctor will have been to see you.'

Barney made some sort of grunt, clearly in pain with his hip reminding him of what had happened. But he'd brightened at the mention of Melissa; perhaps she'd at least call. She owed it to Barney, they both did.

*

The doctor took his own sweet time to get around to see Barney but at last he'd been discharged and they were in Harvey's pickup making their way home to Heritage Cove before midday.

The windscreen wipers swished away the drizzle as Harvey turned off the main road and, driving more carefully than usual, not wanting to cause Barney any discomfort, he pulled into the village. At least Barney wouldn't have the tatty walls of the hospital and greying skies outside to focus on, he could be home in his own place and look out to the trees beyond, the barn that showed off its fine walnut-coloured top when the sun caressed its roof on a fine day.

'Almost there,' he told Barney, who opened his eyes at last. There may even have been a glimmer of a smile there somewhere.

'Good, I need to be home. I'm surprised anyone survives hospital stays, I had a fear I'd never come out again.'

As Harvey made his way along The Street, the main road through the village, he expected Barney to be looking this way and that to see who he could spot. He was waiting for a request to pull over so Barney could chat, but Barney sat quietly in the passenger seat, strangely detached from the beauty of the Cove that he always said was impressive no matter the season. Barney claimed this village had a way of drawing you in, whether it was the appeal of the tea rooms when the fog lay like a blanket across the tops of the buildings and gardens, the lights at Christmas adorning lamp-posts and shop fronts, a waft of spring flowers as winter went away for another year or the salty scent of the sea in summer, drifting up from the Cove. Harvey had always shared those opinions, even after the darker times he'd faced, and he hoped that Heritage Cove would be the tonic to draw Barney out of his current dispiritedness. But sneaking a glance across at him now, he realised it might not be quite so simple.

Harvey turned right into the lane that would take him around the back of Barney's property and before long pulled into the courtyard opposite the barn. 'Home sweet home. Wait, I'll come around to your side.' He'd expected Barney to argue that he didn't need any help, that he could manage just fine. But he stayed where he was and didn't move until Harvey was there to help him out, to hold him under his arm and ensure he had his balance. 'I'll take you inside then I'll grab the walking frame.' At least they'd scared away the rain for the time being and the sun was starting to creep out from behind the murky clouds.

As they walked Barney didn't even take in the beauty of the surrounding fields with their patchwork of greens, mustards and browns. He didn't comment on the smell of freshly cut grass mingled with the distinctive aroma of recent rainfall, nor did he stop to enjoy the rapid burst of song from the wren perched on the big tree stump before he headed towards the house.

'We could sit outside a while…' Harvey suggested.

But Barney wasn't interested. 'I need to lie down.'

Harvey unlocked the door. 'You've been in a bed for days, how about we settle you in the lounge? I could open the window so you can listen to the birds, wait for the rain to start up again.' He looked out at the skies above and, sure enough, there were more unforgiving clouds drifting this way so the sun wasn't likely to be out for long. 'I know how you like to hear the rain pounding the roof of the barn.' They'd seen some great storms in their time and as kids, Harvey and Melissa had knelt next to one another at the window in Barney's lounge watching lightning strikes above the barn, the dark ominous clouds unleashing more rain than they thought possible.

But Barney didn't seem interested in any of that. He shuffled past the sofa and the armchairs and out to the hall before going into his bedroom. When he was safely sitting on the bed Harvey went back to get the walking frame from his pickup. He took it inside and set it near the bed, within reach.

'You don't have to watch me like a hawk,' Barney insisted. 'I moved around the hospital just fine when the nurses made me.'

That was the thing. Ordinarily it would've been Barney instigating the moving, the walking, anything to get back to normal. It was as though he'd lost all his confidence in a few short days.

'I'll be in the lounge if you need me then. Are you hungry? There are a couple of apples in the fruit bowl in the kitchen, they still look passable.'

'I'm not hungry, no. And I've got a phone by my bed, you don't have to hang around.'

Harvey supposed he'd want some time to settle in. 'I'll give you some space, shall I?'

'Please. I'll need an hour or so, maybe two. Why don't you come back then?' His tone had softened, most probably to convince Harvey to let him be.

'Fine, I'll go out for a couple of hours and get a few things done. But do me a favour – call me when you wake up?' He held his hands up in defence. 'I know you don't want the fuss but it's day one of being home, indulge me.'

'I don't suppose you'll ever go unless I agree.'

'You know me well. And I'll get some food organised for you, make you a late lunch. Your cupboards are empty, you're almost out of milk. I didn't realise you'd be coming home today so I didn't get a chance to do a shop beforehand.'

'And so it begins…'

'And so what begins?'

'Being helpless, old, past it.'

Harvey would've laughed if he didn't think Barney truly believed what he was saying. He didn't push the conversation, instead he filled a glass of water from the tap and left it beside Barney's bed. With a couple of hours' freedom he took the drill he'd left in the tray of his pickup over to the house that he and the rest of the loft-conversion team were working on. He'd taken the day off as soon as he knew Barney was coming home, but the other lads wouldn't be able to let up just because he did.

Once he'd dropped the drill off he headed back to Heritage Cove, the clouds above unleashing their worst again as he drove around the corner, past the Heritage Inn, the lane that led down to open fields, the bakery, tea rooms and a gift shop, before passing a set of cottages squeezed together in a tight row, huddled against one another for warmth in the colder months, all of which now, despite the cool and decidedly wet day, had their upper windows flung open to get air circulating. He took the next left turn before the candle shop, the corner shop and the pub beyond and meandered along the bumpy track towards his own home.

Tumbleweed House had been in Harvey's family since before he was born. It had come from his mum's side, his grandparents having operated a small farm on site where they grew elderberry plants. The business had been successful but after Harvey's grandparents had passed away and his mum inherited the house, most of the surrounding fields were sold off. His mum, Carol, had been a stay-at-home mum Harvey's whole life, even when he was too old to need her there, and he wouldn't have changed it for the world. What he would've changed was his dad. Harvey had long suspected that getting rid of the elderberry business was Donnie Luddington's doing, his dad's need for control overriding everything else – he had his wife at home where he wanted her to be while he drove around the country manipulating others with false niceties in his job as a software sales rep. But Harvey knew the truth about him, he couldn't talk his way out of that, and Harvey had no happy memories from his childhood when it came to his dad. Instead, it was the man he'd just brought home from hospital who'd given him a reason to be happy again, who'd helped him be a normal kid while he still could.

The windscreen wipers of his pickup swished back and forth as fast as they could as Harvey pulled up outside Tumbleweed House. The exterior was covered with vigorous purple wisteria blooms that were hanging on before they'd fall again until next year. It had been a crazy few days since Barney's fall, the stint in hospital a stark reminder of how fragile life could be, how important it was to treasure what you had before it was gone. He looked at the frontage of the home that had once been hellish, a house full of bad memories, but was now his solace. A good half-acre of land remained, much of which was taken up with elderberry bushes, and every year his mum would come over from her little cottage to help with the harvesting. He loved how her laughter mingled with his as they plucked the dark purple berries from the clusters that were ready. Most of the hard work had been done when the plants were established so there wasn't much else to do now but maintain and enjoy them. Come late July and early August they'd pick and wash the perishable fruit before freezing and use it throughout the year. And having the elderberries was something Harvey never wanted to change. Too much had disappeared from his life already but, looking up at the house now, he knew some things had changed for the better. He no longer thought of the loft behind those roof tiles as the terrifying place where his dad had once made him go after he accidentally pulled down the curtain rod in the dining room; it was no longer the same top of the house where his brother Daniel had barricaded himself in to avoid the punishment he was going to get from their dad for being found drinking underage with his mates. When Harvey had hidden out up there on too many occasions, he'd covered his ears, rocked back and forth on the dusty boards that stopped him falling through the ceiling, as his dad ranted below, pacing up and down, heavy-footed as always and making the entire house shake, at least in Harvey's imagination. The man had been furious his sons would go off and hide, but his rage was terrifying. Both Harvey and Daniel had regularly been torn between hiding out and going down to face the inevitable beating.

One summer after his father walked out of the family home, Harvey had returned to Tumbleweed House on a break from his job at the time as a builder's labourer with a nearby firm and his mum had commented she had nowhere to dry the sheets. Harvey knew there was an old airer in the loft – it had long become a place to store junk – and so he'd faced his fears and gone up there to get it for her. He'd stepped over full boxes of Christmas decorations that gave the house an injection of cheer once a year and lifted them from their misery, a box of old photo albums, a broken sledge he'd used as a boy and thought he might one day pass to a son. Going up there that day had forced Harvey to confront his demons. He'd dragged the airer down, fixed it, replaced a snapped rod of wood with a new one, superglued another part, putting in a couple of screws to enable it to fold and open easily. And as he'd worked his mind had dwelt on that space at the top of the house. It was time they finally got rid of Donnie Luddington from their lives and that meant dealing with the loft. Harvey researched what could be done to make the area a habitable space and embarked on a project to make it a part of the home, and when he approached a local firm and took more than a passing interest by wondering if he could help them out during the conversion, it was the start of a whole new path for Harvey when he was offered an apprenticeship, something he didn't expect to come by with his mediocre school grades.

Harvey looked up at the top of the house now, the loft space that was as much a part of his home as the rest of it. It was up in that loft that he'd kissed Melissa for a second time; the first had been on the beams of Barney's barn when they were twelve years old, their lips meeting for mere seconds – any longer and they both might have fallen.

Had Melissa read his email yet? Was she even going to bother calling Barney?

With the rain still coming down, Harvey made a run for it from his pickup to the back door, greeted in the usual way the second he opened up. It wasn't easy getting inside the house with Winnie, his nine-year-old Labrador retriever, bounding up to greet him and blocking his way through the narrow porch that led into the large eat-in kitchen. 'Miss me? Course you did, girl.' Harvey had got Winnie as a puppy not long after Melissa left and had put the hours in to training her. He'd needed the distraction, craved the company, and now he couldn't imagine not having Winnie around. He rubbed the top of her head and ears vigorously, the way she liked it. 'I guess you'll want feeding.' He found Winnie's bowl from beneath the sink and dished out some canned food mixed with dried, the only way he could get her to even consider the dry food. Her interest quickly turned from him to the meal.

When his phone rang he snatched it up as Barney's name and number flashed on the screen. 'Everything OK?'

'You told me to call when I woke up, I'm doing as I'm told.'

'Right, don't move. I'll be over in less than half an hour. Do I have time for a shower?'

'I'm not leaping out of bed if that's what you think, I'm not even hungry. Please take your time, I'm happy to lie here a bit longer.'

'Fine, if you're sure. I'll shower, go to the shops, then I'll be over.' He knew when to push Barney and when to back off, and it was time to do the latter, at least a little bit.

In the bathroom Harvey switched on the shower and let the water run across his bare chest, down his torso, and ease the aches and pains from too many hours spent cramped in a hospital chair over the last few days as he waited for news or kept Barney company.

Thoughts of Melissa couldn't be washed away so easily and he was torn between feeling that getting in touch with her had been the right thing to do and worrying that he'd simply got Barney's hopes up for nothing. But he couldn't do anything about it now. The rest was up to her.

He lathered up some shampoo but all he saw when he shut his eyes beneath the water was Melissa, the young girl with fiery red hair who'd been as good at climbing the apple trees at Barney's place as he had, who'd pelted him with rotten apples the day he dared to suggest she was a girl and therefore too weak to lift the logs inside for the wood burner. He'd only said it because he knew she was terrified of spiders, which loved to hang out in the log store beside the barn, and he hadn't wanted one to crawl out from its hiding place and scare her.

Harvey had always tried to be there for Melissa. He'd bought her her first drink when she turned eighteen and they were allowed to go to The Copper Plough, the local pub. He'd listened to her sobs when a boy from school broke her heart by arranging to meet her outside the movies and then standing her up. Harvey had been a friend as well as a boyfriend and the day she'd lost both parents in one cruel hit, he'd been there to pick up the pieces of a girl who was broken with the pain of it all. And when she'd said she wanted to leave Heritage Cove, start anew, see a bit of the world, he'd been there for her by sharing in that excitement and enthusiasm. And he would've gone with her, been by her side, had life not thrown him his own curve ball to deal with.

The day before they were due to leave Heritage Cove, Harvey had wrapped Melissa in his arms and said, 'See you tomorrow, birthday girl.' She'd replied, 'This will be the best birthday present ever, we're off on an adventure of a lifetime.' She'd said those words five years, one week and one day ago. He knew because they'd been due to leave the day after her birthday, May 28th. Every year the 28th and 29th of May taunted him from the calendar. It wasn't that he hadn't moved on – of course he had, especially when he knew she'd done the same – but it still hurt that what they'd once had had fizzled into nothing. Not a word from her, not one single word in all this time, at least not to him. She'd cut all ties. Who did that? Nobody with a conscience, that's who. But he'd put his feelings aside and got in touch with her because if Barney hadn't pulled through this, she would've been heartbroken.

Harvey finished up in the shower and as soon as he had a towel around his waist he picked up his phone to message Barney, but Barney had beaten him to it with a text to say he was fine, he was up and sitting in his chair and he'd had two apples to keep him going.

Harvey wished Barney had waited for him before getting up but at least he'd eaten something. He pulled on his jeans, ready to go to the supermarket to food shop and get those cupboards at Barney's cottage filled again. Then, when he got to Barney's, he wouldn't be pushed away easily, he wanted to see the man eat a decent meal.

Maybe keeping busy could stop him spending so much time thinking about Melissa Drew and how she'd left his heart in tatters.

Chapter Three

After deciding to put off her check-in at the Heritage Inn, Melissa had felt a sense of unexpected freedom as she headed away from Heritage Cove to join the main road and go to the hospital instead. But she'd hit the busiest time, it seemed, and the journey didn't feel too dissimilar to her work commute. The earlier drizzle had turned into heavy rain and she sighed at the speedometer hovering on twenty-five miles per hour until the traffic finally began to progress and the satnav instructed her to take the next exit.

She took a quick call from Jay on her hands-free as she followed the signs to the hospital car park. But he wanted to chat, and she needed to concentrate. She felt terrible ending the conversation before it really got started, because he was missing her. The feeling was mutual. She should be there with him, tucked up in bed or enjoying a leisurely brunch, but instead she was doing something that sent her way out of her comfort zone.

She slowed again to peer at another sign as she attempted to find where exactly visitors were supposed to park. She didn't want to go into staff designated areas or ambulance bays or emergency thoroughfares. It was a bit like a puzzle game, trying to follow the various arrows, some partially worn off on the tarmac, others taking her along thin sections around the backs of monstrous buildings.

Finally, in another area, she found a space. She'd already looked across to see the pay machine said cash only but she scraped together enough coins to manage two hours, the prices exorbitant, which was pretty unsympathetic in most people's hour of need. It wasn't a shopping centre, was it? People didn't come here to have a jolly good time. New mums and dads might be overjoyed and not mind the charges with a new infant in their arms, but everyone else, well, it left them out of pocket.

Maybe she was grouchy because she was so hungry. She'd not eaten since breakfast and it was well after midday by now. She fed the coins into the machine, one by one, too fast, the adrenalin pumping again at the thought of seeing Barney after so long.

She forced herself to slow when the machine spat every other coin out in protest. The weather had changed its mind yet again and the rain abated, replaced by the June sunshine that did its utmost to peep through the weak clouds drifting across the sky, so at least she wasn't getting wet. She didn't want to turn up like a drowned rat, she wanted to make a good impression, show that she was confident and the total opposite of someone who'd fallen apart. She knew deep down that it wouldn't matter a jot to Barney what she looked like but, for her self-esteem, keeping herself together, at least in her appearance, helped enormously. It was the way she coped these days.

Melissa had first met Barney when she was seven years old. She'd gone to the barn one day with a small wicker basket filled with eggs from the dozen chickens her mum kept out back of the family cottage. Barney was outside fixing up a panel at the side of the barn and she'd stood there after he thanked her for the eggs and peered inside. Her eyes had widened at the space, she'd asked what the machine was for, he'd told her it was a juice press and had offered her fresh apple juice as a thank you for the eggs. After that day Melissa began to make regular visits, sometimes with eggs, other times when it was raining and she'd ask to play in the barn. She was into gymnastics when she was little and, according to her mum, who Barney had bumped into the day after her daughter delivered the first basket of eggs, she'd been banned from doing it inside the house after several smashed ornaments and one narrow escape from falling down the stairs after a sequence on the landing involving forward rolls and a cartwheel. When she was older Barney had told Melissa that he'd been instantly captured by her cheekiness, the double dimples, one on each cheek, that spoke of mischief, the fiery red hair that looked almost alight when it caught a shaft of sunshine. And when Harvey turned up after school too one day, the summer's evening stretching out languorously ahead of them, he and Melissa had used the cider press together and spent hours hanging out in the place that felt like home to both of them. It had been the start of an intergenerational friendship that had lasted decades. Or, at least, Barney's friendship with each of them had lasted. Harvey and Melissa's friendship with each other hadn't exactly stood the test of time.

Melissa had come into Barney's life almost as suddenly as Harvey, but unlike him, she'd had a safe and nurturing home life, she'd never wanted for anything until one bitterly cold night an enormous patch of black ice had snatched her happiness away just like that. She hadn't seen it coming and Barney as well as Harvey had picked up the pieces and helped her to function, they'd done as much as they could.

39

Now, Melissa called Jay while she was stood outside the hospital, if only to hear the reassurance of his voice. He'd lined up a game of tennis with a friend later but was missing her a lot and still talking about heading this way to be together. Although it was tempting to have him with her when she heard the longing in his voice, Melissa told him it wouldn't be long before she was home, and for now Barney needed to get all her focus.

Following yet more directions inside the maze of the hospital, Melissa at last found reception, navigated her way to the appropriate ward and paused at the nurse's station, relieved to see it was still visiting hours.

But she wasn't so relieved when the nurse told her Barney wasn't there.

'I don't understand, I was told he was here. Could you check again, please?'

The nurse did as requested. 'He was discharged this morning, about an hour ago, you've only just missed him.'

'Great.'

'Sorry, love.' But she didn't hang around, she was called into the ward.

Melissa pushed her way through the doors a little harder than necessary, followed the rabbit warren, getting lost no fewer than three times, each time firing up her temper, and shoved her way through the main entrance out into the open air. Harvey could've emailed her again to give her the update, or was this punishment? Had the lack of details been his way of tormenting her, and now he wanted to add to that by winding her up and sending her on a wild goose chase? Petty, that was what it was.

When Melissa saw a couple fumbling for coins near the pay-and-display machine she offered up her ticket, which still had ages left on it, and grabbed it from the car. At least it wouldn't go to waste, and she refused to take any money for it. She couldn't wait to get out of here.

Thankfully the traffic was kind. She stopped at a service station and grabbed a banana and a basic sandwich to keep her going, and then it wasn't long before she was back following the country lanes winding between fields, trees canopied overhead in places, other parts of land spread out as though in an enormous painting. Odd, she hadn't taken it all in when she'd done this same drive earlier on today. Her mind had been on the people of Heritage Cove, particularly Harvey and Barney, her vision had been narrowed and she was able to zone in only on the ball of fear in the pit of her stomach. But now she noticed fat bales of hay sat in a field waiting to be rolled on to another destination, a tractor passing in the opposite direction that gave her a strange sense of returning home to the place she'd vowed she no longer needed.

Heritage Cove sat on a mostly forgotten stretch of the Suffolk coast, away from the major carriageways that connected to other villages, main roads and counties. And it had its treasures, especially the cove itself, which could be found by following the small track running parallel to the little chapel, each side of the walkway lined with hedges in some places and in others, brambles reaching at least eight feet high. The track looked as though it led to nothing and more often than not, visitors to the village would turn back when they saw the part-sand-covered steps they'd have to follow down, the wonky thin sloped path with more steps and a dodgy handrail that wouldn't save them if they fell, before they reached the small gateway to the deserted beach. Only accessible by foot, the wide sandy beach of the cove stretched out before you and was a thing of beauty without many beach umbrellas or windbreaks taking away from the tranquillity. And now, on a bright June day, for the first time in a long while Melissa felt sure she could smell the sea as she drove towards the village with her windows wound down now that the rain had given up again. She tried to ignore the niggling thought that on the other side of the track that led to so much beauty was the cemetery behind the chapel, thc place her parents were buried on a day she could barely remember yet every painful second of which had slowly eaten away at her from then on. She hadn't been back to the cemetery since, not once. Not even to say goodbye before she left.

She reached the same lay-by she'd pulled into earlier but this time she didn't stop. Her frustration with Harvey and the one email without a follow-up to let her know Barney had left the hospital chivvied her along because she knew she had to see Barney now. And if he was home, it was surely a good thing.

She drove on past the sign to the village and followed the bend curving to the left. On her right was a bus shelter in the original old stone rather than a modernised metal structure that would never fit in with a village steeped in history and character. She indicated to pull into the car park of the Heritage Inn, where she'd already booked a room via the facility online. Kind of anonymous, but she knew she wouldn't be around here for long. She glanced down at her ring finger, which was naked right now but would soon show everyone she was engaged to Jay. She wished they'd had time to go ring shopping so she had it on for the added confidence, as a reminder she'd managed to move on and she'd changed since she left the Cove.

She laughed when the car's tyres slipped into the same dip that had always been there in the car park of the inn. But maybe it was more nervous laughter than amusement. She hadn't yet seen The Street, the modest-sized strip of road lined with a handful of businesses – a tea shop, a bakery, The Copper Plough pub, a small shop where locals bought their newspapers, a pint of milk, snacks. She'd traipsed The Street many a time with her parents, many more on her own. And she was already dreading the sting those memories would bring with them, the memories that hadn't left her but had been dulled as though behind tinted glass when she was away.

The inn looked the same as it always had as she parked next to a beaten-up old Mini. She'd get settled in her room and then brave walking to Barney's. Assuming he was there, of course. Surely he wouldn't have gone anywhere else – although perhaps Harvey had taken him to his place to recuperate. Wherever they were, Harvey hadn't let her know and she was so annoyed she cursed when, mistiming her exit completely, she stepped out from the driver's side just as a truck swung into the space next to her, its tyres hitting another dip that must've formed over the years and sending a shower of mud in her direction, all the way up the legs of her jeans.

'Seriously!' She tried to brush some of the dirt off but it wasn't working.

'You'll make it worse,' came a gruff voice she'd recognise anywhere.

Her mouth dry, she hadn't expected the confrontation with Harvey to happen quite so soon.

'It's been a while,' was all he said as he strode towards her, his jaw tense, blue eyes unwavering. She

43

suspected those words were almost as hard to get out of his mouth as these stains would be to remove from her favourite jeans.

'Good to see you've finally got a more sensible vehicle.' She couldn't resist the jibe, she'd never liked the motorbike he had.

'More room for my belongings in this,' he said. 'You never know though, maybe I'll get another bike someday.' She didn't rise to the bait.

'You could've told me Barney had been discharged.'

'Sorry, didn't get around to it. And I had no idea whether you'd even call, let alone show up.'

She bristled but she wasn't going to have a slanging match. 'What are you even doing here at the inn?' She tried again to wipe at the mud on her legs.

'I was on my way back from the supermarket and I saw you, thought I'd let you know Barney was home. He'll be glad to see you.'

'I'll take my things inside and then head over.' But Harvey was already walking away. 'Thanks for telling me the details about his fall, by the way,' she called after him. She couldn't stop herself.

He stalked back over. 'I let you know, I thought that's what you'd want.'

'You let me know next to nothing. Barney could've been close to death for all I knew.'

'I think you're being a bit melodramatic there.'

'Re-read your own email, you tell me whether you, in my position, would've assumed everything was going to be fine.' When he started to walk away again she called after him, 'You did it on purpose, I know you did.'

'I don't have time for games,' he called over his shoulder, cocky as you like. 'It might surprise you that I had other things to think about besides worrying what you may or may not take from my message. Be grateful I even got in touch.'

Ignoring him, she got a tissue from her pocket but it wasn't much better at removing the mud than her bare hands had been.

He hadn't finished either. 'Do me a favour, if you're going to run off again, at least give Barney the heads up first.'

'I said goodbye last time.'

'Yeah, you're right, you did.' He'd made his way slowly back over to her, no doubt wanting to keep their bickering between themselves rather than for the rest of the Cove to hear. 'But I don't think Barney realised it was goodbye for five long years.'

Face to face with him in the car park, with the Heritage Inn that looked like it could use a good lick of paint on the outside now she was up close enough to see it in detail, she opened her mouth to speak but nothing came out.

'Five years, Melissa.'

Her voice came out small. 'It was never my intention to leave it so long.'

'But you did.'

'And wait a minute, what about me? What about how I felt? Doesn't that mean anything?' It was as though he believed he'd played no part in any of this. The fact he hadn't shown up to leave with her as promised had given him a lead role in this show as far as she was concerned. No real explanation either, just that he wasn't coming, he'd changed his mind.

The sooner she got back to Jay and her own life the better.

'I called Barney often,' she said defensively, unwilling to let the argument go. 'I wrote to him, sent postcards.'

'I know, he told me.' Harvey's expression gave nothing away. One of his most frustrating qualities had always been to shield his emotions, although right now perhaps Melissa should be grateful. Maybe if he let everything out she wouldn't be able to stand hearing it and knowing that some of it was true.

'I always sent him a card and gift for his birthday, never forgot him at Christmas,' she went on.

'He didn't need all that, he just wanted to see you.' He let out a sigh and his voice lost the accusatory tone. 'Still, you're here now, that's all that matters. Can I help you with your suitcase?'

'I'm not a helpless young thing, you know.'

'Yeah, forgot. You don't need me. Not anymore.' And with an edge of animosity back in his voice he sauntered off, but not without calling over, 'Welcome back,' in a tone that suggested he didn't mean it at all.

She hauled her suitcase from the boot and manhandled it across the car park that's surface wasn't good enough to make use of the wheels. It took her a couple of attempts to yank open the front door but the inside was more inviting than the outside had been and it wasn't long before a girl who looked to be in her early twenties came through from what Melissa remembered to be the kitchen.

'Welcome to the Heritage Inn.' The girl, dressed in a tangerine-coloured T-shirt with denim shorts, took up her position behind the desk.

Melissa introduced herself before the girl caught sight of her jeans. 'A splash from a truck,' she explained.

'I can wash those for you,' she smiled, her olive-green eyes the same colour as the cotton headband holding blonde hair away from her face.

'That would be brilliant, thank you so much.' Melissa felt herself breathe for the first time since she'd arrived in the village.

As the girl turned her attention to the computer to find the booking Melissa couldn't quite place her. She was familiar for sure, but perhaps she was just expecting to know everyone here when in reality Heritage Cove had enough inhabitants that you could never know every single person.

The girl handed Melissa a key. 'You'll be in room eight, up the stairs and towards the front of the inn. Breakfast is between six and nine, continental or full English, and it's included in the price of the room. We use fresh produce here too – eggs, fruit and vegetables are sourced locally.'

The previous owners had always done the same. Melissa remembered bringing fresh eggs here under her mum's instruction. She wondered who was supplying the locals these days because she knew it was these little touches, the attention to detail, that would make this inn a winner if they could sort out that car park and give the place a spruce-up outside. The inside was a definite improvement. A bright, airy reception room with enough glass on two sides to let the sun in most of the day had a floral sofa and two armchairs with a low-lying pine coffee table that was scattered with home style magazines, a couple of newspapers and a menu for the restaurant.

Melissa was about to head on up the stairs when a framed photograph on the side of the desk next to the guestbook caught her eye. It was of her best friend and her husband, and suddenly it all clicked into place. 'Are you Tracy and Giles's daughter?' she asked, before the girl could go back to what she'd been doing before Melissa arrived.

'I am, yes.' She noted the photograph. 'That was taken the day my parents took over this place. Do you know them?'

'I know your mum well, we've been good friends for years.' Tracy was six years older than Melissa but they'd hit it off when they both worked a holiday job at one of the big supermarkets outside of the village. Melissa had never really hit it off with the girls at her school, her best friend had always been Harvey, so Tracy was a refreshing change.

'You're Melissa,' the girl smiled as the penny dropped for her too. 'My mum talked about you a lot, you used to live here in Heritage Cove. I'm Sandy, by the way.'

'I can't believe I didn't recognise you at first, although I've been gone five years.' She was also glad that Tracy didn't appear to have painted her in too bad a light or she felt sure Sandy wouldn't be quite so friendly.

'Five years ago…' Sandy did the maths in her head. 'I would've been twelve, terrible glasses that did nothing for me, curly hair I hated.'

Melissa chuckled. 'Your hair and your glasses never seemed out of place to me.'

'Mum always said the same.'

It was wonderful to know Tracy had settled in the Cove like she always wanted. She'd never been sure of what to do career-wise, she'd drifted from job to job over time, but one thing she'd known was that she wanted to get married, have a family and stay in the village. Even Melissa's postcards of far-flung places had never tempted her friend to travel, she'd much preferred the English seaside to anywhere exotic.

'Does your younger sister work here too?' Melissa asked.

'Violet? Not yet. She's finishing school and I'm not yet sure whether she wants to do this for a living, but I couldn't imagine doing anything else.'

'Well, it's lovely to see you again, Sandy. And if I may, I'll bring the jeans down after I change.' She lifted the handle to her case. Sandy was the spitting image of her mum now Melissa knew who she was, with straightened hair that Melissa already suspected would spring into curls, or at least waves, just like Tracy's had when the humidity outdoors did its worst, and she was the same blonde Tracy had been in her younger years before she naturally went a shade darker.

'Of course, I'll get them washed for you straight away. And I'll talk to mum later, let her know you're here.'

Melissa could only smile. She wasn't sure how that announcement was going to go down. Tracy had every right to give a frosty reception to the friend who'd walked away and not come back. Not even when Tracy's mum had died, because Melissa hadn't felt she could comfort her. She'd tried at first through phone calls and then a letter, but her own grief over losing her parents had snowballed every time and so she'd distanced herself, her much-used coping mechanism. She hadn't come back for Tracy's fortieth party either. She'd ignored the invite, knowing that if she went she'd be faced by a pub full of locals, receive the inevitable hostility. It wasn't necessarily that they would all have wanted to say goodbye or hear from her over the years, it would be far more to do with them feeling protective

49

over Barney, a man everyone liked, admired and looked out for.

'Feel free to enjoy the balcony,' Sandy called after her as Melissa took the stairs, 'it's beautiful in summer and gets the sun all afternoon.'

Melissa smiled. It sounded tempting, but after she'd unpacked and got changed, she wouldn't be putting it off any longer. She couldn't wait to see Barney.

*

Melissa couldn't keep up with the weather – one minute it was sunny, then the rain clouds appeared and the drizzle came, then it dried up again and the sun had another go at convincing them all it was still summer. She pulled on her sunglasses and set off to Barney's, a ten-minute walk away.

On the pavement outside the cottage with its little front gate that was easier to open as a kid than an adult who needed to bend right down, she looked at the place she'd visited more times than she could count. She smiled inwardly at the sight of the barn's roof to the left, beyond the trees that obscured the courtyard in front. She was back and no matter the challenges she faced, it actually felt better than she'd expected.

She bent down, lifted the latch to the gate and it creaked in its familiar way. She knocked on the door but no answer, she knocked again, then a third time a little harder. She didn't use this entrance as a kid, she always came through the gate, turned and passed through the trees and then went in through the back door. This door was usually locked, the back door never was. But after all this time it didn't feel right to come in any way other than the formal front entrance.

When she still got no response she had no choice but to cut down the path, between the trees and across the courtyard around to the back door, where the June sunshine filtered into the large open space that contained the kitchen and lounge area. Barney had always said the kitchen was the heart of the home but he'd wanted guests to be able to talk to each other from the sofa and armchairs, from the large Aga cooker, from the table as they ate, and so he'd had the rooms knocked into one.

She froze as she peered around the doorframe. Barney was sitting in the armchair closest to the fireplace, which had a dried-flower arrangement with purples and yellows to add a bit of colour when it was too warm to add logs and kindling and light the flames. His eyes were shut, his head leaning back, and her breath caught. The house seemed quiet in a way it had never been before. Barney loved noise, hustle and bustle, the craziness of kids racing about, or the radio for company if he found himself home alone. And even though the June sunshine streamed in through the glass, through the open back door where she was standing, the place looked cold and empty.

He slowly opened his eyes as he sensed he was being watched but it took a while for him to realise what he was seeing. 'Melissa?'

'Hello, Barney.' She couldn't help the wobble in her voice as her eyes filled with tears. She raced over to him and wrapped him in a hug before kneeling down on the floor, her head resting on his legs, his hand clutching hers. It was as though she was a little girl all over again.

'I can't believe you came.' His voice caught but he was still able to comfort her, shush her, even as his own tears flowed. The sniff gave him away.

They stayed that way until they'd both recovered, although he got there before her. 'Dry your tears, I'm not dead yet.'

She looked up and laughed, wiping her cheeks. 'Thank God.'

'Came close though.'

She grinned. 'You look like you're going to be fine.' She hadn't wanted to ask Harvey any details, but the fact that Barney was home and Harvey was going about his business told her that Barney was on the road to recovery.

'I had a fall, they replaced my hip, that's all.'

Even though he tried an injection of humour, Melissa could tell he wasn't himself. Or maybe that's what a five-year absence did, it made you forget that ageing waited for no one. 'How long before you're up and about again, properly?'

'No rush.'

'That wasn't what I asked.'

'Who knows? Maybe I'm too old to get back to what I was.' His cold hand covered hers again as though he daren't let her out of his sight. 'Don't look at me like that. Let's face it, I'm no spring chicken.'

She pulled a tissue from the pocket of a fresh pair of jeans she'd thrown on with a creased white T-shirt that could've done with a good iron before she came over. 'Of course you'll get back to normal, give it time, be patient with yourself.'

'I've got a walking frame.' He glanced over at the grey contraption he must've used to get to the chair. 'Ugly thing. What's next? Having to install those thick monstrous safety bars everywhere?'

'I don't think you're at that stage yet.' She watched him shuffle uncomfortably in the armchair. The skin on his hands seemed thinner, age spots peppered the surface, and he'd definitely lost weight since the last time she'd seen him. But she didn't know how much to put down to this setback or how much of it had happened over time.

'I'm old, I'm past it, and I'm cancelling the Wedding Dress Ball too.'

She sat down cross-legged on the floor in front of him. 'Barney, you can't be serious.' She might have been away for a while but the memories of the event still held a special place in her heart.

'It's too much work, too much for me anyway, I've had enough. Let someone else do it, but it won't be me, and it won't happen at the barn either.' He wouldn't meet her gaze.

She opened her mouth to say something else but shut it again. He looked like the Barney she knew but he certainly didn't sound like him. In all the time she'd known him he'd never once said he was fed up with the ball, never so much as hinted that one day he wouldn't want or be able to do it.

Had things changed that much?

'What did the doctors say? What was their advice to get you on the road to recovery?' She decided to steer the topic away from the ball for now; perhaps Barney wasn't thinking straight.

'They've given me a list of exercises to follow when I'm up to it.'

'Then I'll help you.'

'You're not only here for the day?'

'I'm here for three weeks.' If ever she'd doubted he would smile at her in the same way he had when she was a little girl, all doubts were erased now as he beamed back at her. 'Do you think you can put up with me hanging around that long?'

'You really mean it?'

53

'Of course. Now, what are the exercises, maybe I could help you do some now?'

The smile faded as he adjusted himself in the chair again. 'I'm not ready.' He winced.

'What hurts?'

'Everything, and moving around doesn't appeal to me right now so sod the exercises. I just want to sit here in peace.'

When he didn't even apologise for snapping she said, 'I'm so sorry I left it this long to come back.'

'You did what you had to do.'

'It was selfish. Oh! I never would've forgiven myself if –'

His voice softened. 'Stop that now, you hear me, Melissa Drew.'

'You don't need to last-name me.'

The sunlight was blocked as Harvey stepped through the back door. 'He does that when we're in trouble.' Holding a small basket of eggs, he didn't pass comment on Melissa's tears that had begun again.

'That's right,' she smiled back at Barney. 'Remember when I threw an apple at Harvey's head? You double-named me then, at the top of your voice, scared the living daylights out of me.'

'You took aim and were the perfect shot,' Barney confirmed, eyes dancing in amusement.

She'd almost made Harvey cry that day too. She hadn't realised quite how much it must've hurt until she was walking beneath a tree later on and an apple landed plonk on top of her head. She'd wailed, there'd been a smug look from Harvey, and she'd ended up apologising for throwing one at him and causing him pain.

Harvey was in the kitchen area taking out a frying pan, finding a spatula. 'Omelette,' he explained to Barney, 'as requested.'

'It wasn't requested. And I'm not hungry,' Barney grumbled.

'You need to eat,' Harvey batted back. 'Call it an early dinner.'

'I'll bet it'll be so much better than any hospital food,' Melissa assured Barney.

Barney grimaced. 'Don't get me started on that.'

'Was it terrible?' she asked.

He just grunted in response.

'You need to eat, Barney,' Harvey's voice carried over as he began cracking the eggs into a bowl. 'And the eggs were laid fresh this morning, can't ask for better than that.'

Hadn't he just been to the supermarket? That's what he'd told her when she bumped into him at the inn, and there was no need to make things up, no matter how desperate he was to get Barney to eat. 'Laid fresh this morning?' she repeated, looking Harvey's way.

'They came from Nola Green's place,' Harvey answered as though reading her mind and knowing where her comment was heading.

'They keep chickens at The Copper Plough?'

'At their daughter's cottage a few doors from the pub,' Barney told her. 'She's got a lot of land out back. After your family…well, you know, after we stopped having the eggs from your chickens, the few of us who'd been lucky enough to have those fresh eggs had to start going to the supermarket and it was never the same. Nola stepped up and decided to bring the custom back to Heritage Cove herself. She bought a fair few chickens, I'm not sure how many.'

55

'Nineteen,' Harvey called out from the kitchen, where he was grating cheese. 'Was twenty until a fox found them.'

Melissa pulled a face. She remembered her mum's tears when a fox found one of their chickens once. She was thankful she'd never seen the body, ripped to shreds. It was a brutal way to go. 'Good to know someone took over,' she said, even more glad that Barney was one of the lucky few who got to enjoy the eggs that were no doubt richer in taste and colour and creamier than those bought at the shops.

Harvey was on to chopping the tomatoes and a chunk of ham and Barney must've seen her looking over because he whispered to her, 'Have you two spoken yet?'

She smiled, mostly glad that despite his up-and-down moods, he was talking and taking an interest. 'Not properly, it's been a long time.'

'Shame I can't even cook you a decent meal,' Barney moaned. 'Not much of a homecoming with me like this.'

'You don't need to worry about feeding me, I'm hoping the pub still does a good fish curry.'

Barney let out a healthy chuckle. 'Oh, don't, it hurts me when I laugh. But you always did like odd foods. Fish curries were one of them, and what else was it you liked? Peanut butter and jam sandwiches?'

She scrunched her nose. 'Yeah, don't eat those anymore.'

'Thank goodness for that. I'm sure you've eaten lots of different foods on your travels – it sounds as though you've seen most of the world. I can't wait to hear more about it.'

'I'd love to tell you.' When more clattering came from the kitchen she said, 'But all in good time…I'd better get going and leave you to it.'

'But you only just got here.' Another crash from the kitchen and Barney must have read the discomfort on her face as she glanced over there. 'You'll come back soon?'

'I promise,' she said. 'How about I come back again tonight?'

'Oh, would you? I'd like that very much. You'd make an old man very happy.'

'I'll make us both hot chocolates. I've brought some of the most decadent chocolate I picked up in Bruges, I remembered how much you enjoyed a mug on a cold evening. It might not be cold now, but who cares, eh? And so long as you have milk, we're good to go.'

'The only hot chocolate I ever have is from the tea rooms down the road, none of this deluxe stuff. Although they do add crumbled Cadbury Flake on top if you ask for it.'

'Now that sounds pretty good to me.'

'You don't always have to be fancy,' Harvey interjected as he overheard the conversation. He added in that the omelette would be ready in fifteen minutes. Then, 'Sometimes the simple things in life are enough. At least, they are to some people,' was his parting shot and Melissa knew full well the remark was aimed at her.

'I'm not sure us talking is a good idea,' she said quietly to Barney. 'It seems all Harvey wants to do is lay blame and not take any of it for himself.'

'It's a shame you two are no longer the little tykes running riot around my barn. You'd argue and then forget about it the next minute. Simpler times. But you'll work it out.'

She wasn't so sure. 'I'll get going. The smell drifting from your kitchen is making my tummy protest, I only had a small lunch from the service station.' She grinned, keeping her voice low. 'Don't tell Harvey I said that, wouldn't want him to think I'm complimenting his cookery skills.' There had been enough looks passing back and forth between them that she felt the need to escape into the late afternoon sunshine for a while.

'Are you still with your young man?' Barney asked as she picked up her bag.

'Yes, I'm still with Jay.' Without a ring she didn't feel right to announce her engagement yet. They were keeping it to themselves until they'd had a chance to pick something out, make it official.

When Harvey swore after dropping something in the kitchen Melissa took it as her cue to leave. She'd have to talk to Barney again later about the Wedding Dress Ball. Surely he hadn't meant it when he said it wouldn't run this year – and letting someone else be in charge was one thing, but not having it in the barn? That was even more crazy.

'Come back here whenever you're ready,' Barney's voice followed her, 'and could you check the fridge on your way out to make sure we've enough milk?'

'Plenty of milk,' Harvey assured him.

Melissa already had her hand on the door to the fridge. 'You sure?'

'I said so, didn't I?'

She didn't miss his shoulders tense up as she stood so close she'd be able to reach out and touch him if she wanted to.

Glad to get away from the strained atmosphere at the house, she wondered what kind of reception she'd get at the pub. It could be a case of out of the frying pan into the fire, but at least there'd be alcohol on tap to ease her pain should she need it.

*

Harvey shook the spatula enough that the omelette slid onto the plate before taking it on a tray over to Barney. 'There you go, some of my best work – fluffy eggs, ham, cheese and mushroom folded through.'

'Thanks,' Barney mumbled, picking up his cutlery.

Harvey had already helped him to the bathroom, slowly, and now he tried not to stare while Barney ate but rather to watch him surreptitiously while he was clearing up the frying pan and utensils at the sink. That was one hurdle overcome at least, getting Barney to have a proper meal. He'd barely eaten anything in the hospital whereas he usually had a hearty appetite, and if Harvey could make a few meals and be here to see him eat them, it would put his mind at rest.

Harvey retrieved the plate and the tray away to wash up. 'Was it good to see Melissa?' He wondered whether her presence would go some way towards convincing Barney that he should at least try to get better. He seemed to have more colour in his cheeks now, although that could be from the omelette he supposed.

'It was a lovely surprise, unexpected. Did you know she was coming?'

'I had no idea.'

'How was it for you?'

'Seeing her again?' He shrugged. 'I'm glad she's here, for you.'

'You did good, getting in touch with her. I know it must've taken a big swallow of pride.'

'I couldn't do anything else, Barney.'

'What did you do, tell her I was at death's door?'

59

'Hardly, what makes you think that?' When Barney moved to get comfortable Harvey grabbed a cushion from the sofa and wedged it behind his back. 'Better?'

'Much. And the reason I ask the question is because she was pretty upset when she got here.'

'She's been away a long time.' But when Barney gave him a look that told him he wasn't buying it he added, 'I didn't exactly give her many details in my message. It was a rush job, I knew it had to be done.'

'And you wanted to punish her.'

He opened his mouth to deny it but couldn't. 'She should be grateful I even got in touch.'

'She hurt you, I know she did.'

'Ancient history.'

'Is it?'

'I hardly cry myself to sleep over her, Barney.'

'Are you hanging around when she comes back this evening?'

'I don't think that's a good idea. But I'll be staying here tonight.' He held up a hand to stop any argument. 'You're not staying in this house on your own when you've just come out of hospital. And I've already put sheets on the spare bed upstairs.'

'Good job my room is on the ground floor, I suppose. At least I won't have to attempt the stairs myself.'

'We need to get you moving around a bit.'

'Not today, son, not today.' He closed his eyes then, feeling full with food, content to be home.

Maybe with Melissa around for a while they'd be able to convince Barney that this fall was a bump in the road and not an insurmountable roadblock. Barney's lack of interest or enthusiasm for getting back to normal was hard enough for Harvey to see, but for Melissa? It would be punishing, because to her it must seem like she'd lost the Barney she knew and loved all over again.

Chapter Four

Harvey stayed away from Barney's house last night until he was sure Melissa would've left for the evening and by the time he got there Barney was asleep, so he crept up to bed without having to face the inevitable rundown of what they'd talked about and what she'd been up to in her absence.

Harvey had taken leave from his job as a loft fitter for the rest of this week to be around for Barney but he was still following up on existing jobs and when Barney made it clear that he was hovering too much this morning after he'd fixed him a decent breakfast, Harvey had nipped out to walk Winnie and drop some plans from his employer over to the bakery. The owners, sisters Celeste and Jade, lived in the cottage directly behind, which had its own lane to access it winding round to The Street from a smaller road on the other side of the Heritage Inn. The cottage was more of a house, proportion-wise, and had a decent-sized loft space they wanted converting into two rooms and a bathroom, so today he could finally show them the drawings and discuss the next steps.

Back at Barney's place now he held a box of glazed doughnuts aloft as he stepped in through the open back door. 'For the patient.'

'Sugary rubbish.'

'They're from the bakery, compliments of Celeste and Jade.' In exchange for a full progress report on the patient, of course.

'Then you'd better bring them over.'

'Are you sure? I can get rid of them if you don't think they're nutritious enough.'

'Never said that, did I?'

Harvey opened the box for Barney to make his selection. 'Did you see the rainbow yesterday evening?' he asked, satisfied that Barney's appetite was back a bit as he tucked into a doughnut glazed with toffee sauce. Probably not the best diet for recovering after surgery, but at least it made the man happy.

'Melissa and I saw it out the window. It arched right over the barn, best I've seen in a long while,' he smiled.

The good response was probably more to do with Melissa's visit than the act of Mother Nature and Harvey supposed he should get used to her name being mentioned a lot while she was still here. He wondered how he was going to get through the next few weeks seeing her, hearing about her, knowing she was close but no longer a part of his life.

'Did you tell Melissa that you don't want the Wedding Dress Ball to go ahead?' Barney hadn't mentioned it to him again but with the event date looming, Harvey was beginning to wonder how serious he was about calling the whole thing off.

'I did.'

'And what did she have to say?'

'Not a lot.'

Didn't sound like the Melissa he knew, but Harvey sensed he wasn't going to get much more out of Barney today. 'How's the pain?'

'You asked me that this morning.'

'You're right, I did.' He'd forgotten, or maybe he hadn't – he just didn't seem to be able to get a straight answer.

'I've taken my medication as per the nurse's instructions,' Barney informed him, perhaps sensing he was only asking out of concern, 'but I'm still too tired to try moving.'

'Not like you to admit defeat.'

'It's been a long day.'

'You're not even halfway through it yet. Didn't the doughnut sugar rush do you any good?' He held up the box to offer another but Barney waved it away.

'I need a lie down.'

'You might feel better if you stay out here rather than go to bed again.' He'd not been up all that long.

'Put the lid on those doughnuts, they'll keep,' Barney instructed. 'Now, could you help an old man to the bathroom?'

Harvey let Barney have the privacy he needed once they reached the bathroom and was on hand to take him from there to the bedroom, where he held on to him as Barney gingerly lowered himself onto the mattress. With Harvey's help he lifted his legs up onto the bed and settled back against the pillows.

'I'll be around if you need me,' said Harvey. He'd never really been in this room since he was younger, unless you counted the time he'd had to retrieve a dead bird that had fallen down the chimney into the ornate fireplace on the wall opposite the foot of the bed. 'I'm going to go and fix the table in the barn.'

'Whatever for?'

'Because it needs doing. It'll collapse next time you put apples on it otherwise, it's been on its last legs for ages.'

'Leave it.'

'It's no bother.'

'I'm too old to be picking apples and squeezing fresh juice anymore, I should buy it from the supermarket like everyone else.'

'I think we both know you won't.'

'Who says? I might try online ordering.'

'Now I've heard everything,' Harvey laughed. 'Whatever happened to online orders being a sin unless you were housebound? It robs people of jobs working in the shops, you said.'

'I did say that, didn't I?' he winced. 'Well, maybe I'll persuade Lottie from the corner shop to stock some better brands.'

'You do that, although it still won't be the same as the juice you make here.'

'Leave fixing the table, Harvey. I'm sure you've got your own things to be getting on with.'

'It won't take me long. Is there anything else I can get you before I go outside?'

'A blanket, if you don't mind.' Barney harrumphed. 'I hate making a fuss.'

It was unlike him to ask for anything but hopefully this was a temporary state of mind. Surely somewhere along the line they'd reach a turning point and Barney would go back to his normal self.

'You'll find one on the top shelf of the wardrobe. Pop it on the end of my bed,' Barney went on. 'I can pull it over me when I need to.'

Usually Barney protested when things weren't to his liking, he valued independence – he wasn't.the man who asked for a blanket just in case, he was the man who would put himself through pain to get the blanket rather than have to ask for it to be provided. Harvey had envisioned the most difficult patient on earth when they left the hospital ward, the moaning and demanding that he could manage perfectly fine. But those expected traits had somehow been exchanged for this melancholy, this acceptance of defeat, and it had Harvey second-guessing whether Barney was himself at all. The doctors had warned him a fall could knock some patients' confidence, and at the time Harvey had doubted that would happen to Barney. But now? Now he was worried.

Harvey opened up the wardrobe and tugged out the red woollen blanket from the shelf above a selection of jumpers, trousers, a couple of shirts and a lightweight jacket. He put the blanket on the end of the bed, rolled it back so it would be easy to grab, then went to shut the wardrobe doors, but when he did he noticed something long at the end of a rail. Wrapped in see-through plastic, on closer inspection it was definitely a dress.

'Something you need to tell me, Barney?' Harvey pulled out the dress on its hanger. 'I'm not sure it would suit you,' he joked peering at what was clearly a wedding gown.

Barney opened one eye and his lethargy almost didn't alert him to the find but his face turned stony when he saw what Harvey was holding. 'Put that away.'

'Whose is it?' Interest piqued, Harvey wanted to know the story behind the dress. There had to be one, didn't there?

'I said put it away.' Barney shut his eyes again. No other explanation offered, just a tone that matched the one Harvey had heard as a young boy if he did something naughty – like the time he and Melissa had started a small fire near the barn. Harvey had wanted to toast marshmallows on the end of a stick for her but when Barney found the two of them he went mad. They were only teens, he'd said, the whole barn could've gone up, and it was the same voice now, telling Harvey to stop probing.

Harvey put the dress back onto the rail. 'I'll leave you to rest then…do that table.'

'Thank you.' Barney's eyes were already shut; he was either drifting off or determined not to answer any questions.

Harvey shut the door to the bedroom quietly behind him and out in the barn he turned the table upside down. He'd already cut to size a piece of wood to replace the corner brace that had split and so it was a simple job to fix it in place with a couple of screws. It was also a quiet job, nowhere near noisy enough to disturb Barney, and he had no need to be concerned about neighbours either when he was working around here – it had been one of the real perks for him and Melissa as kids that they could run riot without any hassle.

The table finished, he leaned against the side of the barn in the summer sunshine drinking an ice-cold glass of water. This place had always been his escape, somewhere he ran to when his dad was at his worst, where he came when Melissa upped and left leaving him heartbroken. His head could be muddled but coming here helped him to get it straight. The rolling fields beyond gave him a sense of freedom, the row of hardy juniper trees at the other side of the courtyard with an archway in the middle that led through to a small box garden and Barney's front door had always given him a feeling of security and protection as they lined the connection from the barn to the house that was bordered on one side by plump hedges.

Harvey went back into the barn and positioned the fixed table against the wall. There were three other tables and he checked them all, because they'd all be used for apples, vessels for liquid, the apple press itself. It was totally ridiculous to think of Barney giving up and instead of harvesting his own fruit, buying it at the shops. He'd always loved to pluck the fruit as it ripened, he did it year after year as soon as the time was right.

He wondered what Melissa made of all this, he wished he could talk to her. But how could he ask about this when there was so much more to say?

Harvey looked around the barn. He peered up at the beams that were more secure than they'd been years ago when he and Melissa had climbed up onto them so often, using the hay bales to get enough height before they were told immediately to come down before they broke their necks. They'd lurked up there when the annual summer Wedding Dress Ball took place, they'd watched the sea of white dresses, dark suits, wishing they would be a part of it eventually.

Ridding himself of his nostalgia, Harvey packed away his tools, closed the doors to the barn and secured them before making his way quietly into the house. There didn't seem much point in trying to talk to Barney about the recommended exercises to get him on the road to recovery, he was sound asleep, so Harvey left him to it.

He'd try again later.

*

Seeing Barney yesterday had filled Melissa with more joy than she felt possible. But it had filled her with sadness too, disappointment in herself that she hadn't been strong enough or brave enough to come back sooner. She could only be thankful that she hadn't left it too late, that he was going to be just fine. She'd be able to return to her life, the job she loved, the man she was engaged to, and know that life in Heritage Cove went on.

Dinner at The Copper Plough had been far less daunting than Melissa expected. She was used to dining alone anyway, she did it often enough when she needed a break to do her own thing during a stopover for work, and yesterday she'd maintained surprising anonymity with most customers in the pub. It was early, dinner service had only just begun, which meant it was quiet. The owners, Terry and Nola, weren't around and only two bar staff Melissa didn't recognise were working a shift. Benjamin was still the chef and, rather than be standoffish with her for not keeping in touch with Barney, which was going to be the reason for others' hostility, he'd come over the second he saw her.

'You're back!' He'd squeezed her into a bear hug. 'It's been too long.'

He had the same long mousy hair, tinged with a bit more grey than last time and tied back into a ponytail, the same cheeky grin he'd had since the day he started at the same school as Melissa. He filled her in on the menu and how he'd changed it for the better. 'There's plenty to choose from,' he said.

'Please don't tell me the fish curry has been replaced by something else.'

'You were the only one who ever ate it.'

'I'm sure that's not true.' She looked at the choices on this new and improved menu.

'I can recommend the Moroccan chicken, served with seasonal vegetables and chat potatoes.'

'That sounds a good enough alternative to me.'

'I've tried to cater for the more upmarket clientele,' he grinned. 'Talking of which, what are you up to nowadays? You look different – grown up, sophisticated.'

She laughed. 'You saw me five years ago when I was in my late twenties; I was hardly a kid, I was grown up then.'

'Ah, you were, but you're different now, I can tell. You're definitely quieter.'

'I'm worried people will be funny with me, for leaving,' she confessed.

'Well, I suppose this *is* Heritage Cove. But I think you'll find most people won't be any different to how they were before you left. Seeing you might come as a surprise, but they all know what you went through back then. Stop worrying,' he smiled. 'You're not facing a firing squad.'

He went off to the kitchen to get back to work and make her meal as well as others and she hoped he was right. She perused more of the menu and found a list of sumptuous-sounding desserts. She wondered if she'd stay in the village long enough to try any of those, or perhaps she'd come here again when she visited Barney in the not-too-distant future.

Melissa had enjoyed two glasses of wine at the pub, chatted to Benjamin when he grabbed a much-needed break and he'd told her all about the relationship he was still in with his girlfriend, Zoe. He'd briefly touched on the subject of Melissa and Harvey's once-upon-a-time romance to be jealous of but the vibes she gave off must have warned him because he didn't delve too deeply into that.

Now, the day after, leaving the Heritage Inn and heading round the bend to walk along The Street, Melissa stopped to take it all in properly. It wasn't just Benjamin and Zoe who had stood the test of time. The bakery and the tea rooms were still here on the left-hand side, separated from one another by a wide stone archway that led down to a small car park. The bakery had a beautiful Tudor-style exterior – whitewashed stone façade, deep timber panels and criss-cross glass windows. She wondered if the same dark-wood tables were still inside the tea rooms, the biggest table in the bay window, smaller ones positioned along the wall and in the centre.

On the opposite side of the road was the blacksmith's and Melissa could hear sounds echoing from there and wondered, was it Lucy, who she'd met in the lay-by and who was standing in for old Fred, at work? Melissa hadn't known Fred too well; he'd always nodded a hello but was one of those people who seemed content in his own world with a job he loved. Her eyes drifted to the ice-creamery, which was new and almost hidden behind a copse of trees. The building was nothing like the tea shop or the bakery. It was modern, painted a sea blue with white shutters and a huge ice-cream cone on the outside wall. There was a single picnic bench next to the trees with its cherry-red umbrella just visible.

On the other side of the track that took you down to the cove came the chapel, which, despite its quaint stone exterior and wealth of character, didn't hold good memories. The last time Melissa had been there had been the day she buried her parents. And that occasion was the one she remembered the most, not Tracy's wedding, held in the same chapel and grounds, or her children's christenings. Melissa could still recall delivering her first-ever eulogy, standing up on the pulpit, shaking, faces watching her as she did her best to get the words out. Harvey had been at her side that day. She vaguely remembered it pouring with rain and the

71

roof leaking. Before she left Heritage Cove the roof had been covered in a green sheeting as a temporary fix, crying out to be pulled apart and put back together again, the sheeting flapping in the wind whenever it got a chance and making residents wonder whether it would ever be fixed. It looked fixed now. And the chapel's grounds were well tended with delicate pink flowers bobbing in the wind in one of the beds.

Melissa found herself tempted to cross over opposite the bakery and follow the lane next to the chapel, separated from it and the cemetery by a hedge. It was a long time since she'd followed the secret path down to the cove – not that it was really a secret, perhaps secluded was a more appropriate description. The best days weren't necessarily in the summer, though, but rather the autumn months, when the nights drew in and a thick fog wrapped around you like a big blanket. Melissa loved it then because it would be deserted. Sometimes, if you timed it right, the dense fog would lift when you were sitting on the sands, and while all around you and above was grey and impossible to make out, the wine-glass-shaped bay would appear in front of your eyes, stretching into the distance as though a magician had just revealed it from beneath his cape.

As Melissa stood there with the sunlight resting on her shoulders she realised she'd forgotten nothing about Heritage Cove. Even five years couldn't take away the familiarity of this place. Past the tea rooms on this side of the road was the track that led down to Harvey's place, next would be the candle shop she'd rarely been able to visit without coming out with something new, then on from that was the pub of course. The map of this village was as firmly imprinted in her mind as the inscription on her parents' headstone in their final resting place.

In some ways it was as though time had stood still, but she couldn't do the same and so she walked on, unable to resist sneaking a look through the windows of the bakery to see what was on offer. There were pastries – croissants, what looked like pains au chocolat – two wide wicker baskets held loaves of bread, cardboard labels pushed into plastic holders showing what each of them was. There were marmite loaves, bread with chia seeds, wholemeal sliced, white bloomers. Another display case showed off golden cookies next to one with brightly iced cupcakes.

She didn't go inside. She couldn't put it off forever but, boy, it was tempting when she could hide behind her sunglasses like she was doing now. Barney, like Benjamin, had assured her people had better things to do than berate her for her decisions, but she wasn't so sure.

She turned to walk away when the door to the bakery creaked open.

'Melissa?' A voice halted her before she could move on.

Melissa stopped, heard the door to the bakery spring shut behind their latest customer and when she turned, Tracy was standing there clutching three baguettes. 'Tracy, hi.' Her greeting was met with a frown. 'Good to see you,' she tried again.

Tracy adjusted the baguettes that seemed determined to slip from her grip. 'Well, I guess we all know what it takes to make you come back then. Barney, in hospital,' she added at Melissa's confusion.

'Yes, although he's home now.'

'Have you seen him?' Her hair had sprung into those familiar curls of hers and she looked well despite the scowl still in place.

'Of course.'

'Well, forgive me for doubting you, but you can hardly blame me.'

Melissa was about to walk away, but instead she smiled at this woman who had been her best friend, who had done nothing but be there for her, and whose defensiveness was surely because she'd been hurt. 'I'm sorry we lost touch,' she tried.

'*We* didn't lose touch, *you* lost touch. There's a difference.'

'You're right, and I'm sorry.'

'You didn't even come back for Mum's funeral.' Tracy's voice came out small. 'I was there for you when it happened to you.'

Melissa swallowed hard. She felt so ashamed, possibly more ashamed than she was of herself for staying out of Barney's life for so long. 'I know you were. I can't begin to tell you how terrible I feel. My own grief overshadowed everything else. It might sound like a crappy excuse but I couldn't pull myself together enough to be a help. I can't take it back, I can only apologise,' she added with so much regret Tracy's frown lessened.

'I get why you left, you'd said you were going to, but why cut your ties?'

'I guess it was easier to start over.'

'Heritage Cove never was good enough for you.'

'Now wait a minute, that was never the case.' She tried to calm herself but her hackles were rising and it wasn't easy. She tried a different tack. 'I'm staying at the inn. Your inn. I'm really pleased for you, it must mean a lot to have a business here.'

'It does.' And there it was, the smile between friends that Melissa had missed more than she'd ever realised. 'What do you think of the place?'

'It's wonderful, I have a lovely room with the balcony.'

'It's our best room.'

'Sandy has turned into a beautiful young lady, I didn't recognise her at first. She really looks like you too.'

Tracy put a hand to her hair, the mass of blonde curls that came down to her shoulders. 'Same wild curls that don't want to be tamed. She straightens it but in the rain or the humidity, well, it's not a fair battle.'

'No, I don't suppose it is.'

'You're looking well, Melissa.' Tracy's grip on her baguettes had lessened slightly, the tension in her shoulders had given way to a more relaxed and open stance. 'Are you still working with the airline?'

'I am.'

'Are you with anyone? I know you don't need to be, I'm just interested.'

Melissa smiled. 'I'm with a man called Jay. He's good to me. We're pretty serious.'

'So he's the one?'

'Yeah.' She wasn't going to mention the engagement to anyone, not without a ring – it didn't feel real quite yet.

'I was angry you didn't stay in touch,' Tracy said, 'and that you never came back when I needed you, but I also want good things for you.' When Melissa's gaze drifted to the ground she added, 'You know, Barney used to ask me every time I saw him whether I had any news.'

Her heart sank. 'I never realised.'

'You were, and still are, like a daughter to him. Please tell me that now you're in touch, you won't leave it so long next time.'

'I won't, not ever. His fall scared me, I realised how I'd feel if I left it too late.'

'You'd never forgive yourself.'

Melissa nodded in agreement. She most definitely would not.

'How's Harvey coping?'

'I wondered how long it would take you to mention his name.'

'He came to see me, desperate for your contact details that he'd got rid of. I don't suppose he realised he might ever need them again. That day, I'd never seen such a look of fear in his eyes, not even when…well, you know.'

She did know. Harvey had a past, a family history that most people around here were well aware of. He'd run scared from his father on more than one occasion, been known to take solace at the barn mostly but sometimes the bakery, the Heritage Inn, the tea rooms. 'Thank you for passing it on.'

'I never thought you'd move on from Harvey.'

'People change, I guess.'

Tracy smiled kindly. 'How long are you here for?'

'I'm booked in for three weeks, you haven't checked the booking?'

'I don't always get around to looking at names. Blame my efficient daughter.'

'She seems to have taken to it well.'

That seemed to please Tracy. 'She has, Giles too. As a matter of fact, he's been managing the place for me today so I could get a few things done, have a little break. I'll be back in this afternoon so you'll see me around.'

'How is Giles?'

'He's well, he's in charge of the breakfasts at the inn these days and he's loving it.'

'Then pass my compliments on, the eggs Florentine I had was delicious.'

'Eggs came from Nola's chickens.'

'I heard that's where the locals find their supply nowadays.'

Tracy smiled. 'Benjamin put Giles on to a cookery school too. I mean, he could cook already, but we needed better than good to put the inn on the map.'

'And business is going well?'

'It is. And we're looking at more improvements soon – we have the firm Harvey works for drawing up plans to convert the roof space into a penthouse suite.'

'I may have to return,' Melissa smiled, pulling her sunglasses back down. She'd had enough of squinting beneath the June sunlight.

'I really hope you do.'

Melissa stepped forward and hugged her friend, at last feeling Tracy relax. 'Oops, hope I didn't squash the baguettes.'

Tracy wiped away a tear. 'Of course not. So tell me, how's the patient? I haven't asked, which is terrible of me.'

Melissa guessed that seeing her had been shock enough. 'He's doing well.'

'I'm heading over tomorrow. Thought I'd give him time to settle back in.'

'He'll enjoy that.' Barney's place was always open house. You never had to give advance warning, it was the way he liked it, and in turn he visited people whenever the whim took him. It had to be hard for him to be stuck at home right now. Although if he improved his attitude and started doing the recommended rehabilitation exercises it might go some way to getting him out again, along The Street, where he'd be in his element soaking up the concern and catching up on all the local gossip.

'I thought I'd take him croissants from the bakery and some homemade jam.'

'I looked in the window, the bakery seems to have evolved since I was last here.'

Tracy laughed and checked the door was still closed. 'They were always so stuck in their ways, weren't they? It was iced buns, ring doughnuts and vanilla slices from what I remember.'

'And those cream horns.'

She pulled a face. 'Those were revolting, never liked them. You should try their cookies; these days they've made a lot of improvements. Celeste and Jade travelled around Europe for a year and picked up a lot of tips. They did start to do the most amazing coffees but Etna didn't like it.'

Etna ran the tea rooms. 'I'll bet she didn't. I remember when Lottie at the little shop floated the idea of having a coffee machine for takeaway drinks. Etna was livid.'

'She talked with Celeste and Jade and they agreed to leave the beverages out of their repertoire but helped her get a new machine installed for the fancy coffees. Etna resisted it at first but Barney persuaded her to move with the times. It was that or get left behind.'

Here beneath the sunshine, the confrontation had moved from accusatory and upsetting to a friendship that had been there all along, was neglected but still salvageable. Melissa shifted into the shady spot right out front of the bakery. 'I'd forgotten how beautiful summer days could be here.'

'They sure are.' Tracy hesitated before asking, 'Were you worried about coming back after so long?'

'A little…OK, a lot.'

'I wish you'd talked to me more after you left, you might've felt more able to visit then. I missed you. Giles is my husband and I love him dearly, but there's nothing like a girlie night out or trip to the pub to catch up on gossip.'

'I couldn't agree more.'

'So what happened, Melissa?'

She needed to talk and before she could stop herself the admission was out. 'Harvey really let me down.'

'Have you ever asked him why?'

'You think I should've come back before, just to see why he didn't leave with me when we'd planned it all along? How could I? I was humiliated that I wasn't enough for him.'

'Is that what you really think?'

'He chose Heritage Cove over me.'

'Maybe he chose to give you your life, Melissa.' Tracy smiled at her. 'He never spoke to me about it, he's a guy – you know what they're like with their feelings – but I'm reading between the lines. Perhaps there are things that went on that you don't know. Maybe talk to him, give him a chance to try to explain.'

'Maybe it would be better not to rake it all up again.'

'Perhaps you're right, especially if you're with someone else now.'

Melissa looked at the baguettes in her friend's arms when Tracy swatted a fly away. 'What are they for?'

'I'm making lunch for my book club. Hey, why don't you come? I'm hosting it at the inn at midday.'

'Maybe one day, but not today.'

'The only person you'll know is Etna…oh, and Nola, and then there's Lucy – you'd like her, she's the temporary blacksmith.' She took a breath. 'Listen to me trying to give you five years' worth of information in a few minutes! If you're still on the same number, would you mind if I messaged you?'

'My number's changed but grab it from the guest records, you've got your hands too full to add it to your phone right now,' Melissa smiled.

'I'll definitely do that, perhaps we could catch up soon.'

'For sure.'

Melissa went on her way, a sense of relief washing over her at seeing Tracy, although she'd only just waved her on her way when she passed the archway separating the bakery from the tea rooms and almost knocked into a woman coming from the opposite direction.

'Look out!' the woman laughed but any hint of a smile disappeared when she saw it was Melissa.

'Tilly, good to see you.' She didn't look any different. Only a couple of years younger than Melissa, she had the kind of hair that always stayed in place. The middle part never wandered off centre, the bottom of her mid-brown hair curled up evenly around the base.

'I won't say likewise.' Distrusting hazel eyes stared back at Melissa.

It seemed she'd got off lightly with Benjamin and Tracy. Tilly, who ran the candle shop, wasn't about to give her any break at all. Her face had become a dark cloud of disapproval and despite her bohemian dress sense with natural fabrics and earthy colours and patterns, she didn't exactly seem open-minded about what had driven Melissa to stay away for so long.

'Poor Barney had to put himself in the hospital to get your attention,' Tilly huffed. And without waiting for a response she stalked across the road and headed for the bus stop.

'What did you expect?' came a low voice from behind Melissa.

She swung round to face Harvey. 'Look, can we at least be civil while I'm here? I'm in the village to spend time with Barney, I'd rather not fight.'

'It's all about you isn't it?'

'You hurt me as well, remember.' Hands on hips, she snapped, 'It's not all one-sided.'

He opened his mouth ready to disagree but instead rubbed a hand across the stubble on his chin. 'I don't want to fight either.'

A memory of an argument between them came back to her. He'd been working hard as a builder's labourer, she was working as a personal assistant for a solicitor, both earning their own money. They'd talked about travelling and so they both saved, but one day he came home with a surprise. He'd taken her outside and shown her a motorbike, told her he'd been taking lessons in secret. He offered her a helmet and said he'd take her for a ride. He thought she'd be thrilled but instead she saw the dangers, she had a go at him for spending too much money and not being committed to their plans. He'd yelled back at her and the night he took off on that bike in a rage had been terrible. She'd sat with Barney in his barn as he set up for the annual Wedding Dress Ball, sobbing that her last words to him were so horrible, even though she did it out of worry. When the deep rumble of Harvey's motorbike sounded outside the barn she ran out and flung her arms around him, both of them apologising over and over again, her for overreacting, him for not realising that the extra danger of him on a motorbike had sent fear cascading through her, fear that she could lose someone else she loved to a road accident.

Not interested now in bickering for the next three weeks, she changed the topic back to the reason she was here in the first place. 'How do you think Barney's doing?'

'He's eating, he's sleeping, so that's positive. But he still won't do any of the exercises given to him by the physiotherapist.' He pushed his hands into his jeans pockets. He'd always looked good in a simple pair of Levi's and a T-shirt like he was wearing now, a small thread of cotton hanging down onto his bicep.

'It's hard to know whether you're encouraging him or nagging him,' she smiled. 'That's how it felt when I mentioned trying a few exercises – I even offered to help, but he wasn't having any of it. He keeps saying he needs his rest, which I guess is part of it. I'm so afraid of upsetting him I'm not sure what else to say.'

'You and me both. But one of us might have to be more forceful soon if he doesn't come around. The doctors told me his best chance of a full recovery will be to slowly get his strength and mobility back, which means doing the weight-bearing exercises, balance training.'

'Sounds like a gym workout.'

'It does, but it's important and he doesn't seem to see that. Thanks for trying with him, though. Out of the two of us, you're probably our best chance at convincing him. He's pleased you're back – you're a novelty, whereas I'm here all the time and he bites my head off if he thinks I'm badgering him.'

He sounded exhausted with it all. 'I'll try again, see what I can do. He's definitely not himself...emotionally, I mean.'

Harvey sighed. 'I thought I was imagining it.'

'Definitely not. I expect him to be tired but it's the lack of spirit I find such a shock. Maybe I'm overreacting, we did talk a lot last night before he told me he was exhausted and needed to go to bed. But I guess it's a big change going from total independence to having everyone looking out for him, you staying at his house to make sure he's OK.' She held up a hand, pre-empting the rebuke. 'I'm not saying you're wrong to do it – in fact, I think it's the right thing – but he's so used to being on his own that it's an adjustment.'

'I'm not sure how long to keep doing it,' Harvey admitted. 'Part of me thinks I should stay weeks, the other part thinks he'll be better if I go back home soon. It feels like a delicate balancing act.'

'I guess he's only a phone call away when you are back home; do what you think is best.' The look he gave her seemed to suggest he was dubious about her giving him the deciding vote, but he said nothing. 'Maybe he just needs time.'

'Tilly probably does too,' he said.

'She was *not* happy to see me.'

'She got close to Barney after you left. I think after the breakup with her boyfriend she didn't have many people to turn to and you know what Barney's like, he has a knack of magically appearing right when you need him the most.'

She grinned. 'How does he do that?'

'Intuition?' Harvey suggested.

'Well, whatever it is, I hope he's back to it soon.'

'You showing up will do a lot of good,' Harvey confessed, 'as long as you're hanging round for a while.'

'You know I am.'

'Didn't know whether you'd have to get back quicker than you planned, now you know he's home and well.' His gaze lingered on hers. 'I believe he told you he's not going ahead with the Wedding Dress Ball.'

'He did, and I mentioned it to him again last night. I thought it was a knee-jerk reaction but now I'm not so sure.'

'It's a first, I know that much.'

'What about White Clover? He raises a ton of money for them every year.' White Clover was the charity that had benefited from the proceeds of the ball every year, for as long as it had been running. Based on the outskirts of Heritage Cove, it supported families after the death of a child and with Barney a strong voice of the community, he must have been driven to support a local charity.

'White Clover will miss out, I guess,' said Harvey. 'He does appear to have made his mind up.'

'Then we need to change it.' The smile they exchanged made her stomach flip because he hadn't smiled at her like that since she arrived, not since the heady days of the spring before she left the Cove for good.

'I left a handout from the hospital with a list of exercises on the bench in the kitchen near the kettle. If you could get him to at least take a look, I think it would be a start. Maybe he'll see his life isn't over yet, much as he appears to think otherwise.'

'I'll give it my best shot.'

'I'll see you around.' And with a civil wave, off he went.

Melissa made her way along The Street and crossed over the road. She stopped when her phone rang and she smiled to see it was Jay calling. She sat on the low wall that curved around the bend and would lead down to Barney's place and chatted to her fiancé. He was drinking coffee in one of their favourite cafés and sounded lost without much to do until she suggested he finally take his sister up on the offer to go stay with her in Bath. She felt terrible he was having a wasted week and hoped he'd consider her suggestion. She almost wished she was heading down that way with him, exploring the cobbled streets, watching street entertainment, strolling along by the canals. But she needed to be here for now.

Trying not to feel too guilty about ruining their shared time off, she ended the call and continued around the bend, down to Barney's, where she followed the path between the trees and went in through the back door. Barney was in the lounge in the same armchair he'd sat in every other time she'd visited in the last couple of days. 'Harvey says you slept well,' she said, sitting on the ottoman opposite, 'and Tracy asked after you.'

'Well, that's nice. And I'm fine. I always sleep like a log.' He'd pulled a blanket across his lap but pushed it away now, his lips curving into a smile, ready to gossip. 'So, you've spoken to Harvey, and Tracy too. How was it with Tracy?'

'It was awkward, but then it was fine. And we're going to meet up again and talk properly.'

'I told you people around here wouldn't hold a grudge, and if they do, send them to me.'

'Once you're up and about you could tell them yourself,' she tried. But when she got no response she said, 'Tracy said she'll be bringing you treats from the bakery tomorrow, so be warned.'

'Best bakery in the village.'

'The only bakery in the village,' she laughed. 'Now, can I get you anything?' With her parents gone and her brother living elsewhere, Barney was the closest she had to family, and she intended to spend as much time with him as possible while she was here. 'How about a cup of tea?'

'I'd love one.'

The summer was warming up and it was almost at the stage where a cuppa first thing was fine but anything later on was too much, but for now she made them both a tea, his black, hers with a dash of milk, and when she sat down again she asked, 'How are the exercises going?'

'You really did talk to Harvey. Telling tales about me, was he?'

'It's because he cares. He said you slept well and told me you were still refusing to do the exercises. I hoped he might have been wrong.'

'I've had an operation, I should be resting and letting things heal. I'm not daft. It's my hip that was fractured, not my brain.'

'The doctors say it'll speed up recovery.' She picked up the leaflet Harvey had told her about and put it on the arm of Barney's chair, but he simply moved it to the table behind his mug where it wouldn't fall onto the floor. 'They're right,' she went on. 'I did a bit of research myself –'

'Doctor now, are you?'

'No, but it's not hard to find these things out, and increasing your activity gradually will help. I'm not suggesting you take up hiking or mountaineering, but little and often is a start.' And stop slumping in the chair all day everyday like you're doing now, she wanted to add but didn't.

'They'll say anything these days.'

'You know, if you do the work, there's no reason why you shouldn't be on your feet and able to dance at the ball this year.'

'You know how I feel about running it this year. Besides, I'm too old for all of that dancing nonsense, and you won't even be here so what's the point?'

The ball was almost a fortnight after she was due to leave and she'd be flying off somewhere no doubt so couldn't even offer to come back for it when she didn't know her schedule yet. 'How about Tilly? I'm sure she'll want a dance.'

'I hardly think any amount of exercises will have me bopping around a dancefloor,' he grumped.

'Barney, I'm not suggesting you do street dance or even the tango, but standing up, a girl in your arms – you can do it, I know you can.' She had his attention and didn't miss the sheen in his eyes.

'I'm not running the ball this year, Melissa, and my decision is final.'

'I think it's a big mistake not to.'

'I said I'm not doing it,' he snapped.

He was getting worked up and she didn't want to upset him any further. Far more than the physical recovery he still had to face, she was concerned about the emotional changes she'd noticed already. It was as though all of a sudden he wanted to hide away from the world.

She drank her tea and talked about the bakery instead, a safe topic. 'Tracy told me Celeste and Jade travelled and got a few ideas for the bakery. I heard about Etna's reaction to their idea of installing a coffee machine.'

Here was something Barney could get on board with – gossip he could never resist, not in a bad way but he always took an interest and would leap in as a mediator if he needed to. 'Etna was furious,' he chuckled. 'I don't think Jade or Celeste realised how much it would bother her but, to their credit, they backed down and to be honest, I think they were sort of pleased, it was one less thing to focus on.'

'I'll have to go in and sample something delicious soon.'

'Be brave. I know it must be hard facing people after all this time. We're a small village, we look after each other, but most people are only annoyed at you because they care.'

'I'm not sure Tilly sees it that way.'

'Now, she might take a lot of persuading to let you start over. But she's a nice girl underneath.'

'I heard you've spent a bit of time with her.'

'She was lost when that boyfriend of hers took off, don't think she knew which way to turn. I just leant an ear to talk to, that's all.'

'You always did put everyone else first.' He didn't say anything to that so she picked up the hospital leaflet again. 'The exercises are nothing to be afraid of, you know, and you've got so much outside space here, you're in the perfect situation to start slowly and build up.' She spotted the walking frame in the hallway. 'I'd love to see the barn again, would you take me out there?'

'You go ahead, you'll get there faster without me.'

'It wouldn't be the same.'

He rested his head against the chair and picked up the remote control to flick on the television. The Barney she

88

knew hadn't had much time for the 'idiot box', as he put it; he'd always wanted to be outside, or listen to the news on the radio or his iPad.

'Please come out there with me, Barney.'

He set the remote control down. 'I'd rather rest.'

'Come on, I'm back in the village to see you and spend time with you.' And when she kept staring at him, her gaze unwavering, she hit his weak spot. Having her here was enough of a boost to win him over.

'Fine, have it your way.'

She grabbed the walking frame. 'We'll go slow, don't worry.' Positioning it in front of him, she tried to read whether he wanted any assistance or not and when he held out an arm she helped him up before he gingerly put his hands on the walking frame.

They walked slowly to the open back door and followed the path along past the windows at the front of the house until they stepped through the gap between the trees and into the sunny courtyard.

'People love the ball every summer,' Melissa told him as they made their way steadily across to the barn. 'I was so excited when I was finally old enough to go as a guest. I got to put on a proper dress like all the other ladies I'd seen over the years.' She looked at the barn, the buddleia bush to the right that would bloom every August with its rich purple flowers on cone-shaped heads, bringing with it the scent of honey. For now, as they approached the barn doors, the buddleia bush only had leaves of deep green as it lay in wait for the months to roll on so it would have its turn to show off.

'My favourite part was watching the guests arrive,' she went on, wondering whether, if she conjured up enough memories for him, brought to mind the looks on people's faces and reminded Barney how much delight he gave to everyone in the village, perhaps it could persuade him not to abandon the event altogether, to consider that maybe there was an alternative solution. 'I'd analyse their faces – some looked nervous, others excited, a few couldn't stop laughing because they'd managed to squeeze into dresses that hadn't seen the light of day in decades. And don't even get me started on Patricia from Oak Cottage and the expander she told us about.'

Barney couldn't contain a laugh as he steadied himself against the walking frame. The sound bubbled out of him like the softest music, a reminder that the man she knew was in there somewhere.

Encouraged, Melissa continued. 'She went into great detail telling everyone how she'd gained twenty-eight pounds since she was married, had no intention of losing it, so had employed the services of an expert seamstress to let out her dress considerably.' It wasn't funny that she'd put on weight, it was the way Patricia had told the story – complete with actions to mime trying to get into the dress determinedly because she wanted to go to the ball, much like one of the sisters in Cinderella trying to ram a shoe onto her foot. Melissa wondered what Patricia's reaction to seeing her would be when she bumped into her. Patricia worked shifts in the tea rooms, or at least that's what she'd been doing when Melissa left. And better than having had the amusing memory herself, she'd put a smile on Barney's face.

Melissa and Barney were still talking about the ball when Harvey pulled his truck into the courtyard from the lane that led around the fields beyond and sneaked in the back way to Barney's place.

'You seem to have cheered him up,' he told Melissa when he stepped down from the truck as Barney inspected the lavender bush nearby, pulling off a couple of spent blooms that held no colour. 'You got him outside, it's a positive step.'

'Here's hoping.' She kept her voice low and crossed her fingers on both hands, grinning at Harvey.

He seemed to suddenly remember they weren't as close as they had once been and the relaxed conversation was replaced with a stilted, 'Only came to bring some hinges to fix up the door.'

'You work all day,' said Barney, who had come over to join them, his hands resting firmly on the walking frame as all three stood outside the double doors to the barn. 'No need to have to do it here as well.'

'No arguments, Barney, I'm happy to do it.'

The second Harvey pulled open the door on one side, gently, explaining this was the door he needed to fix with the hinge, the smell got her first. The sweet, earthy scent of freshly cut hay scattered across the pale grey concrete floor. She could see where it had come from – the few bales piled in the corner, another couple halfway down the interior, one beside the doors. The barn had been a huge part of her childhood, a play space, somewhere she could do gymnastics freely, a place where there was laughter, a plentiful supply of apple juice, a friendship that had lasted...until it hadn't.

Another memory rose and washed over her as she pictured her mum and dad dancing in the middle of the crowds like they'd done every year. Her mum, who detested the summer heat, had her hair pinned up, a delicate pink flower barely a contrast to the red hair that had faded as she grew older; her dad wore the same suit he'd got married in, the cummerbund a good fit. And they'd both been fine dancers. They'd never had formal lessons but that hadn't stopped her dad teaching Melissa

91

before her first ball – they'd danced in the kitchen, along by the cooker and around the table, as her mum cooked the dinner.

The barn had also been a welcome escape from the sunshine on the days when it beat down upon them relentlessly. They'd had ice-creams from Barney's freezer – he'd gone about his business and let them have the freedom neither of them really got at home. Melissa's family home was too small to run around in, with a modest square garden that her mum had always kept immaculate. The time she and her brother had had competitions on the swing seeing who could go highest and then jump from it into the vegetable patch hadn't gone down well. They'd ruined half of whatever it was she'd planted and that had been the end of the game, and the swing's demise. But here, in this barn, there was more space than they could hope for, and for Harvey it had been a space away from his dad that gave him his sanity. Sometimes Harvey had come here not wanting to talk about his home life; other times he'd kicked hay bales, thrown apples outside, anything to release his frustration. Melissa remembered Harvey turning up one day and Barney handing him a basket of spoiled apples. He'd taken Harvey outside, around the back of the barn where there were the remains of an old six-foot wall, and he'd told him to sling each apple against it. Barney had joined in, Melissa too, and by the end Harvey knew he wasn't alone in all of this. His father could do his worst and he'd still be standing.

'Is it just like you remembered?' Harvey broke into her thoughts now.

'Yes.' But, looking up, she realised there'd been a lot of maintenance along the way. 'The wooden timbers look new.'

'Replaced last summer,' he confirmed as they watched Barney sit down on the hay bale nearest the door. 'This barn takes quite a bit of upkeep, especially with the ball running every year.'

'Except that now it isn't.'

'He still hasn't come around?'

'He seems pretty adamant.'

Harvey exhaled, ran a hand through his hair. Melissa had always loved the way the tufts on top fell in different directions when he did that. He never styled his hair, it just had its own habits. Once upon a time he'd had a long fringe and she'd teased him about it, so much so that he handed her the scissors and told her to cut it. His mum had gone spare. The fringe, jagged and far from a professional job, had prompted his mum to come and have words with Melissa. But all Melissa had thought was that at least it wasn't his dad who had seen it first. He was away with work and it gave Harvey's mum enough time to employ the services of a decent hairdresser and sort it out.

Melissa spotted the old apple press. 'I thought he might have got rid of that or upgraded it.'

'No need, works perfectly well,' Harvey replied, mimicking Barney's tone, before he ducked outside to grab his tools for the repair to the door hinge.

Melissa strolled around the barn, rubbing her hands against her upper arms as tiny goose pimples appeared. It was warm enough outside for the delicate blue T-shirt dress she'd chosen for today, but so much cooler in here.

She squinted. The same slight gap she remembered in the top of one of the doors let in a shaft of sunlight that, if you stood in the wrong spot, hurt your eyes. The stage was still there at the end of the barn nearest to the double doors. Harvey had built it for Barney the year before

Melissa left, around the time they'd been busy making plans to move to London, perhaps travel through some of Europe together if they had enough money. Her need to leave the Cove had increased by the day and they spent hours under this roof discussing what they were going to do, what they could see, how free they would be.

In an odd way, Melissa knew she'd been more trapped by leaving – she'd shut off a part of her life that was very real because that was the only way she knew how to cope. Being here now made her question whether she'd been right to do it that way. But, then again, she'd landed the job that she'd dreamed of, that took her on all kinds of adventures, she'd met Jay and was engaged.

She brought her focus back to the here and now, crouching down in front of Barney as Harvey reappeared and began taking off the hinge on the door ready to replace it. 'Are you feeling all right?' He'd shut his eyes, his legs still in the shaft of sunlight coming in through the open doors.

'Tired, that's all.'

'Thank you for coming out here with me. It's still a beautiful space.'

'You always did like it in here.'

'We got you outside,' she beamed. 'Perhaps we should do little and often when it comes to exercise, we'll get there in the end.'

He took a deep breath. 'I'm not sure it's going to be that easy.'

'Since when have you ever given up?' She toyed with a piece of hay she'd pulled from the bale.

'It might be time I accepted this place is too much for me.'

'The barn?'

'The barn, the house, the garden.'

'You can't mean it…remember you have plenty of people who care and who will help.'

'People look after themselves.'

'Rubbish.' She definitely had, and she didn't miss the irony of her suggesting people did otherwise.

'I've been thinking…perhaps it's time I moved into one of those places.'

'One of what places?'

'For the over-seventies, you know, where there are people of my own age.'

Harvey swore when he caught his shirt on something.

'Everything OK?' Melissa asked.

'Didn't see a protruding nail, caught my shirt, that's all.'

Most likely distracted by Barney's comment, Melissa suspected, as Harvey got his hammer and banged the nail to blame back in again before checking the rest of the surface for anything else threatening.

Her attention back to Barney, she said, 'You and this barn, this house, this land…well, you go together, that's all.'

'I'm getting old, Melissa. In one of those places I'll be looked after.'

Harvey jumped in on the conversation, leaving Melissa in no doubt that's what had distracted him. 'This is crazy talk, you know that. And we'll look after you, Barney. You've no worries on that score.'

'Melissa doesn't even live here anymore, and you have a job and a life.'

'I won't let you down,' he insisted.

'And I won't be a stranger, I promise,' Melissa added.

'Time moves on, for all of us,' Barney replied simply. 'Maybe I need to start realising it and not live in the past.'

'Is this why you don't want to run the Wedding Dress Ball?' Melissa ventured to say. 'You think it's living in the past?'

A look of confusion crossed Barney's brow before he told her, 'I was younger when I first started organising it. Maybe someone else needs to take over, or it should be stopped all together.' He didn't let her get another word in. 'I'd like to go inside now.'

'I can't see it,' said Harvey, who had gone back to working, moving the new hinge into place while he addressed Barney. 'I can't see you leaving Heritage Cove, let alone living with a load of people way older than you.'

While the sounds of a drill filled the air Melissa helped Barney stand up and take hold of the walking frame.

'You kids hang out here as long as you like.' Barney brushed away her hand again when she tried to accompany him. 'I'm fine to go back to the house on my own.'

'We can't let him do this,' she told Harvey the second Barney was out of earshot, across the courtyard and in through the door. How could Barney even think of leaving his home with its special memories, the times he treasured as much as they did?

'Stubborn as anything, that man.' Harvey shook his head and fixed the last screw in place. He tested the hinge by closing the door on that side.

'He was never that pig-headed before, was he?'

'You must've been away so long you've forgotten.' He held up both hands, the old hinge clasped in one

96

before he dropped it into his toolbox. 'Not having a go at you, just saying. He's always been determined.' His brow creased. 'But never quite this adamant on doing something so out of character.'

Looking around the barn as she wondered what to do to convince Barney he wasn't too old for any of this, she spotted a collection of black-and-white photographs lining the wall behind the stage. She went past the hay bales on one side and started working her way along the pictures. Each had a date on the top. There was the summer Wedding Dress Ball of 1997, the first in the collection that she could remember. She would've been ten years old then, too young to attend but not too young to admire those who did. She moved along, recollecting a few of the other occasions, some faces old, some new, and stopped in her tracks at one year's photograph, of a crowd of people dancing. Her parents were in the middle, smiles on their faces, sharing a look only between themselves. She put her fingers to their faces, she knew they'd hate to know she'd left Heritage Cove behind so brutally without turning back.

She moved along, taking in all the scenes, and stopped when she got to the picture of the ball the summer before she left. She was wearing a white dress with a halterneck that she'd found in a charity shop. Harvey's mum had sewn delicate little flowers all over it for her and it felt as special as something she'd had designed for herself. She and Harvey were dancing in this photograph, their faces full of excitement at their adventures ahead. They'd not only talked about moving away and European sights they could finally see, but also about settling in this part of the country, perhaps even back in Heritage Cove, when they returned.

Melissa took another step so she was facing the photograph of the following year. She knew she wouldn't be in that one or any of the subsequent pictures either. 'When did Barney put all these up?' she asked Harvey, who was packing up the last of his tools as she got to the end of the collection.

'I did it for him last year for his birthday.' He came to stand by her and look at the photographs himself. 'This barn has been many things over the years, but its biggest claim has to be the ball.'

'Barney has to see it through again this year and every year.'

'I don't know, maybe he's right, maybe he's getting too old.' When she shot him a look he smiled, 'No, you're right. The Wedding Dress Ball is a part of him as much as he's a part of it.'

'What can we do?'

'To make him change his mind? I'd say, not a lot.'

'Then we'll have to help. With the ball. Between us we'll have to put the event on.'

Harvey laughed until he realised she wasn't joking. 'I've never organised an event in my life – unless you count my mum's sixtieth, which was tea and cakes for a group of eight.'

'Come on, how hard can it be?'

'I'm not being funny, but you're only here for a few weeks, aren't you? So who's going to take charge when you run off again?'

She ignored the low blow. 'I'll hang around for longer.'

'Don't you have a job? A boyfriend? A life?'

'All of that can wait, this is more important.'

He stood staring at her as though he couldn't believe the words coming out of her mouth and she only hoped it showed how much she still cared, how much she loved Barney and this village despite turning her back. A person could have both, couldn't they? They could have roots and wings. You didn't have to sacrifice one for the other.

'Come on, Harvey. We have to do this. What do you say?'

'I say I wouldn't even know where to start. If you want to organise it then go ahead, but count me out.'

She ignored the resistance. 'We could talk to Barney, find out all we can. I think if he sees the event going ahead he won't be able to help himself. He'll want to be involved, he'll realise it can't be the end. And, I think it might stop all this talk of moving into an old people's home.'

'You always did get carried away with plans,' Harvey grinned. 'All right, you talk to him. But I'm not committing to anything.'

'Fine.'

As they walked outside to the courtyard and over to Harvey's truck, where he put his toolbox into the tray at the back, she asked, 'What made you come here so quick today? When I saw you in The Street earlier I got the impression you wouldn't be over for a while. Were you checking up on me, to see if I'd been able to get Barney to at least look at the list of exercises he should be doing?'

'Of course not. I remembered the door hinge, and after he had the fall in here, I don't want anything causing another accident. My mind has been running overtime thinking of things that could possibly go wrong.'

She'd never thought he'd give himself quite such a hard time with this. 'Harvey, anyone could've fallen off a ladder.'

'Doesn't stop me wishing I'd been here for him, though. Both you and I know it could've happened to anyone but Barney seems to think it's his age – it's as though this one incident has drummed into him that he's in the later years of his life. And the more he talks like that, the more I worry.'

'He's got plenty of time left yet. And it's good you keep an eye on him.' But Harvey had always looked out for everyone else. Her, Barney, his mum. He was a good man, she hadn't meant to hurt him, but then again he'd let her down too.

Before he could get into his truck and leave she found herself blurting out the question, 'Why didn't you turn up that day?'

Harvey froze. It took him a while to turn and look at her, his keys hooked around his middle finger. 'Maybe it's not a good idea to dredge all that back up again.'

'Don't I deserve a moment of your time?'

'I didn't turn up that day, but at the same time, you didn't wait,' he threw back.

'Did you want me to?'

He looked ready to argue back but then said, 'No, I don't suppose I did. I knew you needed to leave, so it all worked out in the end.'

'Harvey…' she called after him but he'd already headed off towards the house saying he wanted to make sure Barney didn't need anything else before he left.

By the time she'd caught up with him inside, Harvey was nagging Barney about the rehabilitation exercises.

'It might be a bit much,' Melissa said quietly to him. 'Take it easy.'

'As far as I know, you're not a nurse,' Harvey snapped, far louder than her own voice. He didn't even turn around to face her, all trace of the earlier pleasantries gone. She'd stirred up trouble by mentioning the day she left and now he was taking it out on Barney by going on at him.

Harvey carried on. 'Barney, the more you comply, the sooner you'll be back to normal…we all will.'

Melissa got the feeling Harvey wasn't bothered about sleeping in his own bed so much as getting her out of the picture. That was hardly going to work if they really were going to try to help organise the ball this summer.

'Stop bickering, the both of you,' Barney snapped. 'Now, will someone please pass me my iPad?'

Harvey did the honours, although reluctantly.

'Let me open some windows for you,' Melissa suggested. 'It's stuffy in here, even with the doors open.'

'Be my guest.' Barney didn't bother to look up from his screen.

'I'd forgotten how lovely it could be in the English countryside,' she told him, keen to lift the mood of the room. It had been a long while since she'd woken to the sound of a dawn chorus and the delicate scent of whatever was in the garden at that time of the year but this morning at the inn she'd really noticed it. She'd slept soundly, knowing it must be all the fresh air during the day, and woken to a sweet scent coming through her open window, a bird trilling in the morning sunshine.

Barney didn't respond with anything other than a non-committal murmur, Harvey was busy making cups of tea, and so she gave up trying to get a conversation going and opened up the windows in the lounge as well as the one in the kitchen. 'Mind if I open the one in your bedroom, Barney?' she asked. All she got in answer was a wave of his hand to indicate he'd prefer her to stop asking questions. At least that's how she interpreted it.

In Barney's bedroom the curtains were still closed. Melissa pulled them open, then put the window on its latch and a gentle breeze snaked its way inside. A blanket that must have been on the end of the bed was now lying on the floor so she gathered it up, refolded it and took it to the wardrobe – she assumed that's where it was kept.

She was right. There were another couple of blankets on the top shelf and she stretched up to tuck the blanket alongside the others. But as she lifted it, it got caught on a wrapped garment hanging on the rail below. She wrestled the material away, slotted the woolly blanket onto the shelf and looked at what it was that had caught on it. She expected the plastic to be covering a suit or a winter coat that had been dry-cleaned and wouldn't see daylight until winter came around, but instead it was something white. Too long to be a shirt, she pulled back the other clothes on the rail to reveal a wedding gown hanging at the very end.

'Don't ask,' came Harvey's voice.

She clutched a hand against her chest. 'You scared me.'

'Because you're snooping?'

'Of course I wasn't.' The wardrobe doors were still open and she looked around the bedroom door to check Barney was still sitting in his chair in the lounge area. 'I was putting the blanket away and found this by accident. Why has Barney got a wedding dress?'

'As I said, don't bring it up. When I mentioned it, he soon shut me down.'

She was about to close the wardrobe when a thought occurred to her. 'You know, I've seen this before…'

'You have?'

'It was years ago. At least, I think it's the same one, I suppose I can't be sure. Hang on…' She lifted up the bottom of the gown and pulled aside the plastic covering. 'It must be the same one – see, there's a section of material missing, same as the dress I found before.'

He peered closer to see for himself. 'I never noticed that.'

'I came here one winter's day after school. I'd forgotten my house key and my parents were still at work. Barney made me a hot cocoa but I couldn't warm up. I was shivering and he told me to lie down. He went to find some blankets, I followed him, and that's when I saw this. This same dress.'

'Ah, you're talking about the winter you came down with flu and gave it to me.'

'You have a good memory.' She did her best to ignore the tingle when his arm brushed against hers accidentally. 'I didn't give it to you on purpose, you know.'

'I don't think I even minded at the time.'

She gulped when his gaze held hers. 'I asked him about it back then. He wouldn't tell me anything. And then I suppose I just forgot about it.'

'Perhaps it's a spare, you know, in case someone at the ball has a wardrobe malfunction.' He shrugged as though it was entirely plausible.

'Doubtful.' She put her hand against the dress beneath the plastic. 'And there's a section missing, remember. That would be a major malfunction for anyone's dress standards.'

'Good point.'

'It's such a beautiful dress. Vintage, by the looks of things.' The satin damask gown in rich heavy silk had been heavy to hold on its hanger. Melissa peeked beneath the plastic again to see a ruched neckline trimmed with ruffles, sleeves that had beads sewn on at the edges. 'It looks old.'

Harvey leaned closer again. 'It smells old.'

'There's a little bag that goes with it,' she said when she saw it looped around the hanger behind the garment. 'Whoever owned this dress would've used the bag to carry small items like a lipstick or make-up for touch-ups on their big day. Wait, you don't think…'

'What? I'm clueless on this, Melissa.'

'Maybe this is the reason for the Wedding Dress Ball, the reason it all started in the first place. Perhaps whoever owned this dress is the reason Barney started the event in Heritage Cove.'

'You think he murdered his wife and kept the dress as a souvenir?'

'Of course not, but there's something he hasn't told us.'

'I guess we won't ever know unless we ask him.'

'The mood he's in…' She shook her head. 'I'm not going to push it.'

Melissa checked again that they wouldn't be caught looking, although they'd better get back out to the lounge soon or Barney would get suspicious. Harvey made a show of calling out to say they were opening windows in the spare room and bathroom too, plus the one in the hallway that looked out on a gorse bush that separated the house from a wide flowerbed, a low-lying wall and the road.

'What are you doing?' Harvey hissed when he saw her opening up the little bag.

'Just looking,' she said.

'Hurry up, he'll be in here in a minute.'

'No he won't, he doesn't want to move more than he has to, remember.' She rummaged in the bag and pulled out a piece of paper. But she only got as far as reading "Dear Barney" when Barney's voice prompted them both to leave it alone.

'What are you kids up to?' he called out as Melissa stuffed the letter back and quickly shut the wardrobe.

She went to the end of the hallway and opened the window there while Harvey saw to the one in the bathroom.

'I love that he calls us kids,' Harvey whispered when they met at the lounge door, sending a shiver down her spine.

They shared a smile before joining Barney again. 'Sorry, window in the hallway was hard to open.'

'It always gets stuck, so I don't usually bother,' said Barney, looking up from his iPad for long enough to inspect their faces for signs of mischief in the same way he'd done in years gone by. Finding nothing, he got back to what he was looking at. Clearly they were better at masking their feelings than they'd been back then.

'Let's drink that tea before it goes cold,' said Melissa, heading over to the kitchen bench.

'I'll help,' Harvey added.

In a low voice, as they picked up the mugs between them, Melissa told him, 'We'll have to look at that letter another time.'

'Or we could just respect his privacy,' said Harvey, as though they hadn't been in cahoots moments before.

'But...'

He merely shrugged.

Maybe he had a point. What right did she have to snoop? Especially after all this time, especially after her absence.

Harvey drank his tea quickly enough and left Melissa and Barney to play a few games of cards and although there was no more talk of wedding dresses or the Wedding Dress Ball, Melissa knew that they were going to have to take over the organising soon if they didn't want the event to be cancelled altogether. And that meant she'd need to stay in the Cove a little longer than she'd planned, a thought that would've made her nauseous before but that now filled her with a sense of anticipation that wasn't altogether unwelcome.

Chapter Five

Harvey had a flexible job as it was but with Melissa around he'd been able to return to work confident Barney would be looked out for in his absence, and he was still only a phone call away. She'd spent a lot of time with Barney over the last week, the pair chatting away and catching up, and it instilled a sense of contentment in Harvey that he hadn't had until Melissa had turned up in the cove for the man who was so important to the both of them.

Today, Harvey worked the morning and was close enough to Heritage Cove that he could nip over to Barney's to say hello, check up on him and share a quick lunch.

'It's much nicer eating a sandwich here than surrounded by dust and mayhem,' said Harvey, tucking into the cheese and pickle sandwiches he'd rustled up.

'I appreciate the company,' said Barney, before another voice called out from the open back door.

'Anyone home?'

'Through here,' Harvey replied, recognising Tilly's voice. 'How's it all going, Tilly?'

'Can't complain. I thought Barney might be on his own so I popped out for lunch and came to keep him company.'

'I beat you to it,' said Harvey. 'Can I interest you in a sandwich? Plenty to go round.'

'I don't want to be any trouble.'

'No trouble. I'm making myself another, happy to make you one at the same time. You sit down.'

She rolled up the sleeves of her cream shirt, which she'd teamed with a long red wrap-around summer skirt that reached her ankles, and flopped down onto the sofa. 'First time I've sat down all morning.'

'Candle business going well?' Barney enquired.

Harvey let the pair talk about the business, which had originally been owned by Tilly's grandmother Shirley, a close friend of Barney's who passed away ten years ago – Harvey suspected that had been one reason Barney stepped in when Tilly's boyfriend left her, as well as the fact that Tilly's parents lived in Nottingham so she didn't have any family to turn to. Tilly's dad, Shirley's son, never had much interest in the business and so it had passed down to Tilly, and Harvey couldn't blame him for his indifference, it was a bit feminine with all its wafty scents coming out onto the street, elegant candles of all shapes and sizes fit for the smartest of interiors. Tilly on the other hand had taken to the business as though running it was part of her genetic makeup.

'Enough about me, how are you doing, Barney?' Tilly asked after thanking Harvey for the sandwich, and took a hungry bite.

'As you can see, still standing. Or rather, sitting. Harvey and Melissa keep going on at me to move around, think they want me dancing a jig.'

Harvey looked at Tilly and shook his head before chowing down on his second sandwich.

'Talking of dancing, I have a new dress for the ball.' She set her sandwich down on her plate, needing her hands to help her explain the dress. 'It has beading all across the bodice...' her hands moved across the chest, 'comes down to about here,' she said, touching a hand to mid-calf, 'and if I twirl around it lifts up, *à la* Marilyn Monroe.'

'Now that sounds like a dress.'

'I can't wait to show everyone. And you never know, maybe I'll get a date, it's been a quiet time since Matt left. I'm fine,' she said before Barney could attempt to console her, 'I'm well rid of him, but it doesn't mean I don't miss having someone.'

Harvey knew exactly how that felt. And now was a good opportunity to mention the ball. 'Barney isn't going ahead with the ball this year.'

Tilly's sandwich hadn't even made it to her mouth again. 'You're kidding, right?'

Barney shuffled uncomfortably in his chair, his focus on the model ship he'd had on the mantelpiece for as long as Harvey could remember.

'He thinks he's too old,' said Harvey.

'What a load of rubbish.'

'This fall,' Barney began, 'it's told me I'm not as young as I was. Talking of which, Tilly, doesn't your friend Amber work at Aubrey House?'

'That's right, why?' She scooped up the chunk of pickle that fell from between the slices of bread.

'Could you ask her to pop a leaflet through the door? It's high time I started investigating places more suitable than this.'

Tilly popped the last of her sandwich into her mouth and chewed thoughtfully. 'This is all a bit much, isn't it? No Wedding Dress Ball, moving out to a retirement home? Have I walked into the wrong house?' She looked to Harvey. 'What did you do with Barney?'

Harvey watched Barney pat her hand. 'It's time,' was all he said before he noticed the maroon plastic container with a smaller turquoise one on top that she'd brought with her. 'What are those over there?'

'Oh, golly! I almost forgot about those.' She leapt up and retrieved the containers from the table. 'This is your dinner, tonight or another night. It's chicken casserole plus a side of mashed potatoes.'

'I'm being spoiled.'

'Nothing more than you deserve, Barney. Now, should I put it all in the fridge or the freezer?'

'The fridge is fine. I'll have it tomorrow. Tonight it's roast lamb – Benjamin is dropping it over before he starts the evening shift in the pub kitchen. Maybe I'll have to go into hospital more often if I get treated like this.'

'Don't you go saying things like that. But I'm happy to help. Sorry I didn't make it up to the hospital more than once, the shop has me busy.'

'It's not a problem. You all have lives, no need to concern yourselves with one that's almost over.'

Harvey rolled his eyes at a surprised Tilly as he held the fridge door open for her to try to slot the containers in amongst what was already in there.

Another voice called through the open back door and this time it was Ashley, manager of the White Clover charity, recipients of the money raised from the Wedding Dress Ball every year. 'How's the patient?' Hooked over her arm was a basket filled with muffins.

'The patient is doing just fine and being fed very well.' Barney eyed the latest offering.

'They're mini orange and poppyseed,' Ashley smiled. Green eyes danced and her mahogany curls shook whenever she laughed. She was a jolly character, the sort of woman a charity needed working for them. Even when she wasn't smiling she looked happy and when she spoke personality bubbled right out of her. 'Now, Barney, what's this a little birdie tells me about you wanting to cancel the Wedding Dress Ball?'

Now Harvey was all ears. It was one thing him and Melissa nagging Barney about the ball, quite another for the locals to bend his ear about it. Perhaps this was what was going to do the trick, especially when Ashley had a vested interest.

'It's time I stopped, it's too much for me,' he told her. 'Now, do me a favour. Over there in the bureau there's a folder – if you could get it for me, please.'

Ashley did as she was asked and handed Barney the folder before telling Tilly and Harvey to help themselves to a muffin.

'In here is everything I've organised,' he told her, the folder on his lap. 'There's a list of everything that'll need to be cancelled. There's a list of who I've sold tickets to and I'm going to issue with a refund. Now, I'm sorry, I know this isn't what you want for White Clover, but I've made my decision.'

'Oh, Barney.' Ashley put a hand over his. 'It's a shame for White Clover, but that's not my main concern. You're the priority here, and the whole idea of the ball must be overwhelming – I can see why it would be too much, especially after you've only just come home from hospital.'

Harvey wondered whether he and Melissa had been unfair to push Barney to change his mind.

'Everyone's main concern is you, Barney,' Tilly added.

'Do you need help to cancel things?' Ashley offered, her practical side at the helm.

'I couldn't ask you to do that.'

'Of course you could. But before I go ahead, I have an alternative suggestion.'

'And what might that be?' Barney asked.

'Well, if it's too much for you, why not let someone else take over the organising? It's an event I'd like to see run for decades. It brings everyone together, people look forward to it all year.'

Barney sighed. 'I think it's best that if I'm no longer running the ball, then someone else takes over and moves it to a completely different venue. That's if you can find someone else to do it. People have busy lives.'

Harvey looked out of the window at the large structure looming well above the juniper trees on the other side of the courtyard. 'The barn makes the event, you know that, right?'

'Easy for you to say, son. But I'm done.'

'Why not let someone else run it in the barn?' Harvey wanted to know.

'Nobody else I'd trust in my barn, not a chance.'

'I would offer to do it,' said Tilly, 'but I'm useless at organising.'

'I'm not bad,' said Ashley, 'but between running the charity and caring for my elderly parents, I'm just far too busy I'm afraid.'

Tilly told Ashley about her new dress. 'I was really excited to wear it for the first time.'

'I'm sure you were.'

'Are you bringing anyone?' Tilly wanted to know. She was talking as though there was no way the event would possibly be cancelled. Harvey suspected most of the village would react the same way.

'Not likely,' Ashley smiled. 'My divorce was final three years ago and I'm happily married to my job now.'

112

Harvey went to the ball every year, to support Barney, to be a part of the village where people actually cared about one another. His mum went every year too and to see her happy after all this time was always special, it was one of the rare occasions she did herself up, got outside the house and remembered she was a better person than her husband had ever made her feel.

'What about you?' Tilly suggested, looking Harvey's way. 'Why don't you organise it?' If she was on friendlier terms with Melissa he'd think they'd been talking. 'You trust him, don't you, Barney?'

'Of course.'

Ashley picked up her handbag. 'I have to get going, but please keep me informed. I'm hopeful we can find a solution other than cancelling, but if that's what you choose to do, Barney, then I respect your decision.'

After she left it was time for Harvey to get back to work too. 'Do you need anything before I go?' he asked Barney.

'I can stay a while longer,' Tilly assured him. 'We can chat, but then I'd better get back to the shop.'

'Melissa used to love your little store,' Barney smiled, the folder about the ball cast aside for now. 'She spent a fortune in there.'

'That was then. She's not welcome in there after what she did to you. To both of you, leaving all of a sudden like that.'

'Now that's no way to talk,' Barney admonished. 'She's very special, she's had her problems along the way.'

'Maybe she'll leave soon,' Tilly suggested, 'before she can upset anyone else.'

'Tilly, it really is kind of you to look out for me, to be on my side, but I'm thrilled Melissa is back. Do me a favour and don't make it any harder for her than it already is. If you see her out and about, be kind.'

'Might be a bit late for that.'

'Oh dear. Maybe next time then.'

Harvey left them to it. He'd hoped that Barney could be talked around by Ashley and Tilly, but it seemed the only option they were floating around involved him, and that still didn't sound any better than when Melissa had suggested it in the first place.

*

Melissa had been back in the Cove a week and Jay had missed her incredibly.

'A week off on my own just wasn't the same,' he told her on the phone as she called him before she headed to the pub to meet Tracy. They'd finally lined up a girls' evening at The Copper Plough and Melissa hoped Tracy was looking forward to it as much as she was.

'But Bath would've been a change wouldn't it?' He'd gone with her suggestion of visiting his sister rather than hanging around Windsor missing his fiancée.

'Yeah, my sister was good company. Just not as good company as you. How's it all going with Barney? Have you persuaded him to exercise yet?'

Melissa had told Jay all about the difficulty of getting Barney to come around to the idea that exercise was a help not a hindrance in his recovery. 'Not really, but I'll get there.'

'You've only got two weeks left, do you think you can do it by the deadline?'

She cringed a little. 'About that … I'm thinking of staying longer.' She launched into a long explanation about the Wedding Dress Ball, how important it was to the locals and to Barney, and his reluctance to go through with it for the first time ever. 'Honestly, I've never seen him so down, so unlike himself.'

'I suppose you've been away a long time.'

'It's not that, it's just, well the event is important to him. I've no idea why, it just is.'

'Do you really think you staying will help?'

'I was wondering about stepping in to organise it?'

When he realised she was serious he said, 'Up to you, but for selfish reasons I want you to come home.'

'I know. And I will.' Eventually, when it felt right. She had to do this. She had to be here for Barney this time and not let him down ever again.

Jay did his best to show an interest, asked her what the ball had been like in years gone by. 'What about work?'

'I'll ask for some unpaid leave.' She'd already spoken with human resources but she didn't want Jay to think she hadn't factored him into the equation. 'I wouldn't do it if it wasn't such a desperate situation.'

They ended the call talking about his schedule for the next couple of weeks. Hopefully they'd work out some times to call and if not, at least email. It was hard being apart from each other. Even though they did it frequently, this time it was different, as though being here in the Cove was like being a part of a whole other world.

*

'This place hasn't changed at all,' said Melissa as she picked up her drink from the bar at The Copper Plough and she and Tracy went outside to find a table at the far end of the beer garden. 'The food is still top quality, I ate here the other night.'

'So I heard.'

'I'd forgotten how quickly word travels in Heritage Cove.' Melissa hooked one leg over the bench seat and then the other before sitting down, a glass of cold Chardonnay in front of her. The long, lazy summer evenings were well upon them and would last until the end of August before the seasons prepared to flip and bring autumnal beauty. The ash tree behind them would shed its leaves, which would remain green as they collected on the ground, adding another shade alongside the burnt oranges, deep browns, the golden. The beauty of somewhere like Heritage Cove was that it was surrounded by plenty of countryside as well as offering the added bonus of the water when you ventured down to the sea. Not that she'd managed to make it down there herself yet.

'Do you remember that time a whole load of us gathered up autumn leaves, piled them beneath one of the benches and jumped into them from the table top?' Tracy grinned.

'I remember Terry wasn't too happy about it.'

'I got told I was old enough to know better, I should've set an example.'

Melissa giggled at Tracy's impersonation of the landlord, the gruff voice she attempted. Tall Terry was how they'd known him back then and his height had scared the life out of the lot of them. But he wasn't menacing in the slightest, he was kind-hearted but had a presence that went well with running a pub. It meant he stood for no nonsense and it garnered him unspoken respect.

'Summer is a great season.' Melissa looked around them. 'But it's just as beautiful here in the Cove come autumn and winter.' Only locals dropped the 'Heritage' part of the name when they talk about the village, calling it simply, the Cove.

'I could never leave this place.' Tracy wasn't saying it in a way that suggested nobody else should either, but rather was looking around her and basking in the tranquillity offered by a pub garden, the smells of summer coming from the flowerbeds, the gentle clinking of cutlery as a family ate on the table a few over from theirs, the friendly banter between people out here enjoying the evening.

'I get it, I really do.' Melissa watched a butterfly settle at the end of the picnic bench where Tracy sat opposite her. It wasn't long before it decided not to join the conversation and fluttered off into the trees.

'Ignore me, I get very sentimental.'

'Nothing wrong with that.'

'I want to hear about you instead though. It's been so long.' Tracy's hand wrapped around the pint of cider she'd ordered, her skin disrupting the condensation on the outside of the glass.

'I know it's been a long time and I'm sorry, believe me.'

'I'm not looking for apologies right now, it's a catch-up I'd really like. Tell me, I know you're working for an airline, but what I don't know is: is it as exciting as I think it is?'

'It's very exciting in a lot of ways, but incredibly hard work too.'

'You travel the world, it must feel good to spread your wings.'

'It's a different life for sure and I've been lucky to see plenty of places.'

'Are you still living in London?'

117

'No, I rented there for a while, but then bought my own place in Windsor.'

Tracy's eyebrows lifted. 'With the royals?'

'Hardly,' she laughed. 'I'm in a one-bedroom flat.'

'With your boyfriend?'

'Jay has his own place, it's gorgeous. A Grade II listed townhouse in the same area and we spend most of our time there, but I've kept my flat.'

'Why? Can't be cheap to run two places.'

'I suppose I'm a little reluctant to make the leap, in case it doesn't work out. Pathetic, isn't it?'

'Of course not. I guess when it's right, you'll know.'

'He's been pestering me to move in for ages. I'm thinking I'll do it in time for Christmas.' She took out her phone and showed Tracy some photographs of the house, including the one last Christmas with the wreath on the door. Tied in a big red bow, it really did speak of the luxury inside, the place she was almost sure she was ready to call her home too.

'And what does Jay do?' Tracy asked.

'He's a pilot.'

'Now him, I approve of.' A grin spread across Tracy's face when Melissa showed her a photograph of Jay in his uniform. 'Is he as nice as he looks?'

'He really is.'

'You must miss him.'

'Of course. We were scheduled to have some time off together last week, but then Harvey got in touch…' She broke off at the mention of Harvey's name.

'You'd never have forgiven yourself if Barney had gone before you saw him again.'

Melissa hid behind her glass sipping her drink, the crisp liquid cooling as the words sank in. 'You're a hundred per cent right.'

'So why *did* you leave it so long?'

'When I first left I was angry that Harvey didn't come with me as we always planned. I was upset but then I became determined. I'd wanted to leave for a long time. After my parents died I almost broke apart.'

'I know.' She covered Melissa's hand with her own. 'Losing a parent is hard and you were hit with a double whammy.'

'I'm sorry I wasn't there for you when your mum died.'

'I know you had your reasons.'

'None good enough not to be there for a friend.'

'Now you'll get me all teary in a minute and I don't want that. And I had Giles and the kids, I wasn't on my own.'

'If Barney hadn't had the fall, I wouldn't be here now.'

'I suppose it must be what you call a blessing in disguise then,' said Tracy. 'And he's so glad you're back. He worried so much for you when you left. But he was also one of the few who didn't berate you for doing it.'

'Really?'

'Some people ranted about it, saying you'd upset him, you'd thrown his goodness in his face. They worried about Harvey, said he was too good for you.' She stopped.

'It's nothing I didn't expect so carry on.'

'With all the moaning that went on, Barney never once joined in. He didn't once say you shouldn't have done it, that you should have stayed.'

'Being here was painful. Every single day.' She gulped, the memories assaulting her from every angle. 'I had this unbearable sadness hovering over me like a fog

119

that never lifted. It stopped me seeing any of the good things. I'd walk along The Street and see Mum coming out of the bakery – I'm not suggesting it was a ghost of her, but I'd see someone who looked so much like her that for a moment my mind would trick me and it was like being pulled to the top of one of those big-drop amusement rides and then dropped down from a great height. Any moment when I felt like my parents were still here was like a giant slap in the face. Some days I'd dream Dad was downstairs in the kitchen at their cottage and I was in bed, woken by the sound of him tapping out a melody against his cup with a metal spoon, something he did every time he made a cup of tea. It used to drive me crazy when he did it. And when I woke up from those dreams, I'd sometimes even call out to tell him to stop it, before I realised it wasn't real.'

'Surely the pain followed you,' said Tracy. 'I know when I went on holiday, up to Scarborough, I still felt the loss of Mum enormously I barely wanted to go out some days. I felt so sorry for myself. All I wanted to do was talk to Mum and I had to make do with Giles. I told him that too,' she smiled, 'and he apologised for being such a poor consolation prize.'

'You're both still really happy?'

'We have our moments, every marriage does, but I love that man to bits.'

She almost told Tracy about the engagement then, touching her right hand to the fourth finger on her left. But she had to hold back, it would be more special when they had a ring to make it official.

Melissa waited for the family who'd been eating nearby to walk past their table and back towards the pub before she carried on. 'I guess being away from here, there were no constant reminders for me. I had to focus on finding my own way around a big city, I had to navigate the tube in London, which I'd never done before, and slowly the adventure distracted me enough to make me feel as though a weight had lifted. It was still there, of course, but a lot of the pain was eased. And then came the change of career. I lined up interviews for cabin crew and the application process kept me busy. Finally I wasn't turning street corners feeling sad – instead, I was full of hope. I felt that at last I could start over.'

'It sounds as though getting away really was the solution for you. Tell me, since you've been back, have you been down to the cove?'

'Not yet, but I will. I suppose I wanted to find my feet first.'

'And the cemetery?'

She toyed with a beer mat that looked as though it had already been fiddled with plenty of times. 'I'm not sure I can do it.'

'I know it'll never bring them back, but it might be nice to put some flowers there, sit a while.' Tracy didn't push it. She'd always been good at dishing out advice and then taking a step back to let you process. 'How's it going being around Harvey after all this time?'

'It's not been terrible, but we haven't talked, at least not properly. I think we're both afraid to. Like I said, I was angry at him for a long time for not leaving with me as we'd planned. I called a couple of times but he never answered and then I got so furious, I stopped trying.'

'You were punishing him.'

'Yes, I suppose I was. Maybe I needed to find myself on my own without someone holding me up. I think it made me stronger, does that make sense?'

'It does, but listen, he's not a bad man, quite the opposite. Try talking to him again.'

She nodded. 'Another drink?' She'd finished hers and found she was enjoying herself here as much as she'd hoped she would.

'Yes please.' Tracy grabbed Melissa's wrist before Melissa could pass by and go into the pub. 'This is nice, I've missed this.'

'You've no idea how much I've missed it too.'

When Melissa returned with the drinks and settled back into her spot she told Tracy, 'I came back, you know.'

The pint glass didn't reach Tracy's mouth. 'Here? To Heritage Cove? When? I never knew and nobody ever let on.'

'That's because nobody knew. No one saw me – I hired a car, I kept my head down.'

'What, so you drove into the village and straight out again?'

'Not quite. I pulled up near the bus stop trying to think of where I'd go first. And that was when I saw Harvey.'

'But he didn't see you?'

'No. He was in The Street, going about his life as though everything was normal. He was chatting and laughing away with Tilly. It was then that I realised perhaps he was better off without me. He'd never wanted to leave the Cove, not really. I instigated it and he went along with the plan because he loved me. His heart was never in it as much as mine was. I couldn't be selfish by turning up and begging him to come with me, and at the same time I couldn't stay in the Cove for him. It was as though with a new career and a new city

122

entirely I'd found a part of myself again. So I turned the car around and went straight back to London.'

Tracy was shaking her head. 'You never were one to hang around and ask for explanations.'

'That's because explanations usually involve excuses, explanations usually end up hurting someone. And I'd been hurt enough. I'd managed to stand on my own two feet, pull myself out of a deep, dark hole that I never wanted to disappear into again. I figured me driving away was probably best for everyone.'

'Harvey would've done anything for you.'

'And that was part of the problem. We both needed to be on our own to figure out what we really wanted, we needed to be ourselves for a while.'

'What a mess.'

'It was back then.'

'And it isn't now?'

'I'm with Jay, I've moved on. I suspect Harvey has too, although he hasn't mentioned a woman in his life.'

'There have been women along the way, I've seen him hanging out with several –'

'I don't need the details,' Melissa protested.

'He's never got serious about anyone else as far as I know.'

Perhaps Harvey not being with anyone was the hardest thing of all, it made her question the 'us' that they'd been once upon a time and it was difficult not to look for signs that something may still be there between them. Or was it no more than nostalgia playing tricks with her?

'So, how long are you staying?' Tracy asked after a good swig of her cider.

'Initially it was to be three weeks but I'm extending my stay.'

'Barney's recovery is going well, isn't it?'

'Physically, yes. But he's not himself.'

'You must be concerned if you're thinking of hanging around a while longer.'

'Barney's saying he doesn't want to do the Wedding Dress Ball this year.'

Tracy looked even more shocked than she had the day she saw Melissa in the street for the first time in years. 'You can't be serious. He does it every year and raises a lot of money for charity.'

'He's being really stubborn.'

Tracy laughed. 'You know, sometimes it's odd to think you two aren't related.'

'Very funny. But joking aside, I've never known him to be like this. Remember the time he dropped the planter pot that lives outside his front door onto the fingers of his left hand while he was attempting to move it?'

'Do I ever? He swore, and not quietly either.' They'd been helping hang the curtains Tracy's mum had made for his lounge windows, the sort with the insulated backing that would keep the heat in during the winter.

'Do you remember after he'd been to the hospital and they'd found one finger was broken, the other badly bruised, he was adamant he didn't need two women running around after him?'

'I do remember. I remember him going crazy at me when I saw him at the bus stop and offered to carry his groceries home. He was so mean, I cried my eyes out – pregnancy hormones at the time. He came to the house later with flowers and a box of chocolates and apologised.'

'My point is,' Melissa continued, 'he hates sitting back and letting anyone take the lead. Or at least he did.

124

Remember the Wedding Dress Ball the year I finished high school?'

'The one where gale-force winds saw warnings on the radio telling people not to venture out?'

'That's the one. He wouldn't accept it. He still had the ball, in the barn. It was as though it would be the end of the world if the event didn't go ahead.'

'I remember my mum talking about him being pig-headed,' Tracy recalled. 'She said he reminded her of my younger brother the year they cancelled the Wizard of Oz performance at the school because of snow. He wanted everyone to go there no matter the danger, he howled for days, I remember it myself.'

'I'm worried about Barney and this fall taking away his independence.'

'But he was up a ladder, could've happened to anyone.'

'Everyone else seems to know that apart from Barney, who sees it as a sign of worse to come, that it's the mark of the beginning of the end.'

'Sounds a bit dramatic.'

'I thought that too but now I'm not so sure. I've looked it up on the internet and his reaction is quite common in older people.'

'You know, investigating things on the internet is often asking for trouble. I made that mistake when Giles wasn't well last winter. I was horrified by all the things that he could have when it was a bad case of the flu combined with the worst cough I've ever known.'

'Are you sure it wasn't man flu?'

'No, he really was sick. And I honestly thought the worst after looking it up online.'

'But you agree, this isn't like Barney at all, right?'

'Of course I agree, and for selfish reasons I want that ball to go ahead. This year I've dieted enough that I'll easily get into my wedding dress – might need a bit of padding around the boob area – and Giles has taken up running so is already looking forward to pulling on his tux.'

'You won't be the only ones disappointed. I think if this event doesn't go ahead, it'll have a worse effect on him than he realises. I did mention to Harvey about taking over the organising, but already Barney has said he doesn't want it in the barn.'

'At least you're here with him now – that's got to help, surely. Perhaps he'll come round about running the ball.'

Melissa smiled, until it dawned on her. 'Unless…'

'Unless what?'

'Unless it's like they say, you know, when someone is dying they hang on to see those they love before they let go.'

'Enough of that talk. And you know what? If you're extending your stay it means you can come to the ball.'

'If it happens.'

'I'm sure Barney can't be serious about not having it this year.'

'I'm afraid he is. He's already on about cancelling things.'

'Then you'll have to step up, you owe it to him. And yes, I am trying to guilt you into it.'

'It's working.'

Tracy stood and picked up her pint. 'Come on, let's get some crisps, I'm starving. And it's getting chilly out here. We'll go inside and you can tell me what you're planning to wear to the ball this year, because mark my words, this event will go ahead.'

She was right. This ball had to run or Barney would regret it, and perhaps stepping in to ensure it did would go some way to making up for the hurt she'd caused.

Chapter Six

This morning the heavens had opened and shrouded the village in a damp cloud that didn't appear to want to shift. Not that you'd know it now, as Harvey returned to Tumbleweed House after his early-morning start on a loft-conversion project. He unloaded his tools from the back of his pickup beneath a bright sky now that the sun had emerged from whichever cloud it had been hiding behind. The only sign of the questionable weather was the waxy leaves on the bushes that still held drops of rain in their palms.

As Harvey walked up to the front door he could hear Winnie's tail thwacking against the other side of the wood. Winnie, predictably, launched herself at Harvey the moment he opened up and he crouched down in the doorway, his face in the dog's fur, his hands ruffling Winnie's coat the way she liked. Local girl Gracie, who lived at Hollyhock Cottage, was on hand to come in and walk Winnie on days when Harvey had to work longer hours than expected, and at least it gave the dog a change of scene.

'You missed me, I know you did,' he laughed, still fussing over Winnie. He'd be back out soon, to go and check on Barney, see if he could coax him into at least trying to follow the rehabilitation program. Talking with his mum yesterday as they sat in her gloriously sunny courtyard behind the tiny cottage she now lived in, he'd listened to Carol Luddington's opinion that Barney just needed time. She'd always approved of her son's bond with Barney, the man who'd been a father to him when he'd needed a positive male influence in his life. He certainly hadn't had that from his own dad or his brother.

Filling a glass of water at the tap in the kitchen, he told Winnie, 'You can come with me to Barney's, if you behave and don't get in the way.' Winnie had already been out today, he knew because Gracie had texted, but she loved company. She'd been a rescue dog and he figured she'd had enough rough days along the way, so now he wanted to spoil her. But the last thing he wanted was for her to trip Barney up if she got excited and playful. He'd never forgive himself if Barney landed up in hospital all over again.

A gentle tap on the front door announced a visitor but Winnie was already on it and Melissa didn't flinch when the dog ran straight at her.

'Not interrupting, am I?' She'd crouched down to fuss Winnie, who now had a fresh, captive audience. Melissa had always loved dogs, Harvey remembered. She'd once taken in a stray, convinced she would need to give it a home, only to find it belonged to someone who'd come into the village earlier that day and the dog had wandered off. There had been tears when she'd had to return the canine to its rightful owner. She got attached quickly. Shame she was also capable of detaching at the same speed.

'Not at all. What brings you here?' He pushed the toolbox he'd brought inside further under the wooden bench in the porch, out of the way.

'I need to talk to you and thought a house call was better than over the phone.' Her voice followed him as he walked back through to the kitchen.

129

'Fair enough. Come on in.' Having her in his space felt odd but he distracted himself by freshening up Winnie's bowl of water. From the corner of his eye he saw Melissa sit down at the battered oak table running parallel to the bench that looked out onto the gravel courtyard and the fields beyond Tumbleweed House. On the same bench was the butler's sink that added character to the property, and above the island that separated him from the table and Melissa hung the same period wrought-iron saucepan rack that had been here since the day he first invited Melissa over and his mum made them elderberry milkshakes as their short legs dangled from the now-tatty chairs with the same patina as the table. Melissa had thought it was fancy having all your pots and pans hanging up – he'd thought it was an odd thing to notice, but he hadn't cared, he was just happy he had a friend over and his father wasn't around.

'What's her name?' Melissa still only had eyes for the dog. Perhaps it was her way of dealing with the awkwardness of coming to the place where he lived after all this time.

'This is Winnie,' he smiled, glad of the shift of focus too. 'Can I get you something to drink?'

'That would be lovely, thank you.'

'Tea? Or coffee? Or I could do you an elderberry tea.'

She looked surprised. 'I never thought…'

'That I'd keep up an interest in the elderberry bushes?'

'Well…yes. I assumed that side of things would stop.'

'Never, it's part of this place.'

'I suppose it is.' Memories hung between them until he broke the silence.

'Mum still enjoys coming over when the berries are ready to pick, we do it together.'

'How is she?'

He thought about how his mum had tried to read his face earlier when he mentioned Melissa's name. He'd shut her down quickly enough, he didn't need to rake over the past – at least not with anyone other than Melissa. 'She's good, settled in her own cottage now rather than pottering around in this place. And she's finally free of my father, so enough said...'

'I'm glad she's happy.'

'She asked after you, she heard you were back in the village. She always liked you, you know that,' he added when a strange look crossed her face. 'Mum isn't one to hold a grudge, no need to worry about that if you bump into her.'

Relieved, she accepted the offer of elderberry tea. 'I remember your mum talking about how elderberries –'

'Boost your immune system,' he finished for her with a chuckle. 'She said that all winter long. Who knows if it ever worked. But I've maintained the bushes, the berries are picked in season and dried out before freezing so we have plenty of supplies year-round.'

He set about the task of making her a cup of elderberry tea. He put a few teaspoons of dried elderberries into a glass teapot he didn't often use but brought out if he had a guest, which he supposed she qualified as. He added a cinnamon stick the same way his mum always did, topped it up with boiling water and while it had a chance to steep on the table, found out two decent china cups. The last time he'd done this was about a month ago when Barney was convinced he was getting a summer cold. He'd come round for what was locally known as the Luddington go-to winter remedy even though the sun was almost on its highest rung of the ladder to the sky, the days were long, with not even a hint of autumn in the air.

'Have you done much to the house?' Melissa asked.

'Nothing major. I repainted, carried out a few repairs, redid the floor in here, and the loft is a great additional space of course. I still go up there to listen to the rain hammering down on the roof some days.' She'd know his memories of the loft and hiding out from his dad, he'd told her about it more than once.

While he poured the tea she went to the kitchen window and gazed out beyond the elderflower bushes to where trees lined the rear of the land that then dipped down so you couldn't see any further. 'It feels as though you're in the middle of nowhere.'

'That's what I love about living here.' He took both cups over to the table.

The second Melissa came to sit down again Winnie put a paw up onto her knee, demanding attention. Melissa put her hands either side of Winnie's face and rubbed beneath her chin and around her ears.

'Just tell me if she's annoying you,' he said.

'Not at all. She's got a lovely temperament from what I can see. I'll bet she misses you when you're at work every day.'

'I think she does.' He laughed as Winnie rolled over and Melissa was prompted to bend down and rub her tummy. 'She's got you wrapped around her little finger…or should I say paw?'

'She's adorable.'

'She loves company. I have Gracie on hand to take her out for walks when I'm working longer hours, so that works well.'

'Gracie from Hollyhock Cottage?' She gave an appreciative nod when she tried the tea.

'You remember her?'

'Of course, she was finishing school and started work in the pub from what I remember.'

'Well, she's no longer at the pub, she's working in Cambridge three days a week as well as studying.'

'Good for her.'

'So she can get away from the small-village life, you mean?'

'Harvey, I –'

He sighed, irritated by his stupid comment. He wished he was better at letting things go rather than bottling them up. He guessed he'd got used to doing that when he was a kid and the habit had followed him. 'That was unnecessary, I apologise.'

'I came to talk some more about Barney.' Winnie nudged her arm again and she laughed, this time focused on her tea while it was still hot.

'I am sorry, it must be the long days. In the winter she's happy to be inside by the fire, but in the summer she wants to be out all the time.'

'Like someone else,' Melissa remembered.

Thrown by her recollection of something else she knew about him, a part of his character, he focused his own attention on Winnie and got her a treat from the cupboard. Melissa was totally right, though, he'd loved to be outside as a kid, a teen, and still to this day. During the long summers of his childhood Harvey had left the house the second he woke, only going home when it was almost his curfew, and when his dad was away working he'd relished the freedom, staying out until night fell. His mum had given him free rein, knowing how imprisoned they all felt with his father around.

133

'We could take Winnie for a walk,' Melissa suggested, finishing off her tea. 'It's a lovely day for it now.'

'Winnie wouldn't care if it wasn't…Gracie took her out in the belting rain this morning, said she loved every second.'

'You strange thing,' Melissa told Winnie. Her hair caught a shaft of sunlight, making it glow a deep red as she bent down again to rub the dog's tummy. 'What do you say, Winnie? Walk?'

'Oh, you've done it now.' Winnie's tail was thumping against the floor, head raised, eyes looking from him to Melissa and back again. 'Never mention the W word unless you're totally serious.'

'Of course I'm serious.'

Maybe a walk was a good idea. They could talk at the same time and it would certainly be a lot less awkward than this. He finished up his cup of elderberry tea too, the rest in the pot would keep. 'Winnie, it's your lucky day.' All it took was picking up the lead and the jangle of the chain to send Winnie into a frenzy, chasing her own tail in excitement. When she was in this mood, getting the lead on wasn't all that easy, but finally they bundled out of Tumbleweed House.

'May I?' Melissa asked, hand outstretched for the lead Winnie was tugging on in her enthusiasm.

'Go for it, she's strong though.'

Laughing, she agreed, as Winnie tugged her forwards and she wound the lead tighter. 'Slow down, Winnie, anyone would think you'd never been outside.'

'Have you been down to the cove yet?' Harvey asked when they reached the top of the lane that led from his home up to The Street. On the left was the candle shop, on the right the tea rooms, and opposite was the chapel, adjacent to which lay the path they'd followed so often down to the sand and the sea together.

She cleared her throat. 'Not yet. Is it still the same?'

'Of course it is. Not much changes around here.'

'I wondered whether flocks of tourists had found it.'

They began to cross over. 'I think the brambles usually put them off, especially the lazy ones who won't go anywhere without a car. Most tourists favour the car park further on from the village and the nice easy walk down to the beach.' He surreptitiously glanced at her. 'Why the hesitation about going down there? Don't tell me you're a city chick and you can't clamber down to the sand anymore.'

'Of course not. Just been a long time, that's all.'

They'd often raced down there, laughing and panting hard by the time they jumped onto the golden sands. But he had to remember the pain she'd been in when she left the village, the reminders she faced being here every day. She'd hurt him by leaving and never coming back, and it was easy to be encompassed by that rather than anything else, but he could tell by her reaction to his question that this was harder than he'd realised it might be for her.

As they reached the top of the track he decided distraction was a good idea. 'Can I interest you in an ice-cream? I've got some cash in my pocket. My treat.'

'Sounds good to me.'

Melissa met Zara, who ran the ice-creamery, and with a chocolate honeycomb for each of them they set off for the cove.

'I wonder who bought the old shop,' Harvey speculated, briefly turning to glance back past the bus stop at the almost hidden derelict building at the far side of a big patch of grass. Zara had been talking with another customer about the place that had once sold buckets and spades, inflatables, and other beach paraphernalia.

'You'll have to keep me informed of any developments.'

The reminder she wasn't back here permanently was sobering. 'Here, hold this.' Harvey handed his ice-cream to Melissa while he removed Winnie's lead. 'She's good to go from here.'

'She knows where she's going,' Melissa laughed, watching Winnie run off as fast as her legs could carry her. The sound of her laughter rolled with the breeze that already carried with it the smell of the sea, the distant swoosh of the waves, the screech of the gulls.

'I bring her down here a lot. She's had me panic more than once, running into the water.'

Harvey led the way, battling the brambles and careful not to let them ping back in Melissa's direction. Although he came down to the cove often he hadn't come here with Melissa in a long while and already it felt different. This had always been their special place. It was where she'd come to grieve after her parents died, where he'd come to yell away his frustrations over his father, a place they'd shared a romantic picnic of croissants, fresh cream and strawberry jam as a surprise for him when he'd landed his first job. He could still remember Melissa shrieking when a seagull snatched his croissant from his hand. She said the seagull had ruined the picnic; he thought it had made it. To see the expressions on her face had always got to him in a way he couldn't explain. And the night he hadn't gone with her as planned, when he hadn't met her at the bus stop to leave Heritage Cove behind, he hadn't seen the look of

136

sheer disappointment on her face but he hadn't had to, it had still been embedded in his mind ever since.

The track got even narrower as they went the same way as Winnie. The sounds of the sea, the salty tang in the breeze grew stronger the closer they got. There was nothing like it. He'd thought that back when he and Melissa floated ideas of cities around the world they could visit – London, Tokyo, New York, Paris, Sydney – the beaches they could lie on in France, Spain, the Maldives if they were lucky. Their list had been endless but when circumstances had forced him to stay in the village he'd realised that he hadn't been all that sorry. He would always regret the way he'd let Melissa down, but at the same time he'd had to let her go. She might have resented him if he hadn't because, given how long she'd been gone, it was clear she was more suited to a life away from Heritage Cove than he ever would be.

He stopped at the best vantage point to look out at the sea as it broke and crashed down below on the shore. Finishing up his ice-cream, he turned to Melissa when she came to his side brushing away a few crumbs from her cone that had fallen on her top. He tried to ignore the soft wisp of sweet-smelling hair that blew against his cheek when she stood close enough to share the view, the waft of light and flirty perfume he didn't recognise.

He started to head on down when Winnie, impatient, bounded back up to get them both, tongue hanging out with exertion. 'Come down when you're ready,' he told Melissa, venturing further to follow the crooked path down towards the sands. Narrow, uneven with small rock formations catching the least suspecting out, there was a rickety wooden rail on one side that probably wouldn't do much if you reached out and expected it to hold your weight, but Harvey didn't need it anyway, he knew this place too well.

By the time Melissa joined him on the sands he was on to the third game of throwing a stick for Winnie to retrieve and bring back to her master.

Melissa took off her sandals to feel the cool water between her toes. 'I'd forgotten how beautiful it is down here.' The cove, despite its restricted entrance leading the way here, opened up to a wide oval coastal inlet with golden sands and a calm, shallow sea that only got deeper when you waded farther away from the beach.

'You must see stunning beaches all the time.'

'I've seen plenty, but travelling takes it out of you. The time between flights isn't always long either.'

He threw the stick again and this time watched Winnie take it over to her rather than him. 'Thanks, Winnie, nice to see where your loyalties lie.'

She laughed but picked it up and threw it in the other direction. 'She's a great dog, I'd love to have one eventually.'

'Might not fit in with the job.'

'No, it wouldn't.'

They had the whole cove to themselves, the way it had been more times than Harvey could remember. The way they liked it. And when she stood smiling, face tipped up to the sun, it shocked him back to the day he'd gone to London after her, many months on from when she'd left. Tracy had heard from Melissa, had her new address, and he went to find her – if only to explain why he hadn't gone through with their plan, why he'd kept his distance for so long, and the reasons he needed to stay in the Cove. He'd been about to cross the road when he saw her come out and stand on the top step leading up to a house that was probably made up of several flats.

Head tilted up exactly like it was now, she was smiling at a man, she kissed him, their bodies close, before waving him goodbye. Harvey had frozen on the spot, she hadn't seen him, and so he'd left. She had a new life and one he wasn't a part of. He'd gone back to Heritage Cove, asked Tracy not to mention his little trip, and he'd done his best to move on.

'So…Barney,' Melissa began, throwing the stick once again for Winnie. 'How do you think he's doing?'

'Same as last time we had this discussion.'

'Exactly as I thought. I haven't mentioned us organising the Wedding Dress Ball to him yet.'

'Whoa, hang on a minute, who said we were definitely doing that?'

'Please, Harvey, I think this is the only way the ball will go ahead and I also think he needs the event as much as everyone else does.' She turned to face him, one hand holding back the lengths of hair that the wind insisted on wrapping across her face. His hand twitched and almost reached out to lift her hair and hook it behind her ear for her.

He didn't argue because, he suspected, she was right. 'You're not the only one to suggest I help,' he admitted. 'Tilly and Ashley both seem to be thinking along the same lines.'

'Barney agreed to it? He'll let it go ahead if he doesn't have to be the one organising?'

'None of us agreed to anything and I haven't mentioned it since. I didn't want to upset him, you know what he's like.'

'He does seem to get wound up when the topic of conversation isn't one he approves of.'

He grinned. 'I never thought I'd see the day he'd tire of any topic of conversation.'

'Me neither. And I want to ask him more about that dress too. Don't you think it's weird?'

'I do, but don't go there, I'm telling you. The look on his face the day I asked is one I'll never forget. Whatever he's hiding, he doesn't want any of us to know.'

'I really think it might give us some answers though.' She picked up the stick and threw it for Winnie yet again. 'He was a bit odd last time I was there too.'

'In what way?'

'It started when I accidentally knocked the model ship off the mantelpiece. I caught it just in time, but when I was dusting the shelves in the kitchen I looked over at him and he had it on his lap as though it was precious, as though it has memories attached with it.'

'He used to sail, I suppose that's why.' He let the calming sounds of the sea wash over them both. As much as he was worried about Barney, one of the positive things to come out of all of this was that the shared common ground when it came to the man who was so important to them both was helping to bridge the distance between him and Melissa. They weren't focused on what had happened between them, they were too busy trying to move things forward for Barney, and he wasn't all that sorry.

A memory came to him. 'Do you remember when you were younger, burning your hands on the rope that used to hang from the tree beside the barn?'

'How could I forget?' She clasped the palm of her hand instinctively even though the mishap had happened a long while ago. 'It hurt like hell. Barney took me inside, washed my hand, applied some special lotion. He started talking about sailing and the ropes that would chafe his hands, how he dealt with his skin afterwards. I could see the love he had for boats, he told me how much time he'd spent in a local marina as a boy.'

'He hasn't mentioned any of that to me for years. When I was building the stage in the barn, he talked about it a lot. He told me about hauling boats out onto the water, the strength needed to sail, how he was frustrated his strength wasn't what it used to be. But then, it was as though something clicked and he stopped talking about it just like that.' He threw the stick for Winnie this time. 'What else did you think was odd about him the other day, apart from his staring at the model ship?'

'He started saying how he understood exactly why I'd left the Cove. He told me I shouldn't put off making peace with those I love. He said "My biggest regret is that I didn't try harder".'

'Try harder with what?'

'I've got no idea. But then he told me not to do the same, he said he lost something and it was his own fault, he hadn't fought hard enough and he'd let his pain get in the way of everything else. I was so focused on not talking about the reasons I left, my own pain, that I moved the conversation on. It was only later on that I wondered what he'd meant by all of it and what he hasn't told us. Because it's obvious now that there's something. You don't think...'

'What?'

'Perhaps he lost someone in a sailing accident – it would explain the sadness and the way he's had that model ship in prime position ever since I've known him.'

'Most people would keep a photograph front and centre if that was the case, surely.'

'You're right. I keep Mum and Dad's photograph in a frame beside my bed in my flat.' Her voice caught. 'Maybe I'm grasping at straws with all this.'

'Maybe. But only Barney can tell us the truth.' He took a deep breath and let it out on a sigh. 'He's said he doesn't want to talk about the dress and it looks like the same goes for the marina. I don't think we should push it, not while he's in his current state of mind anyway.'

'No, I suppose not.' She hooked her hair behind her ears again but it didn't want to stay put in this wind.

'The fall has changed him. He's detached, he sits in that chair way too often.'

'When I'm with him I'm torn between letting him recuperate and nagging him to move,' she admitted. 'Then I think about mentioning the dress and the letter that was written to him, but I'm not brave enough. I guess now I'm here I don't want anything to come between us.' Winnie brought the stick back, dropped it at her feet and then settled down on the sands, gnawing at the wood. 'Perhaps I'm making more out of that dress than there actually is. I mean, it could be a spare for a guest at the ball, couldn't it?'

His expression said otherwise. 'Doesn't explain the letter.'

'I wish I'd read all of it.'

'I felt bad that we were prying, it felt wrong.'

'Do you ever wonder whether he was married once? He's never said, not in the whole time we've known him, but he must have had someone special at some point.'

'He probably has, but not everyone ends up married. Some people would be better off if they weren't.' His mum certainly would've been. 'It doesn't mean there's some mystery we need to solve.' He took a step back as the sea crept a little closer along the shore line. A seagull circled up again, higher and higher until it reached the path they'd followed to get down here. 'Apart from asking Barney, I don't see how we can find out anything more.'

'I think that if we found out more about the dress, we'd find out why he started the Wedding Dress Ball in the first place. It wasn't something either of us ever questioned, but what if it's what's holding him back now? What if it isn't just the fall, or old age, what if it's something buried in his past that still has a hold of him? Maybe he won't be right until he lets it go.'

'Perhaps we should leave it be. Maybe we don't have the right to snoop.'

'I don't want to snoop either. I want to respect his privacy but at the same time I want him to be back to his old self, and I don't think he can be unless he sorts his head out.'

'Are you that convinced there's something lurking in the background?'

'I honestly believe that whatever it was that made Barney start up the Wedding Dress Ball in the first place is the key to all of this. And if we understand his reasons, we may be able to get through to him and make him realise what the event means to him, why he can't give up on it or anything else.'

He didn't miss the sheen of tears in her eyes. His arm lifted briefly, he almost reached out to her but at the last second he drew his hand firmly to his side.

'I'm convinced there was a Mrs Barney once upon a time,' she went on.

'Your imagination is running away with you. But I suppose it's possible.'

'See,' she grinned, 'you agree.'

143

'And maybe,' he said with as much seriousness as he could find, 'maybe he got rid of her, perhaps she's buried in the old barn and he runs the ball every year to dance on her grave.'

In true Melissa style she gritted her teeth and stomped away back towards the steps. 'If you're not going to take me seriously I won't bother talking to you anymore.'

'I'm sorry,' he called after her, he'd only been trying to add a bit of humour into the moment. She looked like she was getting all wound up and worried and her homecoming or whatever this was shouldn't be like that. 'Come on, Winnie,' he said when he realised Melissa wasn't going to stop and wait.

*

Melissa had forgotten how pig-headed Harvey could be but she couldn't be too annoyed when Winnie caught her up and trotted by her side. She stopped before they reached the road, waited for Harvey to put Winnie's lead back on, and together they all set off for Tumbleweed House.

Harvey reheated the elderberry tea and poured both of them another cup as Melissa tried again to work out a way forwards with Barney. She was well aware she wasn't going to be here all that long. 'I don't want to leave without knowing he's back to normal.'

'I get it, you have a timeframe,' said Harvey. 'But not everything can work to your timetable.'

'I wouldn't even suggest that it could.' She refused to rise to it. She wished he'd just come out with it and tell her what he was thinking, but as usual he kept it all in. 'I've extended my stay, which means I'll be around for the ball. I've taken unpaid leave, booked in for longer at the Heritage Inn, I'm doing everything I can. I just want

144

that ball to go ahead, see if it's the secret ingredient to get our Barney back.'

Phrasing it that way seemed to calm Harvey down. 'I hope you're right. And it's good you're staying, for Barney I mean. He'll be happy about that if nothing else.'

She relaxed a little with fewer accusations flying her way, whether in words or the way he looked at her. Sometimes it was hard to guess what he was thinking. 'It's the talk of the old folks' home that scares me the most,' she confessed. 'I saw a brochure for Aubrey House residential care home at his place, it must've come through the door.'

Harvey shook his head. 'He asked Tilly to have her friend who works there drop it round.'

Her heart sank. 'I didn't realise he'd requested it.'

'He's still our Barney, whatever happens,' said Harvey. 'Perhaps it's you and I who need to accept that things change.' He laughed at his own remark when he saw her reaction. 'Didn't think for one minute you'd agree with me.'

She let out a groan of frustration and gave her tea another stir to mix in the tiny pieces of dried elderberry that had slipped through the strainer.

'Trying to persuade Barney to do the rehabilitation exercises is impossible,' Harvey went on. 'Have you had any luck at all?'

'What do you think?'

'If he does them, he'll feel better, and if he feels better, he'll be back to himself. It's a vicious circle he's stuck in.'

'Look, I know you don't want to, but I really think we need to step up and take on the task of the Wedding Dress Ball. If it was already suggested to you it means he'll be on board, and I can't see him objecting to my help.'

He groaned. 'How did I know you were going to mention that again?'

'Because you know I'm right. If we tell him we'll take on all the work to get the barn ready, he won't have to do anything, he might just agree.'

'You know there was a time he would've hated not being involved.'

'And maybe that time will come again, but this year it'll be down to us.'

'I haven't got a clue where to start.'

He looked about as panicked as any other man left in charge of an enormous wedding-related event. 'We'll manage.' She smiled tentatively, unsure whether he was going to agree or push her away. Since she'd arrived and bumped into him on and off, she'd found herself permanently trying to read his moods, his reactions, his words. She put down her empty tea cup. 'I know you may not believe me, but I have felt guilty over the years, about not seeing him.' She felt guilty about not seeing Harvey too, but talking about that was much more difficult. She still wasn't ready to tell him how she'd felt a part of her ripped away when she left, then how let down she'd felt that he hadn't gone through with their plan. She wasn't ready to admit how she'd pictured him by her side many a time enjoying a new life away from Heritage Cove, one she'd pined for and thought he'd wanted too.

'Why don't we both go over to Barney's and start making firm plans?' she suggested when a tiny muscle in his jaw tensed and he made no further comment. 'No time like the present. I just hope he hasn't officially cancelled everything already or it'll make our job so much harder. And the barn…I mean, it looked fine when I saw it the other day, but is it in a good state of repair or is there work that needs carrying out?'

She almost jumped out of her skin when his hands settled on her shoulders reassuring her. 'One step at a time. First, I'll pick us up a sandwich each from the bakery.'

'Sounds good to me. It is lunchtime after all.' She sounded hopeless, giving away the effect his touch had on her.

'Then we'll go to Barney's. I need to inspect the barn and work on fixing up a couple of wobbly beams, check there's nothing else to take care off. It'll need to be one hundred per cent safe for the ball.'

'It's hard to believe we once climbed up onto those beams,' she whispered, still aware of his touch. 'I doubt kids would do that now. I have a friend in London who has twins and she's fussing over them all the time, I can't imagine her ever letting them run loose in a barn with an old man for company.' She was rambling, nerves getting the better of her.

'We had a good childhood. The Cove saw to that.' He finally took his hands away and it felt strange to no longer be beneath his touch.

But it was time to go to Barney's now. And she only hoped their plan would work out, that the both of them organising the ball, might just be the key to getting Barney back to being himself.

147

Chapter Seven

'How are you feeling?' Melissa asked Barney the second they arrived at his cottage.

Barney didn't answer at first, he was too busy looking behind her at Harvey coming in through the back door not long after she did. 'I'm fine, but what are you two up to?'

'We've come to see you, of course,' Harvey replied.

'Together?' He looked doubtful.

'We've been talking,' Melissa explained.

'About time.'

'Talking about you, she means,' Harvey clarified.

Barney grumbled, 'It sounds like you've come to nag me some more and you think that if you both do it together, it might work. Well, I'll tell you now –'

'Just hear us out,' Harvey interrupted.

'It's about the Wedding Dress Ball,' Melissa began.

'I've told you, not happening this year. What's the point? It's a lot of hard work, I can't face people being everywhere, invading this place.'

Harvey sat on the chair to the side of him, leaning forwards, arms along his thighs. 'How about we run the entire event?'

'Now that's ridiculous. You weren't interested the other day when Ashley tried to suggest it to you,' he directed at Harvey. 'And you're going back home before it'll even take place,' he said to Melissa.

'I've already extended my stay and cleared it with work,' she explained.

Barney couldn't hide his surprise. 'And you're intending to work on this together?'

'As crazy as it sounds, yes.' Harvey sat on the arm of the sofa.

'Ridiculous,' Barney countered.

'Hey, it's not that bad an idea,' said Melissa. 'We're both grown adults, we both know the event well enough.'

'I don't think it's a good idea, you'd argue or not talk. It's not easy to coordinate, you know. And it's too late now, I left it too late.'

'Since when did you give up?' Melissa demanded.

Barney shrugged and shut his eyes as he listened to Harvey suggest they got a bit of paper and a pen to write down what needed doing. Melissa had already pulled out a chair at the table that had one end folded down and was only opened up when there were more guests.

Barney stayed where he was. 'I'm comfortable right here,' he said from the armchair.

'Not to worry.' Harvey's rummaging in the bureau produced a notepad and a pen. 'Melissa and I will sit here at the table and you listen in, we'll need your input.'

'Suppose I could do that.'

'What's the first thing we need to do?' Harvey asked. 'The date is set, but do people think it's cancelled?'

'I may have started spreading the word.'

Melissa wrote down at the top of the paper, 'Re-publicise'. They'd need to make sure everyone knew the ball was in no way cancelled. 'Have you issued any refunds yet, Barney?'

'No, all the money is still safely stashed away. I just hadn't got around to dealing with it.'

'Good, one less thing to think about,' said Harvey. 'But we'll need to quash any rumours, make sure we publicise enough that we sell even more tickets to people who were hesitating until now. Most of the village residents jump right in and get a ticket but people who pass through might grab one later on, a few extra sales won't go amiss to cover costs and raise even more for the charity.'

'Do you have a list of people coming already?' Melissa asked.

'There's a folder in the bureau, the list is in there,' Barney told her. 'You might want to get the word out quickly that the ball is on or people could make other plans, then want their money back, which creates a whole load of admin to deal with.'

'Don't worry, we've got this.' But Melissa exchanged a doubtful look with Harvey. She'd never been up for organising large events, she panicked in case she forgot something, and Barney, although injecting the odd comment, wasn't exactly enthused with all of this or buoying them along. 'And if people have made alternative plans,' she went on, 'then they can unmake them.'

'Bossy,' said Harvey, but with a smile as he found the folder.

'We'll need music.' She picked up the pen to add it to the list.

'Cancelled,' said Barney from his assumed position in the armchair.

Harvey frowned and rifled through the folder to find the contact information. They went through the other details too: flowers to decorate the barn, a suitable raffle prize, raffle tickets, which would have to be sold before the event, catering, portaloos to be delivered and go behind the barn.

'We also need a cake,' Harvey sighed. 'There's always a cake,' he smiled at Melissa.

'Cancelled,' Barney called over.

Melissa shook her head. 'Add it to the list.' The list was already long enough. It was going to keep them busy and again she felt guilty about all the time she'd be spending away from Jay. Perhaps she'd send him a nice long email later before she fell asleep. That way it didn't matter if he was working or sleeping, he could enjoy it when he was ready.

When she and Harvey had at last compiled the list of everything that had to be done to organise the Wedding Dress Ball this year, they played board games with Barney, they talked about the ball, and if Melissa wasn't mistaken Barney's spirits did appear to have lifted a little already by the time she took charge of cooking dinner for them all. Maybe she'd been right all along, this event was going to be what brought the real Barney back to them.

*

The next day, Harvey went to have flyers for the event made up ready for a leaflet drop to remind people the ball would be happening and to drum up new ticket sales. Melissa headed for the bakery after she finished chatting with Jay who would shortly be flying off to Singapore. She'd emailed Jay last night and this morning they'd had a FaceTime call. He'd told her off for apologising yet again that she wouldn't be home for a few weeks and he seemed happy enough himself as he prepared to go to work, which made her feel much better about being away for so long.

Unfortunately, before she could open the door to the bakery, Melissa bumped straight into Tilly, who emerged from inside with a wrapped sandwich she'd just bought. It didn't look as though Tilly had mellowed in any way since they'd last crossed paths and so Melissa disappeared inside without a word, ready to sort out the predicament of a celebration cake for the ball.

'Welcome home,' said Jade with a smile.

'Thanks, Jade.' She told her all about Barney's lack of interest and subsequent change of heart, and she asked about the possibility of doing a cake in time for the event.

Jade's lips twisted awkwardly. 'I want to help, I really do, but I'm not sure I can.'

'But he gets the cake from here every year.'

'These things take a lot of planning and time.'

Melissa wondered whether the welcome-home greeting and smile had all been for show. 'Is this about me?'

Jade came around to the front of the counter, hooking her black bobbed hair behind both ears. She still had the freckles she'd had since childhood, across the bridge of her nose and peppering those high cheek bones. Kind green eyes understood Melissa's distress. 'We all love Barney, but we all think a lot of you too, and leaving couldn't have been easy after everything you went through. Please, don't think I'm being difficult because of anything you've done.'

Melissa sighed heavily. 'I'm sorry, it's just I really want this to go smoothly.'

'I know you do. I'd normally have started making the cake about now, but as soon as Barney cancelled I took on other commitments. It's a busy time of the year for weddings, the summer.'

Melissa's heart sank. 'Do you know anyone else who could help? I don't mind driving somewhere, working with a bakery outside the village.'

'I suspect other bakeries will be in the same situation, some plan much further ahead than I do.' She hesitated a moment. 'Wait here a minute, let me see what I can do.' She went out back and returned with a ledger, bits of paper sticking out everywhere. She opened it up against her red apron with its sprinkling of flour dust and ran her fingers thoughtfully down one of the pages. 'There's a chance…'

'Really?' Melissa's hopes soared and she clasped her hands against her chest.

'Yes, I think I might just be able to squeeze you in. I don't mind putting in some late evenings to get it done,' she nodded, 'as long as you promise it won't be cancelled again.'

Melissa threw her arms around Jade. 'It won't be, I swear to you.'

Jade flipped through the same ledger, to the back. 'You're lucky, I still have the details in case the event went ahead next year.'

'At least that's one thing off my mind.'

'You don't have long to get everything ready, are you sure you're up for it?'

'Completely, one hundred per cent in.'

'It'll be good to have you around for a while longer. And even better when Barney is back to himself, walking down The Street, bossing us all around.'

'I hope he's back to doing that soon.' Melissa hated hearing that others also thought Barney had changed since his fall, but it was all the more reason to ensure this event went off without a hitch. 'What's the cake going to be like?' she ventured now she knew this part of the conundrum was sorted.

'You know Barney, he could get a more impressive cake elsewhere but he wanted to keep it local. We went for a very simple strawberries-and-cream cake.'

'The taste of summer, as always,' Melissa smiled. 'Barney said that in the early years of running the ball he'd put out a traditional white-iced fruit cake but he always had a lot left over after the event. On a whim he tried something different and never looked back.'

'That's right,' Jade remembered. 'We've made lemon drizzle, there was a peaches-and-cream cake once, and another year it was a lemon-and-elderflower cake.'

'I'll confirm exact numbers when we've spread the word that the event is still on.'

'Great, but for now I'll base it on the numbers from before plus extras in case. And between you and me, there's no way anyone will back out. Barney is well-loved around here, and the same goes for the ball. It's one of the best fundraisers out there. If you have some flyers, bring one in and I'll pop it in the window.'

'That would be amazing. Harvey is off getting them printed now, I'll drop one in.'

'Bring a whole pile, I'll hand them out to customers.'

'Thank you. Perhaps we'll get some interest from outside the village as well.'

Jade was more sceptical. 'It's good to see new faces unless you get the rowdy lot we had in three years back. Almost wrecked the barn, they did. We would've had to call the police if Harvey hadn't stepped in – he was like a bouncer, throwing them out on their ears then guarding the door. Nobody dared mess with him after they'd see him in action.'

'I can imagine.' He'd do anything to protect Barney and his property, as well as the community, and he'd probably have had women falling at his feet. She could just picture him dressed in a tux, looking the part. The first time Melissa had seen him wearing one, when he took her to her first Wedding Dress Ball, she could barely speak. Jaw-droppingly handsome, Harvey Luddington was the catch of the village, and once upon a time she'd been the girl every other single female in Heritage Cove envied. 'Well, let's just hope we don't get anything like that this year.'

'Remember to contact the local newspaper about the event too, they usually cover it.'

'We don't have that on the list but I'll make sure we contact them,' said Melissa. 'It should be a year to remember.'

'It always is. I can't believe Barney even thought about cancelling it altogether.'

'He's quite infuriating when he makes up his mind about something. He seems to think he's past it because of this fall and won't be told it could've happened to anyone.'

'It must be all the more frustrating after not seeing him in so long.'

'It is,' Melissa said, looking down at the display cabinet instead of at Jade.

'Hey, I didn't mean anything by it, people around here know that everyone has their own story to tell. None of us can write the endings for someone else.'

'Nobody ever put it like that. I appreciate it, thank you.'

'Anytime. And here – take an orange-and-poppyseed muffin, on the house.' She lifted a muffin out with a pair of tongs, dropped it into a bag and handed it to Melissa. 'It's been lovely to catch up, don't be a stranger.'

'I promise I won't.'

Back at the inn Melissa made a couple of phone calls – one to the florist, the other to the portaloo company to confirm their booking, which thankfully was one that had survived the cull. Then she moved straight on to her next task, driving to the caterers who she didn't seem to be able to get hold of over the phone. Every call went to an answer service and she wasn't interested in leaving a message. They were based in the next village and it was quicker to go there in person, but when she arrived at their premises she realised why they'd been incommunicado. They'd closed down, a big sign plastered across the door telling everyone who showed up that that was the case. Barney had booked them at the start of the year and left a phone message to cancel, so he probably had no idea.

Melissa drove back to Heritage Cove wondering what on earth she was going to do about the food. Usually there was an enormous spread, a range to please everyone – plates of delicate finger sandwiches, goujons, dips, pork-and-apple sausage rolls, breaded prawns – a whole list of foods prepared by the professionals. Melissa had sat outside the closed-down caterers and made a few calls but had no luck finding anyone.

She parked up at the inn as Sandy came outside to water the hanging basket at the front entrance. 'You look stressed,' Sandy began, stretching up and tilting the watering can into the basket. The surplus trickled down and splashed onto the concrete.

Melissa explained how she and Harvey had taken over organising this year's ball.

'I went last year,' Sandy smiled, watering the other side of the basket to get even coverage. 'It was my first time. I'd watched my parents go every year and couldn't wait to join in.' Her blonde hair tied up in a ponytail today, she hadn't bothered to straighten out the curls she'd inherited from her mum. 'My boyfriend panicked when I first brought out a white dress. He's not from around here, I think he thought I wanted to trick him into a wedding.'

Melissa laughed. 'I can see why he'd be worried.'

'No way am I ready for that.'

'Good for you, go spread your wings first,' she smiled, just as Tracy came outside to help an elderly guest with her suitcase before she could go on her way.

'Don't go putting ideas into her head,' Tracy said after she'd waved the guest away.

Sandy rolled her eyes and went back inside now she'd finished watering the hanging basket and the window box filled with vibrant pinks and purples.

'I wasn't filling her head with silly ideas, I promise,' said Melissa.

'I'm kidding. Much as Heritage Cove is for me and I secretly harbour a wish that my kids will stay here while I grow old, I'm taking a leaf out of Barney's book and they'll get my blessing whatever they decide to do. Would you like to join me in the garden out back for some lunch? I can have Giles whip us up a chicken salad.'

'That would be lovely.' She could use a break from all the rushing around and they first went inside to escape the heat that at this time of the day made the parking area out front feel like it had been transported to the Mediterranean rather than being on the east coast of England.

In the kitchen Giles took their orders for salad, Tracy filled a jug with traditional lemonade and plenty of ice cubes, and they took it outside to the bistro-style table and chairs.

They'd only just sat down when Melissa excused herself to take a call from Jay. They'd only just spoken but he'd forgotten to remind her to go and check out her little cottage while she was here. He'd seen a stunning house for sale in the Loire Valley and when he fired the photographs her way she couldn't disagree, it was beautiful, a real escape. But mentioning her cottage again, she knew she wasn't feeling the same way about getting rid of it as she had when she first arrived in Heritage Cove. Talking with Jay earlier and again now also reminded her that she had a very different life outside the Cove with a faster pace and detachedness from somewhere like here, an existence that hung in the background like a safety net protecting her from all the uncertainty. Since getting back to the village the lines were becoming increasingly blurred and it was hard to think straight on some days. She found her feelings for Harvey swung between regret and longing some days and, on other days, hovered between frustration and a need to finally draw a line under everything that had happened.

Giles delivered the salads and cutlery to the table and Tracy poured two glasses of lemonade, handing one to Melissa.

'This salad looks good,' Melissa smiled. 'Giles seems to be enjoying the catering side of the business.'

'That he is.'

She tucked into a mouthful of chicken with cajun seasoning, juicy red peppers, peppery rocket mixed with crisp, fresh lettuce. 'Compliments to the chef,' she reiterated.

Tracy, cutlery in hand as she enjoyed her lunch, hadn't missed a thing. 'Was the phone call from your other half?'

'It was, he's missing me. I'm away for quite a while now I'm hanging around for longer.'

'I'm sure he understands. It is Barney.' Tracy obviously thought Melissa had shared a lot more about her life in Heritage Cove than she actually had. 'Why don't you invite him up here? I for one would love to meet this mysterious pilot of yours.'

Melissa wasn't sure she wanted to share this part of her with Jay. She'd separated her new life in Berkshire and Heritage Cove successfully so far, and it worked. Jay knew she lost her parents, he understood she didn't want to dwell on what had happened and he let her disappear into her own thoughts whenever she needed to. What he didn't know was that when she'd left the Cove five years ago, she'd also left behind the man she thought she'd spend the rest of her life with. By the time she and Jay became an item, she no longer wanted to look backwards, only forwards.

'Talking of men…' Tracy adjusted her chair so the sun wasn't right in her eyes. 'How's Harvey coping with you being back and the two of you having to spend time together to organise the ball? I saw Barney today and he filled me in on everything. Thank goodness you both stepped in is all I can say.'

'We had to, but it's crazy busy trying to work out what was cancelled and what wasn't, what still needs to be done.'

'You still haven't answered my question.' Tracy speared a piece of tomato. She wasn't going to let her get away with avoiding the focus on Harvey.

'Awkward is probably the best description of how it is between us.' She recapped on what they had to organise, what they'd already taken care of.

'I can help you out when it comes to caterers.' Tracy put her cutlery together now that she'd finished her salad and pulled out her phone. 'I would suggest Giles but party catering isn't his thing unless you're really desperate. Let me send you a couple of contacts I have – try them, mention my name. I've used both of them before when the oven at the inn went on the blink just in time for a guest's eightieth birthday event and then again the week after we had it fixed and were supposed to cook Sunday dinner for twenty-five people to celebrate owning the place for a year.'

'That sounds like a nightmare.'

'It was, let me tell you, never been so stressed.' Melissa's phone bleeped as the contacts appeared via text message on her phone. 'Both of the caterers I'm putting you in touch with are wonderful, their food is top notch – book them in for a tasting if you can.'

'I will do, and thank you.' She pulled an awkward face and Tracy knew where her mind was going.

'Go ahead, do it now, I need to take these empty plates inside and make sure I'm not needed in reception. I'll be back.'

By the time Tracy returned Melissa had been in touch with both caterers. 'One already has a booking, I've locked in the other on your recommendation and on the condition we get a tasting beforehand. I'll sort something with Barney.'

'Great, another thing ticked off the list, I'm relieved I could help.' She clinked her glass against Melissa's in a toast. 'My parents used to talk about that ball all the time, you know. They loved putting on their finery and heading on over. Mum was always thrilled she still fitted into her gown and Dad bought himself a new suit for the occasion – his had seen much better days. They went every year until Mum died and Dad went into a home.'

'It's a shitty time losing a parent.'

'The worst. But it's the circle of life. I guess I'm lucky I had them both around for so long, they got to meet their grandchildren.' She covered her face. 'I'm sorry, I didn't think.'

'Never apologise. We're all in different situations, I was lucky in other ways. Mum and Dad gave me the best childhood I could wish for, that doesn't happen for everyone.' She knew they were both thinking of Harvey's upbringing, a dad who dominated the family and gave very little love in the process.

Melissa relaxed with the lemonade and shut her eyes. The sun was behind her now and it warmed the back of her sundress, kissed her pale skin that was protected by sunscreen so she wouldn't burn. 'I made it down to the cove the other day.'

'Finally. And…?'

'It was as beautiful as I remembered. Dipping my toes in the water after all this time, well, it felt like coming home. Is that weird when my home is no longer here?'

'Your home will always be here. You spent decades living in the Cove, that isn't something that disappears just like that.'

'I suppose you're right. And Winnie certainly loves it down there, she chased up and down the sands for a stick, had me working hard.'

161

'Winnie?' She made a face. 'Yes, I know who Winnie is, what I'm asking really is how come you were at the cove with Harvey?'

'We were talking about Barney.'

'Of course.'

'Don't read anything else into it, Tracy.'

'I won't.' Her look suggested otherwise. 'Have you been to the cemetery yet?'

'Not yet.' Melissa turned away as someone else came out into the gardens and settled at a table on the other side of the grass to read the newspaper. 'I'm a terrible daughter, aren't I?'

'No, you're not. I could go with you, if you need me to. You may even find it helps. I know I feel closer to my mum when I visit.'

Melissa would've preferred to scatter both her parents' ashes into the cove, let the water take them away, but each of their wills had instructed they were to be buried at the cemetery. People were always going on about how nice it was to have somewhere to visit, so perhaps that had been their thinking all along, maybe they'd done it for her and her brother. Not that she thought it helped at all. She hadn't been to the cemetery since the day her parents were laid to rest. Billy had moved away and despite Harvey and Barney being there for her, she'd been unable to make sense of the world and her part in it without someone else who knew the exact pain she was going through.

Tracy brought the conversation back round to what they'd been talking about before. 'Do you remember your first Wedding Dress Ball?'

'I do. I found a white debutante dress from a second-hand shop in Norwich.'

'That's right, and you were so pleased with it, you wore it year after year. Harvey couldn't take his eyes off you.'

She remembered. And the feeling had been mutual.

Tracy waved over at Sandy who'd come outside to cut a few extra pale pink roses like those Melissa had seen in the little vases on the tables in the restaurant area. 'You know, I was jealous when you left. I knew that I'd already settled down, my time for travel and fun had well and truly gone.'

'You've found other things in your life.'

'That I have…and I couldn't leave the Cove. I could go away for a holiday, but not for good. It's the kind of place that grabs hold of you and refuses to let you go.'

Home had always been a feeling rather than a place for Melissa. After her parents died she'd found being here painful, little reminders waiting to jump out at her at any moment. But it was only now she realised that after some time away and with her focus on Barney and getting him back to normal, since arriving here she hadn't been faced with quite the confronting reminders she'd once dreaded. Instead, there were smaller moments, pangs of nostalgia, and not all of them bad. She had one right now, sitting here in the pretty little garden, remembering Sunday lunch with her parents on Father's Day one year. Her mum had been nagging her dad to get out of the sun so he wouldn't burn, he'd argued back that it was the first sunny day they'd had in weeks after severe storms had bashed the east coast and he was going to make the most of it.

Before she fled Heritage Cove a memory like that would've had Melissa sobbing, returning to the cottage that had once been her parents' and hiding out under the duvet as she tried to sleep the hurt away. But, now, here

163

she was, still listening to Tracy chat away about the Cove, and she hadn't fallen apart.

'How's Barney going with those exercises you said he has to do?' Tracy swatted a fly away from the rim of her lemonade glass.

'As far as I know, he's not doing any of them. He has a rehabilitation program and the stubborn old goat won't comply. It's frustrating.'

'It's a shame, I miss bumping into him on The Street or him coming in here for a chat.'

'What worries me is that he can't see it himself, he can't see that with a little bit of effort he can go back to exactly what he was doing before. You'd think he'd want to get better but it's as though he's given up. And I'm happy to help with the Wedding Dress Ball, but what I dread is…I worry that it won't be long before…' Her voice caught and she couldn't finish.

'Steady on, love.' Tracy's hand reached out and covered hers. 'None of us is immortal but Barney's got years in him yet. We keep an eye out for each other around here too, nobody will let him suffer in silence, and he still has Harvey locally.'

'I'm glad Harvey's here for him.' It gave her some comfort to know that they were both still close and when she left here Barney would have someone keeping a watchful eye on him.

'That man would move heaven and earth for Barney. He'd likely move those things for someone else I know.'

Melissa shook her head. 'Once upon a time, yes, but not now. Some days he seems pleased I'm here, others he seems to be counting down until I leave.'

'I doubt that's true.'

'Why didn't he come after me, Tracy?'

'Remember what I said last time we talked about this? You need to ask him. Only he and you know what you were both feeling deep down. It's no use second-guessing or having others speculate.'

'I suppose you're right. But I think I'll try to get through organising this ball first. Speaking of which, I'd better carry on.' She finished up her lemonade but before she headed up to her room to freshen up before meeting Harvey and distributing those flyers, she had another question. 'I meant to ask you before, does anyone ever want to come to the Wedding Dress Ball but can't, for whatever reason, find an outfit?

'Strange question, and isn't an outfit kind of a prerequisite? If the dress or the suit don't fit or if you don't have one, you're not coming in,' she laughed. 'It says it clearly on the tickets. It's part of the event.'

'Harsh,' Melissa laughed back. 'But I'm serious, does it ever happen?'

'Not that I can recall. Several people, myself included, couldn't fit into their wedding dresses no matter how much dieting we did, but we've all had our dresses altered for the cause – taken in or let way out in sections where we've changed shape. Some dresses are probably unrecognisable from what they once were, but everyone gets on board and has fun with it. It's all part of the event, and a definite ice-breaker for anyone on the shy side – we start talking and laughing about gown- and suit-fitting struggles and it's all we need. And anyone old enough but without a gown, they pick up a dress just like you did. May I ask where your mind is going with this?'

They made their way back inside and into the lovely cool kitchen. 'I found a dress, at Barney's house. It was tucked away in his wardrobe. Beautiful it was, gorgeous in fact, something I'd pay a small fortune for now if it didn't have a section of material cut out from the bottom.'

'You sound like you've got your eye on it. Are you and Mr Pilot getting serious?'

'I don't have my eye on it. But don't you think it's weird, that it's there in his wardrobe and he hasn't mentioned it? I saw it years ago when I was a lot younger too.'

Tracy shrugged. 'Maybe the dress was left at his place and the person never reclaimed it.'

'What, they came to the ball wearing it but went home naked?'

'Good point. Well, the only explanation I can see is like you said, it's a spare, just in case. And perhaps the cut-out section meant he picked it up somewhere for next to nothing, meant to have it mended, then didn't get around to it.'

'You could be right. Perhaps I'm trying to read too much into it.'

'Probably, and you've got enough to focus on with the ball coming up,' she smiled. 'And Barney will come around, I know he will.' With a cloth she wiped some crumbs from the chopping board on the side and emptied them into the bin inside the kitchen door. 'It's really good to have you here, Melissa.'

'I'm glad to be here,' she smiled at her friend, and she was.

But that was the problem.

*

Between them Harvey and Melissa spent most of the afternoon and early evening delivering flyers for the Wedding Dress Ball to local businesses, houses in the

Cove and a slightly wider area, before meeting up back at Barney's place.

Harvey watched Melissa after they'd shared a cup of tea with Barney and headed outside toward the barn. While the red of her hair had faded, it still shone as though she were years younger, that same girl he'd fallen for. He wished he could switch off his feelings, but it was getting more difficult to do by the day. Until she'd shown up in the Cove again he would've said he was over her, but now she was here, he knew he was anything but. The more time he spent with her, the more he remembered what they'd once had and what she now had with someone else.

'I phoned the table-and-chair-hire company,' she told him as he opened the doors to the barn and folded them back. 'We're almost there.'

He positioned a stepladder at one end of the barn. His job now was to inspect all the beams, something he did periodically to check for rot, mildew or any deterioration. Catching things early was key and some beams had been repaired, pieces had been replaced, and at least he didn't have to worry about the concrete floor, which pretty much looked after itself. The only other scan he'd need to do was of the sides of the barn in case there were nails protruding or splintered wood that could catch an unsuspecting person or their outfit.

'Let me hold the ladder,' Melissa insisted when he climbed up to the topmost step.

'No need.' He wanted to get rid of the cobwebs above the barn doors. There'd be more soon enough but it didn't hurt to keep the place clean as they went along.

'If you fall too, I'll have to organise this whole event on my own and I'm really not up for that.'

He smiled down at her. 'Fine.'

When he finished up and climbed back down the ladder her body was so close he brushed past it and the jolt between them was something he knew they both felt.

'I'll go back inside and try to see if I can get Barney to do at least one exercise with me,' she said, scurrying off in the direction of the house.

She might be with someone else but he wasn't sorry he still had an effect on her. 'Good luck, make him listen.'

'I'll sweep the floor when I get back,' she called over her shoulder as she left.

He carried on checking for splinters of wood and exposed nails and dealt with each in turn.

'Knock, knock!' came a voice from the barn door and when he looked up from his position in the corner of the barn, it was Casey, a girl who'd moved to Heritage Cove with her family a couple of years ago and who he'd dated a handful of times.

'Hey, Casey, how's it going? What brings you here?'

'I wondered if you'd had a chance to think about my proposition.' When he pulled a face she added, 'Being my date to the ball.'

'Ah, that.'

'You forgot, didn't you?'

'No.' He grinned. 'Yes.'

'I knew it.'

He was about to think up an excuse to turn down a girl who was striking to look at with her sharp green eyes, angelic blonde hair and curves she wasn't afraid to show off in fitted clothes that didn't leave much to the imagination. But when Melissa appeared with a broom, ready to sweep – clearly she'd had no joy convincing Barney – he had no choice but to introduce the two women.

Casey looked between Harvey and Melissa. 'I hear you two are in charge of this year's ball.'

'Word certainly got around fast,' said Melissa. 'I think we'll be able to pull it off.'

'I don't mind helping out if needs be. Harvey has my number,' Casey added cheekily.

Harvey didn't miss a flit of something in Melissa's eyes. Jealousy? Part of him hoped it was. 'Well, I'm all finished here for today,' he declared. As friendly as this was, it was awkward more than anything. 'Everything looks good and the stage is ready for the band.'

'Did they call back?' Melissa asked.

Confused, he told her, 'I thought you were dealing with it.'

'No.' Before he could add anything else Melissa spun on her heel, calling behind her, 'I'll do it now.' She mumbled something else too but he couldn't quite make it out.

Casey, perplexed at Melissa's sudden departure, got back to the reason she'd come. 'Please tell me you need a date. I can't turn up to the ball on my own, it's lame.'

'So you're happy to use me?'

'Hey, feel free to use me back,' she grinned.

She'd like that but he wasn't going to. If there's one thing he knew about women it was that leading them on was a bad idea. Which is why things with him and Casey had never gone further than a bit of fooling around and a couple of late nights in the pub. She didn't deserve to be messed around, especially not now when his head was elsewhere.

'I mean it, it's a genuine offer,' she went on, reaching out to touch his arm with her fingers that trailed up the skin. She took her hand away when she got no reaction. 'You're turning me down because of the redhead.'

169

'Melissa?'

'Don't even try to deny it,' she said good-humouredly. 'I've heard about the pair of you and probably wouldn't have thought you were still hung up on her if I hadn't seen it with my own eyes.'

'Melissa and I are ancient history. She's with someone else.'

'You're not, you're single.'

'Nothing's going on with her, I assure you.' He dropped his hammer back into his toolbox.

'I saw the way she looked at you, how you looked at her, blah blah blah.' Casey had never been backward in coming forward and she was a lot of fun to be around. Her sparky persona tended to have a way of carrying you right along with it. 'I'm pleased for you, pleased she came back, I mean.'

'She's not back, she's just visiting.' Outside the barn he told her, 'And she has a boyfriend who she'll be going back to in a few weeks' time.'

'Well, I hope her new guy realises his girlfriend is still in love with someone else.'

Shaking his head at her claims, he put his toolbox into the tray of the truck. 'I'll see you around, Casey.'

'Don't go all broody on me. How about a drink at the pub? Just friends, I know the deal. Come on, there's nobody around. And I'm bored.'

He sighed between his teeth. 'You'll get me into trouble.'

'I'll try to.'

'OK, you're on. Let me go and tell Barney, I'll drop the truck home, meet you there.'

And when Melissa came outside and overheard him tell Casey he'd see her at the pub, her reaction told him perhaps Casey was right about the girl who'd once broken his heart.

Maybe both of them had fallen in love a long time ago and neither of them had truly let the other one go.

Chapter Eight

Melissa was pleased with progress when it came to organising Heritage Cove's event of the year. Despite her plummeting mood after she saw Casey with Harvey last night, inviting him to the pub and hanging off his every word, she'd turned her attentions to everything else that still needed to be done for the Wedding Dress Ball to go off without a hitch. She'd confirmed flowers with the florist, managed to get hold of the band, and she'd contacted the newspaper. She'd had a few emails back and forth with Jay, although ignoring any mention of her little cottage in the Cove, and she'd been for a long walk around the countryside filling her lungs with the fresh air that had a calming effect.

At least it had until she went over to Barney's in time for dinner that day. Giles had made a lasagne that Barney took one look at and claimed it was enough to feed a family four, he suggested Harvey come on over, and when Harvey turned up he'd gone on and on about Casey and how she wanted him to join their pub quiz team, he was a hidden weapon apparently. Melissa had begun to wonder whether Harvey was going to bring her to the ball, and it didn't put her in a particularly good mood.

After the dishes were cleared, Harvey headed to his mum's place to fix her shed door that had come off its

172

hinges, and Melissa busied herself emptying the dishwasher for Barney.

It wasn't long before Barney called over to her from the armchair. 'What's with the crashing about? I won't have any crockery left if you're that heavy-handed with it.'

She took a deep breath and slowed down. 'Sorry, Barney.'

'What's he done now?'

'What's who done?' She stretched to slot a pile of four plates onto the corner shelf near the cooker.

'You know full well who I'm referring to. Harvey, that's who. He must be the reason for the sudden bad mood.'

'I'm in a perfectly good mood, thank you. And Harvey hasn't done anything.'

'Could've fooled me,' he batted back.

'Cup of tea?'

But her question was interrupted by a knock at the front door and Barney grumbled, 'Who's that? It's after eight o'clock.'

And he thought she was in a bad mood? 'I'll get it.' He usually reacted well to visitors and she hoped his frame of mind would shift sooner rather than later. But when she answered the door, she knew from the uniform that this visitor wasn't going to help matters.

'I do apologise,' said the woman as she followed Melissa through to the lounge. 'I'm the health visitor. I couldn't get here earlier, my schedule has been ridiculous.'

Harvey had mentioned the health visitor was coming but it had completely gone out of her head.

'What are you here for?' Barney snapped.

'Barney…' Melissa laid a hand on his shoulder. 'Be nice,' she whispered. 'She's not the enemy.'

She turned to face the health visitor and mouthed the word, 'Sorry.' The woman just smiled and took a seat opposite Barney, ready to take charge. Melissa hoped she'd have better luck than she had in trying to convince him he wasn't too old to make a full recovery if only he'd comply.

Melissa picked up a pile of sheets she'd laundered yesterday and left them to it while she went to make up the spare bed that Harvey had stayed in a few times to keep an eye on Barney. He was still staying here some nights but mostly he'd gone back home at Barney's insistence, and the only signs he'd left behind were a spare toothbrush and toothpaste.

She leaned against the window frame and looked out past the peaked roof over to the barn. Although enjoying her solitude at the inn, she wondered whether Barney might have been better had she stayed here. She'd be around all the time then and maybe have half a hope of persuading him to take on board his part in the recovery process.

She thought back to the times she'd stayed here as a kid. She and Harvey had begged for sleepovers in the barn every summer, arranging hay bales to sleep on, positioning their sleeping bags and pillows on top. They'd only ever had the sleepovers when Harvey's dad was away with work, but it had always been fun, a big adventure for them even when booming thunderstorms came with a vengeance. Barney had often stayed in the barn to keep an eye on them, and the night of the big storm Harvey and Melissa had giggled away at his snores competing with the chaotic weather outside until a long, low rumble followed by an almighty clap of thunder had Melissa so scared that Harvey reached out to hold her hand and tell her everything would be fine. They were safe, they always would be here.

As she came down the stairs after making up the spare bed and walked along the corridor it was a relief to hear the gentle murmur of voices. Barney was at least talking to the health visitor and Melissa hung back, not wanting to interrupt. She wondered whether she and Harvey had been crowding Barney and perhaps someone impartial was exactly what he needed.

Stopping outside Barney's bedroom, her mind flipped to the dress again, hanging in the wardrobe with a section missing at the bottom. She had to get a look at the letter she'd found before and so, sure she wasn't going to be caught red-handed – not unless Barney sprinted from his chair to here – she tiptoed into the room and opened the wardrobe slowly in case the door creaked. She unzipped the plastic and reached into the material bag to pull out the letter. She unfolded the single sheet with a partially faded blue symbol that looked a bit like an anchor and she began to read.

Dear Barney,

It is with much pain and regret that I write this letter. And it is cowardly of me to do so while you're not here, but I have to, because I know you would not let me go otherwise.

As I write this you are at work doing your best to build a future for the both of us. But it is one I can no longer be a part of. After everything that has happened I feel I have no choice but to get away, to find out where I fit in the world. I truly believe we can both be happy again but I'm no longer sure it is something we can achieve together. Our pain has broken us in a way we cannot get past.

Be happy, my love. You are the kindest man I have ever known, please don't ever change that about you.

With love always,

Your Lois x

Melissa stuffed the letter back into the little bag, tucked the bag next to the dress and checked again that she wouldn't be disturbed. And though she hated herself a little bit for doing it, she got down on her hands and knees to look through what else he had hidden inside the wardrobe. She fished through umpteen pairs of shoes, a couple of rolled-up leather belts, the odd faded receipt, a tub containing spare buttons, and when she lifted up a pair of slippers with holes in the sole and wondered why he'd never thrown them away, there underneath was a photograph. Black-and-white, not very big but in a frame, she pulled it out, holding back a sneeze that sneaked up on her when she brushed the dust away.

Heart thumping, she studied the photograph. It was definitely Barney, she'd seen other pictures of him at around the same age, one sitting on a boat wearing a life jacket and holding on to the rope from a sail, another with his mother sitting on a beach eating fish and chips. The woman standing next to him in this picture had to be Lois, surely. She was classically beautiful with delicate features, dark hair wound up at the top of her head and curly tendrils hanging either side of her face. She held a small posy of flowers and was smiling into the camera as

Barney looked at his bride as though there wasn't anyone else there at all. And there was no doubt about it as she compared the top of the wedding dress in the photograph to the one hanging in the wardrobe, this was the same dress, it had to be Lois's dress.

Melissa put the photograph back where she'd found it and covered it with the old slippers. She piled up the shoes, the belts and everything else and hoped it didn't look as though it had been disturbed. Her head all over the place, she was desperate to get outside and so without a word she passed the closed doors and went out of the front and around the side of the house to the courtyard. She sat on the big tree stump and tried to text Harvey, but no response. She wasn't sure what she was going to tell him anyway, but she wanted to talk to someone. Why had Barney never mentioned Lois? Melissa doubted she'd died given that she'd left him the goodbye note, but plenty of people married and split up, it was hardly anything to be ashamed of.

When the health visitor emerged from the house Melissa snapped out of her reverie. She went back through the gap in the juniper trees and peeked in the side window near the door to make sure Barney wasn't looking out this way. But she was safe, it looked as though his focus was back on the television. 'How's he doing?' she asked.

'As well as can be expected.' The health visitor, a tall rangy woman called Penny who'd had to duck at the low ceiling to pass through the hallway into the lounge, deftly did up the leather buckle on her bag with one hand and with the other clutched a folder to her chest. 'He's as stubborn as my father-in-law, a no-nonsense man, who will cope with things in his way and nobody else's, and in his own time come to that.'

'That doesn't tell me much.' Melissa helped Penny with the latch on the low-down front gate and waited for her to put her things onto the backseat of her sky-blue Peugeot parked on the street.

'His hip is mending slowly, maybe don't push him too much, be there for him. I'm sure we'll notice a difference soon. He's lucky it's summer. The winter months are hard, especially for the elderly, some of them struggle with hospital stays and a long recovery.'

Melissa wanted to shout after Penny as she drove off that Barney wasn't old, there was plenty of fight and spirit in him, but little by little she was realising how long she'd been away and that perhaps it was time to accept change. And if this was the last year that the Wedding Dress Ball would run, if Barney had really had enough, then she owed it to him to make this the best one ever.

*

Harvey shared a beer with his mum after fixing the shed door, and by the time he got home the sun had already set.

As he approached the front door the outside light was on and Melissa was sitting on his doorstep, waiting for him. 'Everything all right with Barney?' he asked straight away.

She realised her mistake, that she'd made him panic. 'I'm sorry, I didn't mean to worry you. Nothing has happened, Barney's fine, the health visitor came.'

'Ah, I meant to remind you about that.'

'Not a problem, he seemed to talk to her at least and she thinks he'll get there in the end.'

He let them both inside the house and Winnie didn't waste time getting Melissa's attention. 'So what's with the late visit?' he asked.

'It's about the dress.' Melissa fussed Winnie around the ears in the way she liked.

Harvey switched on the lamp in the corner near the kitchen table. 'And you need to talk about this now? It couldn't wait until tomorrow?'

'I read the letter, the one in the bag.'

Frowning, he shook his head. 'It's none of our business.'

'Maybe not.'

'Come on then, out with it, what did it say?'

She recapped almost verbatim. 'He's never mentioned a Lois, has he?'

'Not as far as I can remember.' He went to sit down and tried to focus on the subject matter rather than Melissa, here, in his home again. He'd imagined it a few times over the years, especially since he bought the place and made it his own, but he always snapped back to the present and stopped his mind going too far down that particular road.

'Barney has been through more than we know,' she went on as he sat down. 'Whoever Lois was, she must've broken his heart and we've no idea why.'

He still wondered why this couldn't wait until the morning.

'I don't think Barney has ever truly moved on from whatever happened between them. And I think…well, I can't help thinking that Barney's mood, his lack of desire to get back to normal, is also something to do with Lois.'

With a sigh he said, 'Whatever happened would've been years ago, before he came to the Cove. I know I'm a man and I'm not supposed to understand feelings as well as you women, but I'm pretty sure he would've

179

picked himself up from a woman dumping him and moved forwards.'

'You don't have to sound so heartless about it.'

'It's not heartless, it's reality. I think you're reading way too much into this. Now, it's late, I have to be up early for a job.' And the more she sat here opposite him the more he wanted to reach over and touch her hand, pull her to him and pick up where they left off. Perhaps she was right. Perhaps moving on wasn't so easy for Barney, it certainly wasn't for him. But he wasn't going to let her know that. 'Not everyone bounces back from a broken heart,' he said instead.

'Are we talking about Barney and Lois here, or us?'

'Maybe both.' He didn't take his eyes away from the dog, who had turned her attentions to her master.

After a while she asked, 'Should I say something to Barney?'

'Then he'd know you were snooping.'

'I'd hate him to resent me.'

'He'd never do that.' He quickly changed the mood when her gaze lingered on his by telling her, 'Well done for doing so much organising today – the band, the newspaper, the florist,' he elaborated.

'I feel better now it's all done. The band was a worry. I called them, they said they were already booked up after the cancellation as we suspected they might be, but they phoned back less than an hour later. I don't mind telling you I was sweating a bit, I don't really have any idea where to start when it comes to hiring a band and some I looked into were way too expensive or the members all looked about fifteen years old and I suspect would put on a heavy-metal gig that wouldn't go down well at all.'

Harvey was amused by that. 'Doesn't bear thinking about.' Silence fell between them again until he said, 'I wonder why Barney never mentioned this Lois.'

'Ah, so you're curious too.'

'OK, I'll admit it, I am. It's weird, you're right. Especially with our history, particularly with me, when you left. I'm not having a go at you,' he said when she flinched, 'but it would've been the perfect example of a breakdown in a relationship and a man who has carried on regardless.'

'A perfect example? Or a bad one? I mean, he doesn't ever talk about what happened, he's got a wedding dress in his wardrobe. Perhaps he didn't want to share it with you in case you went down the same road as him and never moved on.'

'You can check my wardrobe if you like, I only have men's clothes, no dresses.'

'I don't think that'll be necessary.' He loved the way her whole face got involved when she smiled and she couldn't hide her expression even if she tried. 'Perhaps I should leave this alone. Winnie, what do you think?' She ruffled the dog's fur, but Winnie just rolled on over for a tummy tickle. 'Maybe Barney just left the dress and forgot about it, perhaps he did keep it as a spare or to give to someone. You know what he's like about including people. He's big on community relations, keeping local businesses going, making sure new residents don't stay anonymous.'

'Even if they'd rather,' Harvey smiled. 'I hear Lucy, the new blacksmith, resisted getting to know everyone at first until Barney insisted upon it and had her over for afternoon tea to give her the low-down on the Cove. He accosted her on The Street and left her little choice.'

'That sounds like our Barney. And I've met Lucy, she seemed nice. I wonder if she's here for good.'

'Knowing Barney, he'll treat her as though she might be.'

She waited a while and then said, 'I know you think I'm trying to find explanations that may not be there, solve a heartache that may never be mended. But something about the dress, the Wedding Dress Ball, it all niggles me. And I think that whatever it is that Barney doesn't talk about has affected him without any of us realising and I think it's affecting him now, making him want to give up.'

'I get where you're coming from but we're doing all we can by running the event this year. And Barney said he'll be there watching from the sidelines.'

'Are you going?'

'To the ball? Of course. I've been every year since I turned eighteen.'

'Even after…'

'Even after you left,' he finished for her.

'Life goes on, eh?'

'Something like that.'

'Remember one year we climbed up to those beams and shuffled along until we broke a part of the wood?' There was that smile of hers again.

'We didn't break it, it was rotten.'

'It might have been rotten, but we were the reason it fell down.'

'You know, I think it's the first time I'd really seen Barney angry. I ran off and hid.'

'And it took him two hours to find you,' she reminded him. 'He was frantic.'

'My dad used to get angry like that, no way was I hanging around for Barney to do the same.'

'He talked to me about it, you know.'

'About my dad?'

'About the night you ran away from him. He was in pieces thinking you were worried he might hit you.'

'I don't think I ever really believed it, I just freaked out I suppose.'

She gave Winnie one last fuss before she stood up. 'I'd better get back to the inn. I just wanted to talk to you and let you know about the letter.'

'Were you waiting for me for long?'

'No, not at all, and it was probably more torturous for Winnie than me, I could hear her on the other side of the door, desperate to find out who was here.'

'Sounds about right.' He stood up too. 'Let me walk you back.'

'Harvey, it's not far, and this is the Cove, I'm safe.'

'No arguments.' He grabbed Winnie's lead and the dog was well up for an unexpected late-night walk as he locked up and they set off down the lane.

He put out his hand and pulled Melissa to a stop outside. 'Do you hear that?'

Her eyes sparkled beneath the moonlight. 'Crickets,' she beamed. 'I love that sound. It makes me feel as though I'm on holiday.'

Her comment sent a weird feeling cascading through his body. She was technically on holiday, but would she ever see that Heritage Cove was still the same place she'd once loved? Talk returned to the Wedding Dress Ball and the organisation they'd done so far.

'It's all coming together,' he said. 'We've had a fair few extra ticket sales from the flyers I had made up.'

She crossed her fingers on both hands. 'Almost there. It sounds as though everyone is getting really excited – Tracy and Sandy don't stop talking about it, Jade too whenever I see her. Celeste can't wait to dance. Mum always said it was the only place she got to dance after she was married, I used to love watching them get ready, her and dad setting off together as though they were newlyweds and not a couple who'd been together for years.' She looked across at him. 'You and I always reminded ourselves when we were younger that one day we would go, we'd drink champagne from those tall skinny glasses that wouldn't let your nose in the top and we'd be the last ones dancing at the end of an evening.'

Heritage Cove was quiet at this time of night and Winnie's paws gently tapped their way along in a constant rhythm as they walked down The Street talking about the dances they remembered, people in the village who'd loved an occasion to dress up, until they rounded the corner and came to the inn.

Melissa bent down to give Winnie one last bit of her love and attention. Lucky dog. 'Do you know what I think we should do?'

'Something tells me you have a plan,' he smiled.

'I don't think we should wait until the date of the ball to show Barney what it's all about. We need to get him in the mood, remind him, get him excited for the evening before it's upon him. It might just make him want to get up out of that chair and move.'

'What do you have in mind?'

'Pick me up from the inn when you finish work tomorrow and you'll find out

It almost sounded like they were arranging a date. And whatever might happen between him and Melissa from now on, the one thing he knew for sure was that her being back in the Cove couldn't have come at a better time for Barney. If anyone could work their magic on him, it would be her.

Chapter Nine

Two days later, after a ridiculously early start to pull off this surprise, Melissa had expected Barney to be sitting in his chair by the time she knocked on the back door. Thank goodness for the set of keys he'd passed her the other day or she'd have been running to Harvey to grab his set when she'd got no answer.

'I'm through here, in the bedroom,' the voice called out and she dashed through, hoping he hadn't fallen or hurt himself. But she needn't have worried, he was lying in bed looking perfectly fine.

'I did knock at the door,' she explained.

'Don't look so worried about me, nothing wrong with a sleep-in once in a while.'

'Fair enough, but it's not like you, that's all.'

'Things have changed, Melissa, you know that.'

She did but she wasn't going to humour him. 'How about I make your favourite breakfast?' She didn't wait for an answer before heading to the kitchen to do just that. She and Harvey had shared bacon butties this morning at first light before they quietly arrived at Barney's property and put their plan into action. Yesterday after Harvey picked her up from the inn, they'd dashed about collecting supplies to decorate the barn, and after a good four hours of hard work this morning there was only one thing left to do. Show Barney.

Thirty minutes later and Barney was seated at the farmhouse table he'd had ever since she was a little girl, back when it had been him cooking the eggy bread.

'So to what do I owe this pleasure?' he asked when he was almost done with the surprise breakfast. She'd squeezed some fresh apple juice using the press too and he took a thirsty sip. 'Are you so bored over there at the inn that you have to come and see an old man this early?'

'I'm in Heritage Cove to see you, so it shouldn't be a surprise. And it's nine o'clock, hardly early.'

'In all the years I've known you, Melissa, you were never a morning person. And you're worse in the winter.'

'True fact. But I've grown up, got a job, you know, responsibilities as an adult.'

'I still like to remember you and Harvey as kids, more fun that way.' He'd only just picked up the final piece before she whipped away his plate and plunged it into the soapy suds in the sink. 'What's the urgency?' He observed her looking at her watch for the umpteenth time.

'You'll see,' Harvey grinned, coming in through the back door before Melissa could answer the question. 'Now go and get dressed.'

Barney rolled his eyes and with the help of his walking frame shuffled off to do as he'd been asked.

When he came back to join them Melissa decided to take charge and do without the frame, instead linking her arm through his before heading outside, through the gap in the trees, over to the barn.

186

Harvey waited in front of the wooden doors. 'Are you ready?'

'What is all this?' Barney had never liked being kept in the dark.

Melissa still had a hold of his arm in hers. 'You know you mean the world to the both of us and this year we are honoured that you trust us to organise the ball. I know you were hesitant to let it happen here, but we want to show you how special it's going to be.'

When Harvey opened up the doors Melissa watched Barney's reaction. It was clear he hadn't expected to see anything all that different to the usual empty wooden beams up above, the odd hay bale lying on its side here and there, straw strewn across the floor, the apple press in the corner with the side table, a basket of apples waiting to be dealt with. Eyes wide, he took in the scene that looked set for the annual ball already. Instead of bare wood everywhere, white linen had been wound around the rafters hanging low enough to create a makeshift ceiling with the effect of clouds billowing, the gaps between like a vast sky of possibility. Harvey's mum had helped them out with sourcing the material, she had a contact who'd jumped at the chance to help the local community. Hay bales were piled more strategically than usual, the stage had been cleared of detritus – empty apple trays, a few tools, an empty wicker basket or two – and instead had three music stands as well as a chair, and it was easy to envisage a band playing first the songs that got everyone up and moving, then those that spoke of the love in the room as they slowed the tempo right down.

Melissa had sourced white bunting, which looped along the walls, as well as fairy lights, running across horizontal beams and wrapped around those that were vertical. On top of tables Melissa had arranged vases of delicate lisianthus that wouldn't last until the day of the ball but she'd replace them, it was worth a bit of added expense to have the floral decorations here now. The chairs had big white bows tied around their backs, Benjamin from the pub had donated two old wooden barrels that he and Harvey had brought down here earlier than anyone else in the Cove would've been up this morning while Melissa kept watch to make sure they weren't sprung by Barney. Now, the wooden barrels had tealights in mason jars on top and one would, on the day of the event, also have a collection box for any further donations to White Clover. A couple of days ago at Melissa's request Tracy had donated a big photo album that had never been used, and now it was sitting on the second barrel by the doors to the barn, along with a pen pushed into a wooden holder ready for guests to sign in and leave a message marking the occasion.

Melissa began to walk backwards, hand outstretched. 'It won't be long before this barn is once again filled with people from Heritage Cove, everyone you know and love, Barney.' She went over to him. 'This year while you recover you can be as involved as you like. We won't force it, but I'd really like to follow tradition. You always dance with me. I don't care if you need holding up, I want that dance.'

'Well…' he cleared his throat. 'I suppose I can't argue with that.'

Harvey was letting her take the lead but was watching the exchange the whole time and she smiled over to him. Had their efforts paid off?

She turned back to Barney. 'Would you try, for me? Maybe go through the exercises some more, make an effort?'

'I can do that for you.'

She smiled. 'Some of my fondest memories are of this barn and the ball, I'm only sorry I missed out on so many years before coming back to see it again for myself.'

'You're here now,' Barney replied, taking her hand in his, 'that's all that matters.'

*

Seeing Barney's reaction this morning had justified this visit even more strongly for Melissa. Barney and Heritage Cove were very much a part of her, she'd just shut them away for a little while, a bit like hiding under the bed covers when you were scared. She'd been frightened to confront a place that held not only special memories but painful ones she wanted to run away from. But being back here, she realised she couldn't do that any longer.

She left the inn after having lunch out in the garden – a ploughman's Sandy had piled with cheese, ham, pickles and chunky wedges of bread. She'd had her lunch with sunglasses on, the newspaper laid out in front of her as though she was reading, but her mind had been on what was coming next.

She walked down the gravelled path leading to the chapel itself, the grass too long on one side and swaying in the wind, begging for a cut. She continued on the same path alongside the chapel and to the back and didn't stop until she reached the very end of the grassy area where the single headstone stood solidly. Crouching down, she laid an arrangement she'd bought at the florist tucked away in a side street beyond the pub. She placed it down as delicately as if the stone beneath were able to feel her movements, arranging the ivy that surrounded white carnations and large-headed yellow roses so it nestled perfectly.

She sat on the grass for a while, nothing but silence and the odd cry of a gull to keep her company. When an ant ran across her skin she got up, brushed the strands of grass clinging to her dress and stood next to the headstone again. She put a hand against the surface, she reached out and ran her fingers across the epitaph, the simple words, the goodbye that would never be enough, that would never let her have another moment with her mum or her dad, the centre of her world.

She thought about all the times as a kid they'd run along the adjacent track to head down to the cove, her mum fretting she'd fall she took the track so fast, her dad laughing and encouraging her to keep being a kid and never worry about a little bit of dirt.

When had life got so hard? When had being an adult eclipsed everything else, all that was fun, all the freedom you had when you were young without really realising?

'I miss you,' she said quietly, her hand still on the headstone. And it was only when she spoke that she realised the tears had snuck up on her. She couldn't stop them. She looked upwards to try her best at halting them in their tracks, but they were adamant.

A bird swooped across the sky as though it hadn't a care in the world and she looked back at the place her parents were buried again. 'Why did you have to leave me? It's not fair…it's not fair…it's not fair…' She no longer cared about the tears, they'd been collecting for years, trying to find their way out.

She hadn't realised anyone else was nearby until a hand rested on her shoulder. The person hadn't even scared her, she'd been lost in the moment, still was. 'It's so unfair,' she repeated as the visitor folded her into her arms.

Tilly let her cry against her until there were no more tears left.

'Better?' Tilly asked when the sobs subsided at last.

She looked up. 'I'm sorry, I've cried all over you.'

'Don't worry, although if there'd been snot I'm not sure I could forgive you.' She sat down on the grass cross-legged and slipped off her beaded flip flops in the summer heat.

Melissa followed suit and sat down next to her.

'Is this the first time you've been here since you left?' Her hair was wound up in a high bun, she had on a floaty paisley dress, a typical uniform she wore at the shop and one that suited her for its informality and comfort.

'First time since the funeral. I didn't even come here the day I left.'

'You say it like you're apologising.'

'You don't think it's terrible?'

'Why do you care what I think?'

'I know you're not happy with me for what I did to Barney.'

Tilly took a deep breath. 'I may have been a little rash going off at you like that when I first bumped into you. It wasn't nice.'

'Don't pity me because you've seen me cry.'

Tilly smiled. 'It's more than that. Barney has been there for me a lot over the last year. I'm not sure why he was so much easier to confide in than anyone else, but he was, and in turn I look out for him. I know how much Barney misses you, he never hid the fact, and I guess when you came back all I could think was that you were going to leave again. Not that you can't – it's more that I know it'll be hard for Barney all over again.'

'I know I hurt him, but I think he understands why.'
Especially if Lois had done the same thing to him.

'Sounds about right. He's always been fair,
understanding too.'

'You know, my parents would be so mad if they
knew I'd done a runner from the Cove. They were as
hooked into this village as Barney is.'

'I bet they'd be proud you came back when you were
needed.'

'You think so?'

'I know so.' She groaned and pushed herself to
standing. 'Now, I've got a numb bum sitting on the
ground for so long, fancy an iced bun from the bakery
and then a browse in my shop? I've got a lot of new
things since you last came in.'

'You're on. Just give me one more minute here.'

Tilly nodded and left her to it.

Melissa sat there a while in quiet contemplation, and
when a breeze disrupted the flower arrangement she left
the cemetery knowing she wouldn't ever leave it so long
before she came to visit again.

*

Melissa saw far too many things she liked in the candle
shop – a pair of beautiful teardrop ivory candles set in
glass stands, burgundy and corn-yellow floating candles
to put in elegant glass bowls, scented candles in orange
pomander and thyme and mint, and the most gorgeous
earthenware to hold tealights. She came away with the
earthenware to take back to her flat in Windsor and
suspected she'd be back in the shop before long, giving
her credit card a good workout.

After her tears earlier Melissa felt a strange sense of
relief. She hadn't expected to cry, she hadn't expected to
bump into Tilly, never mind to call a truce with her.

She'd expected to go to the cemetery, feel incredibly sad, and to want to run. But she hadn't. She'd happily gone to Tilly's shop after the bakery, they'd talked more about inconsequential things – her flat, the trendy shops in her local area, Tilly's new stock – and then Tilly had taken charge by telling her she couldn't avoid people any longer. They would all see her at the ball, it was time for both her and those who judged her to get over themselves. She'd taken control and made her go to the tea rooms, where they'd seen Etna who ran the show and Patricia who worked there. Both had acted as though Melissa had only been in there last week, asking no questions apart from whether they wanted tea or scones, both of which they'd declined for now. Then it had been heads held high and a walk along the length of The Street, anyone they knew nodding a hello in passing, everyone else going about their business just as they were.

By late afternoon after a phone call from Jay, she was feeling the most relaxed she'd been in a long while. He hadn't mentioned the idea of a bolthole in Europe again, she'd been too busy blabbering on about the Wedding Dress Ball and how the plans were coming together so well. But even still, Melissa knew it was time to stop putting off the inevitable and go see her little cottage.

She walked from the inn, past the bus stop and to the road beyond that led down to the riding school, past the paddocks where horses grazed and a group of riders saddled up preparing to go out on a hack, and, finally, she stood outside the cottage where she'd gone from being a baby to a toddler, an unsure teen to a woman, a happy daughter of two doting parents who had the world at her feet to a grieving adult who didn't know which way to turn. The path still had the wobbly brick right on the edge where it met the pavement – she put her foot out to test it. The flowerbeds in front of the downstairs window had kept the familiar curve her dad had dug one summer for her mum to plant bulbs to add colour to the otherwise neat and tidy tiny patch of lawn. Only one cluster of tulips remained, the rest had died away for another season and now bright orange marigolds and a row of rich blue delphiniums had begun to spring up to take their turn. The front door had once been the same blue as those delphiniums but over the years it had faded, the paint had peeled near the letterbox, and her mum never had planted those roses across the door. She wondered, did the tenants love to light a fire in the winter months, cursing as they cleaned out the grate the following morning, but realising as they cosied down in the room and watched the flames flicker that it was worth it every time? She wanted to know whether the stairs still creaked on the second step up unless you stood on the edge that wasn't carpeted, and if, when you opened the windows at the back of the property, you could hear the distant braying of the ponies at the riding school.

Melissa had so many good memories caught up in this cottage. It was funny to think that part of her life was contained in those walls that no amount of repainting would gloss over. So much was the same, yet everything had changed. She thought about the holiday homes she and Jay had looked at on the internet, including the latest one he'd found, and realised she had never wanted anything less. She might not live here anymore, but somehow she didn't want to cut her ties with this little cottage. Maybe she would one day, but for now, she wasn't ready.

When a little boy's face popped up at the window investigating who had taken such an interest in the cottage, she went back the way she'd come.

Back on The Street there was only one place to go now, the cove, where she'd done so much of her thinking over the years, and when she turned down beside the chapel she smiled and didn't feel that tug of pain or brace herself when she knew she was parallel to the cemetery. Instead, she felt a sense of peace.

Her smiled widened when she got to the part of the track from where she caught her first glimpse of the water. She made her way down to the sands, picked up a handful of stones and walked down to the water's edge.

She stood, breathing in the salty tang, letting the breeze caress her skin. The sound of the waves made her shoulders drop and she relaxed. She loved the feel of the sea air on her skin. After the last time she'd come down here she'd got back to the Heritage Inn and tried to brush her hair, tugging at the tangled strands bound together with salt residue. She knew it would be the same after this visit too.

She tried to skim the stones, one after the other, none of them managing to come up from their initial immersion. She'd only just run out of stones when one came from past her right shoulder and expertly hopped from one part of the water to the next, the next and the next after that.

'You never were any good.' Harvey came to stand beside her.

'And you could always do it,' she answered with a smile. People seemed to be springing up when she least expected today. 'It frustrated me no end.' She didn't have to look to see he was grinning.

'May I?' He took hold of her wrist when she picked up another stone and when she didn't move her arm away he showed her how to rest the stone on her second finger while making a backwards C shape with her thumb and first finger. 'You want to angle it at about twenty degrees, give a side throw, flicking the wrist.'

'Like this?' She moved so it was at the correct angle.

'Go for it.'

She threw again, tried another and then a third, which skimmed twice and then plopped into the depths of the water.

'Practice,' he said.

She sat on the sand as the water gently lapped a few feet away. It was cooler this afternoon as though the summer had already had enough for one day but with a cardigan on over a navy-and-white-striped cotton dress it was pleasant enough. 'Why aren't you at work?'

'I was, I went after we showed Barney the barn, but now I'm done for the day – it was a very early start, remember.' He let the quiet between them settle.

'You must like having varied hours.'

'I do, especially when I get to enjoy time down here.'

'I've been to a lot of countries, you know I've seen my share of beautiful beaches,' she told him, 'but this is special.'

'You can't beat the British seaside. It's got character. Pity we can't make the cove like one of those fancy gardens in London where you need a key to gain access. Residents only.'

'I like the way you think,' she grinned.

He picked up another stone and toyed with it before skimming it across the water. 'How are you feeling now, about being back here?'

She could tell from his voice he wasn't all that sure about asking the question. 'Better than I was, put it that way. I went to the cemetery today.'

'And how was that?'

'Traumatic.' But she was smiling. She told him how Tilly turned up, how they'd talked, how they'd spent time together and Tilly had made her go into the tea rooms, walk The Street with her head held high and get over it.

'She's a good sort, Tilly. Bossy, but I'm pleased she's giving you a break.'

'I spent a small fortune in her shop, maybe that was her ulterior motive.'

'You'll be going back to Windsor with an extra suitcase if you're not careful.'

'Don't joke!'

'Are you missing home?'

'I'm getting fed up with living out of a suitcase and in one room. I get bored unless I'm with Barney.' Or with him, but she wasn't going to admit that. The other night when she'd gone to his house to tell him about the letter she'd found, she knew deep down it was an excuse. She'd wanted to see him, she wanted to know he hadn't met up with Casey after going to his mum's, and her relief when he'd turned up alone had wracked her with guilt when she thought of Jay. At the start of her relationship with Jay she'd got the feeling that complicated emotions weren't a thing with him and it was a relief after everything that had gone on. But now, spending so much time with Harvey was making her question herself and it was hard to know which way to turn. Part of her longed to leave and head back to familiarity, her job, Jay; the other part of her felt as though she really did belong here, and the more time she spent with Harvey, the harder it got. She knew that her being in another man's company wouldn't faze Jay but the history between herself and Harvey might. And the longer she kept his name out of any of their conversations whether by phone or email, the harder it got to mention him.

Harvey gave up skimming stones and sat down beside her, watching the gentle waves coming in to the cove, splaying out and clutching every grain of sand they could before fading away again. 'Did you see the tears in Barney's eyes this morning when we showed him the barn?'

'I did. And I'm glad.' She nudged him when he pulled a face. 'Not because we made him cry but because he's all in. He might not be running the show, but I think perhaps it might go well and make him want it to run next year.'

'And where will you be next year?'

She shrugged and then asked, 'What brings you down here anyway?' He wasn't walking Winnie so she wondered whether he'd followed her down her. Her suspicions were correct.

'I saw you head down this way and I wanted to talk to you about Barney. I've been thinking about what you said, the reasons behind Barney hosting the ball in the first place.'

'You don't think I'm being ridiculous?'

'No, I don't. It didn't occur to me before but after I left his place, after we'd shown him the barn, I remembered a conversation I had with him a few years back. I'd seen the newspaper coverage about the event and for some reason I asked more questions, I wanted to know what gave him the idea and why he picked that charity.'

'Can you remember what he said?'

'He always insisted he got the idea from somewhere else and it just seemed a good idea for a community event. He didn't answer the bit about the charity. From what I remember he avoided that part of my question and changed the subject. He said helping the community was the most important thing.'

'He always did have everyone else in mind.'

'He did, still does. You know, he hated that you'd left here and gone to London, not just because he never saw you, but because he said you'd be one in thousands, you probably wouldn't know your neighbours, nobody looked out for each other anymore.'

'He told me all that before I left too, but he never once tried to stop me.'

'He wouldn't have, he thinks too much of you.'

'Why didn't you stop me, Harvey? I mean, you didn't go with me, but you never told me not to go either.'

The muscles in his forearms twitched when he stood and brushed the sand from his jeans. 'Let's focus on Barney, shall we?'

'We need to talk, Harvey.' She followed after him when he began to walk away, close to his heels to close the gap. 'I'm not looking for an argument.'

She hadn't expected him to turn around so suddenly, their bodies almost touching, the wind lifting her hair and blowing it across her face. She could smell a mixture of the lavender shampoo she used and something more earthy, masculine, a part of him.

He reached a hand up and hooked her hair away from her face and in that moment she saw the regret in his eyes, the love that might still be there. Or was she making up stories in her mind that weren't really there at all?

'Hey, you guys!' The voice behind Harvey broke the moment and it was Tracy coming down onto the sands with her dog, Mischief.

'Hey.' Melissa reached down to fuss the dog but it was more intent on barrelling towards the water.

The wind had picked up and Tracy was struggling to keep the strands of her hair away from her face too. 'Mischief loves it down here, she's the boss some days when I just have to get her outside.' She looked from Harvey to Melissa and back again but if she picked up on anything she didn't mention it.

'I'll leave you women to talk,' said Harvey, waving a goodbye and making his way back up the sands towards the steps that would take him away, back up to the track.

Melissa watched him go as Tracy encouraged Mischief out of the water so they could walk along the shore. The dog had boundless energy but was obedient with it.

'I've already walked her around Heritage Cove,' said Tracy, 'but I knew coming down here to the beach would wear her out. She'll likely sleep all afternoon in the garden.' She threw a ball she'd brought with her some distance in front of them for Mischief to chase after.

As they walked along Melissa told Tracy all about Barney and his reaction to what they'd done with the barn. 'I think I may have been right to suspect the ball is more important to him than he's ever let on.'

'How so?'

'I don't want to talk about him behind his back, but trust me, there's more to this than we realise.'

'Does Harvey know you're thinking that way?'

'We talked, yes. And get that look off your face, it doesn't mean anything.'

'Sure it doesn't. You two looked pretty tight when I got down here a minute ago.' Tracy threw the ball even further when Mischief dropped it at her feet again. She'd always been a solid cricket player at school, much to the boys' chagrin when she could throw the ball much further than any of them managed.

'We're friends again, I suppose.'

Tracy let it go. 'If you have a hunch about Barney – and I won't pry – then why not ask him about it?'

'Barney isn't the easiest person to get information out of.'

'I can well imagine.'

'He has shared things with us. He's talked about being a young boy, his school days, the pranks he and his buddies used to play. He's talked about when he first arrived in the Cove and moved into his house, the barn that was part of the attraction. But there's a great big gap between him being young and living elsewhere and his coming here that he never talks about. There's a sadness somewhere and I think that's what's got into his head since the fall, the things he's lost or missed out on. He keeps warning me not to do the same, not to have regrets. I can't help thinking that if we can get to the bottom of it, have him deal with whatever happened, then he might let it go once and for all and be back to himself.'

'We would all love that in the Cove. I was only saying to Etna this morning that I miss seeing him wandering up The Street, she misses talking with him over a cup of tea and a scone.' Tracy grimaced at the amount of slobber on the ball when Mischief brought it to her this time but threw it again and rinsed her hand off in the sea. 'Let's face it, if anyone knows Barney well, it's you and Harvey. You both do what you think is best.

If you want to know more, why not do some investigating. Barney obviously isn't going to give you anything if he's refused so far.'

Melissa smiled. 'I'll bet you're a great mum, you sound so wise.'

'I doubt my kids would agree.' She laughed and scolded Mischief, who'd lost interest in the ball and instead run into the water before coming up close and shaking her coat all over the both of them. 'Did she get you?'

'A little, but I don't mind. So you don't think we're being nosy and prying into Barney's private affairs?'

'He's not leaving you any choice. And you're doing it because you care. That makes it all right in my book.'

The only problem was, Melissa had no idea where to start.

Chapter Ten

Two days after he saw Melissa down by the water's edge, it was breakthrough day at the house Harvey and the rest of the crew were working on. The family had cleared out for the day to let the team get on with the task of cutting through the ceiling and installing the new stairs. This was the most exciting part for the owners, because rather than disruption and banging all day every day, they got to finally envisage what the finished result would be. Harvey remembered this stage at Tumbleweed House, it had been the mark of a new beginning, a fresh start to rid the place of tormenting memories.

Harvey and workmate Bruce went outside to the garden and between them carried the new main stair length up to the first floor. The corner steps had already been fixed in position and with a little manipulation and a couple of swear words from Bruce when he almost trapped his fingers – he seemed to do all his cursing when he was away from his kids – the stairs were a perfect fit. Harvey took the drill and fixed the screws in at the very top before wiping the back of his hand across his brow.

'I need a beer tonight after all this,' said Bruce after one more swear word for good measure when he knocked his funny bone on the edge of a wall.

'I'm with you there, mate,' said Harvey, fixing a screw lower down on the staircase. He set down the drill when one of the lads passed him a mug of tea. 'Cheers.'

After a couple of thirsty gulps he stood back to admire their work. 'Looks good, even though I do say so myself.'

'Always the best part,' Bruce confirmed. 'And one of the hardest.'

'I don't know, I'd take lifting that staircase over getting those steel supports into place.' The tea went down very well, gave him the impetus to carry on. 'You got your tickets for the ball yet?' As well as flyer coverage, he always mentioned it at work to make sure everyone knew about the event of the year and was reminded that it wasn't all that far away.

'You mean ticket, singular,' Bruce grinned. He set down his own cup and began to prepare to finish the plasterboarding now the stairs were in place. He found the adhesive they'd use to paste onto the wooden frames.

'Not got anyone to take?'

'Working on it,' Bruce laughed. He'd had few dates since he and his wife split up, although he'd smartened up his image and worked out at a gym as well as doing a physical job. He'd told Harvey it was a good place to meet women, but so far he hadn't proven his point. 'How about you? You and Melissa picking up where you left off?'

'Hardly.'

'Who's getting lunch today?' Tim called out from wherever he was working on the floor above.

'That'll be me,' Harvey called back. 'I'll go after I've helped lift the plasterboards into place.' And just like that Bruce's quizzing about Melissa had been avoided as they both concentrated on lifting an end of the board each and put it against the adhesive.

Harvey made notes on his phone of the orders from the others and left the semi-detached residence on the outskirts of Heritage Cove to drive the short distance into the village and to the bakery. There was a chain bakery in the next village, but Celeste and Jade did the best sandwiches around. And besides, in Heritage Cove they supported each other and that included the small businesses that operated there. If they didn't, the village would lose its character and personality. It wasn't that any of them liked living in the past or were blinkered to changes, it was just the way it had always been.

At the bakery Harvey reeled off the orders – the usual ham and cheese for Clarke, egg and cress for Tim, a roll filled with roast beef and horseradish for Bruce. And for himself, Harvey humoured Celeste who loved to experiment with flavours. Last week it had been a poppyseed bagel with smoked salmon, capers, juicy tomato and red onion, today it was pulled pork with portobello mushrooms and lashings of chipotle sauce.

Celeste, in her usual white apron with a cloud of bakery dust puffing against her forearms as she loaded more bloomer loaves into the rack, memorised his order and pulled on plastic gloves ready to handle the long ciabatta roll and position the fillings. She slit the bread down the side just as the door opened and let in a welcoming cool breeze from the outside.

Blacksmith Lucy had come into the bakery and watched Celeste making up Harvey's part of the order. 'That looks interesting.' After a brief recap of what it would be she said, 'I'll take one of those too please.'

Harvey laughed as Celeste generously added the chipotle sauce. 'You might want to go easy on the sauce,' he warned Lucy. 'Rumour has it, it'll blow your head off.'

'I can handle it,' she smiled.

'How are you enjoying the Cove?' He didn't see her around much but when he did she seemed content, always polite without giving too much away.

'I'm slowly getting used to it. I found it a bit quiet at first but there aren't many villages or towns that have this kind of character anymore.'

'Fred better watch out, you'll take over completely one day. How's he doing?'

'He's still with his sister in Cambridgeshire, he checks in every now and then, but he's dropped more than a few hints that he might not want to come back permanently.'

Celeste's ears pricked up as she added Harvey's wrapped lunch to the bag with the others and then pushed pulled pork into the second ciabatta roll for Lucy before scooping up more of the portobello mushrooms. 'Fred said he'd work until he was no longer standing.' Head tilted to one side, she said, 'It'll be a shame not to see him return.' When Lucy pointed out she had flour in her hair a smile stretched out the freckles that ran along the bridge of her nose and across high cheek bones. Both she and Jade were tall and willowy with the trademark Irish porcelain skin and darker-than-ebony hair, and the flour stood out more than it would on anyone else.

'For what it's worth he sounded jolly enough on the phone and he intends to come back for the ball in a few weeks,' Lucy assured her as she did the honours and brushed the flour away for Celeste, who still had her gloves on and wouldn't take them off until she finished handling the ingredients. 'When I first took over, he seemed strung out, perhaps he needed the rest and some time away has made him see that working late in his life is good in some ways but not others.'

'He's better off with his sister,' said Harvey after paying his bill by contactless and slipping the card back into his wallet. 'She's only a couple of years younger, they'll be good company for each other.'

'It's nice he has someone,' Lucy smiled.

Harvey wondered what Lucy's story was, he hadn't seen or heard of any men hanging around. Did she have someone too? She was attractive but she clearly liked to keep her private life just that, so he didn't grill her. 'Thanks, Celeste.' He picked up the big paper bag filled with his orders as Celeste and Lucy chatted away in the way women did, speculating about what the old beach shop would possibly become. According to Celeste the new owner planned to demolish it and put something else in its place. But Harvey left them to it. He'd never been good at small talk and always envied Barney for his ability to chat to anyone and everyone. Barney was one of the few men Harvey knew who could talk as much as any female.

He climbed into his pickup out front but before he could drive away a voice asked, 'What are you smiling at?' It was Melissa, she'd poked her head through the open passenger-side window as he put down the sandwiches and started up the engine.

'I'm hungry and in about twenty minutes I get to sink my teeth into a blow-your-head-off-chipotle-sauce-laden lunch.'

She looked down at the bag and the wrapped-up parcels tucked inside. 'I tried that yesterday, you'll like it. She made the sauce herself, you know.'

'A woman of many talents.'

'Do you have a minute or are you racing back to work?'

'I've got a minute.' For her he had so much more. 'Hop in.'

She climbed into the passenger seat and held the lunch bag on her lap but not before he got a welcome glimpse of the top of her leg as her shorts rode up. 'I think we should find Lois,' she said without preamble.

His first reaction was to ask why bother but instead he went for, 'Nice idea, but how do you suggest we do that?'

'I'm not too sure, but…will you help me?'

'You're serious?'

'Never been more serious. Barney saw the barn transformed ready for the ball and we both saw the emotion on his face. The fact he has this dress, the note, that he has never told us anything about Lois but has said he regrets not making amends with his past, all tells me he never got any kind of closure. It's holding him back. I know it is. It's what's behind his warnings for me not to have any regrets either, and I think it's why he can't be bothered to even try to get back to normal. And let's face it, he's never going to tell us anything.'

'You're right about that.'

'So you'll help?'

He puffed out his cheeks. 'You don't think we should take the hint, that he really doesn't want us to pry?'

'This is too important to ignore, Harvey. I might be grasping at straws but I'd rather try something than nothing.'

'You're worried he'll get worse when you leave.'

'Maybe. And I'm not big-noting myself or anything like that.'

'I didn't mean to imply that you were. I get it, you're worried that if he's not pushed, he'll keep on the path he's found himself on and give up.'

'Exactly. Whatever happened to him and to Lois, he needs to deal with it and then move on.'

'Ever the optimist,' said Harvey.

'Pessimist,' she batted back.

'He might be angry if we interfere.'

With an accepting smile she replied, 'If we get nowhere then he'll never know, will he?'

'I can't help wondering whether at seventy-one years old, he's got a right to be left in peace, a right to make his own decisions whether we approve of them or not.'

She thought about it but not for long before she lifted up the bag and climbed out, then settled the bag back onto the passenger seat for him. Leaning in through the passenger window again, she said, 'Seven o'clock tonight in the beer garden at the pub, we'll talk. Enjoy your lunch.'

And with that she left him to drive back to his job and attempt to concentrate.

But this time it wasn't Barney occupying his thoughts, it was her, the closeness he hadn't felt in a long while and that had been building up ever so slowly since she showed up in the village. And the way she'd talked to him just now? There was no tension, just a sense of togetherness, maybe a light flirtation even, working towards something they both wanted.

Or was he kidding himself and very soon she'd jump into her car, drive back to Berkshire and forget all about this brief hiatus?

*

Melissa often shopped when she was overseas, it was a good way to fill in time until the next flight, you got to find bargains and unique items. As a result the wardrobe in her flat was bursting and it meant that when she came away to the Cove, she'd been able to fill her suitcase with plenty of outfits so that she wouldn't have to constantly face doing laundry. But it also meant that she had options and she'd tried on three different dresses in an effort to decide what to wear to the pub to meet Harvey. Cursing herself for her indecisiveness, she settled on a polka-dot ruffle-neck dress that wrapped around and tied at the waist.

Today hadn't been a scorching summer's day as it could sometimes be at this time of year, but the evening was muggy, the temperature hadn't dropped much at all, and as she walked over to where Harvey was already sitting at a picnic-style table in the beer garden of The Copper Plough, she went from feeling comfortable to unnerved as he watched her. It was almost as though time had stood still and they were exactly the same Harvey and Melissa who had come here after work to meet for drinks, the same couple who had won the pub quiz more times than they could count, the same people who'd thought they'd be together forever.

She was going to ask him if he'd like a drink but as she got closer she saw he'd already bought two beers.

'Thank you.' She sat down and clinked her bottle against his. 'Cheers.'

'Cheers. Nice evening for it.' He took a swig. 'You look good. Sorry, am I still allowed to say that?'

She smiled. 'Of course you are.'

'You never used to wear your hair that way.'

She'd pinned it all up loosely into a bun with strands hanging down. 'It's laziness, I really should put it up more neatly.'

'Don't.'

Uncomfortable at the focus she moved the subject on to Barney and what they should do.

'I'm still not completely convinced we should start trying to unearth Barney's secrets,' Harvey admitted, 'but I'm trying to stay open-minded.'

'I don't want to upset Barney either, and I do have my reservations, but I'm only here until a couple of days after the Wedding Dress Ball and I can't waste any more time.'

'What if we can't find anything out at all?'

'Then we let it go.'

She tried to ignore the zip of electricity through her body when he finished the rest of his beer and tilted back his head, revealing the stubble that ran part-way down his throat. She could remember scraping her face against it as they lay next to one another, the feel of it when it got softer if he didn't get around to shaving.

He caught her staring but she was rescued when he had a brief exchange with a couple of men who walked by. Harvey introduced her and told her they worked for the same company he did. They were out with a group at the other side of the beer garden helping one of the men to wet the baby's head after his wife delivered a second son earlier that day. As they talked Melissa watched the men. This was one of the reasons she didn't talk to Jay about her life in Heritage Cove. He wouldn't understand. He'd never lived in a small village or town where people knew one another and quite often the intricacies of their lives. They'd never taken the time to get to know anyone else on their own streets, not even their neighbours. Everyone was so busy going about their everyday lives, they didn't have the time to stop and say a simple hello, a smile in greeting was as far as it went. Jay wasn't much of a fan of cosy pubs like this one either, preferring modern and spacious rather than quaint and characterful, restaurants and bars that erred on the pricey side with portions that left you somewhat wanting rather than a pub with hearty meals that made a half-empty stomach an impossibility.

'I think he'll be soaking the baby's head before long,' Harvey said when the men went back to the group.

'I'm sorry, did you want to join them?'

'I can do that any other time.'

She looked over to where the group were getting well into the celebrations, pints lined up in wait on the table. 'I hope that guy's wife doesn't mind him being that merry when he gets home.'

'She's in hospital for a couple of days so I think he may well be making the most of his freedom while he can, he has his dad babysitting. How about you?' He sipped his beer. 'Do you see kids in your future?'

Where had that question come from? 'Hadn't thought about it.'

'No? Not even with your other half, you must talk about it? I always imagined you with a family one day.'

'I could say the same about you.'

'Not met the right person.'

She gulped back her beer. 'We need to make a plan, about Barney.'

With what could've been a faint eye-roll, she wasn't sure, he asked, 'Where do you suggest we start?'

'I've been thinking about this.' In between deciding what to wear and applying her make-up ready to meet the man who wasn't even her boyfriend let alone fiancé. 'Do you remember him telling us that he lived in a Norfolk village?'

'That narrows it down,' he harrumphed.

She plonked her beer bottle on the table, missing the cardboard mat entirely. This was what was hard between them, the not knowing whether he was happy to be spending time with her and trying to help Barney or whether he was still so angry with her for how things worked out that he couldn't move past it. 'Look, maybe we should forget it, you're obviously so sure we won't find anything that you don't want to try.'

'I never said that. I apologise for the sarcasm. Continue.'

Tears began to form, something she hadn't predicted, certainly not tonight on a balmy summer's evening in one of the prettiest beer gardens she'd seen in a long while. The rear windows of the pub had flower boxes filled with the brightest petals, variegated ivy covered the walls, blue flowers on the wisteria going over the back door added a pop of colour and well-tended flowerbeds added a sweet seasonal aroma to the air.

'Melissa, I really am sorry. I'm being a dickhead.'

'You are.' But her tears weren't because of the way he'd bitten her head off, she could handle a bit of attitude, it was more to do with her mounting confusion. Lately it was as though she had two lives, one here, one in Windsor. And it was as though she'd passed the optimum mourning for her parents by going to their graveside and dealing with her emotions, and next in line to process was her feelings about this man sitting opposite her.

Her voice wobbled. 'We have to do this before I leave. I can't bear the thought of this being the start of the end for Barney.'

'You always were good at drama,' he teased.

'If you're referring to my god-awful performance in *Aladdin* at the playhouse then please, I beg you not to bring that up. Not my finest moment – I forgot half my lines.'

'You did just fine.' He took a swig of beer after smiling as he remembered the night she was talking about. 'Right, what do you have in mind to get going with the search for answers?'

'I think we should go back to the village in Norfolk. Barney has talked about living there, we know how much he loved to sail, he's never made a secret of going to a marina and hanging out there a lot as a kid and as a teen. What we don't know is what happened to bring him to Heritage Cove.'

'I can't remember what the Norfolk village is called.'

'Me neither. So we're going to have to do some detective work to find out where it was.'

'Challenge accepted,' he grinned, bringing out his phone as she did the same.

Between them they found maps and lists of towns and villages in Norfolk online, but none of them stood out as having been a place Barney had mentioned. There was one that kind of did but both Harvey and Melissa remembered it had been somewhere Barney holidayed several times as a boy, another stood out until Harvey recalled that it was only because there had been a street festival there and Barney had supplied apples for the cider-making contest.

They were well through their second drinks when Melissa's phone rang and Jay's name popped up on the caller display. She let it ring out but felt guilty. 'I should really call him back.'

'It's fine, you do what you need to do.' And if Harvey was bothered he didn't let it show. 'The name of the village might come to one of us when we least expect it. Maybe sitting here trying to remember is making it harder. You go and make your call, I need to get back to Winnie, she's been on her own for a while today.'

'I can always take her for a walk when you're too busy.' Was she offering for Winnie's benefit or so she could be more involved with Harvey? She didn't want to think about the truth behind that one.

'I appreciate the offer, I'll let you know.' He picked up the empty bottles. 'I'll visit Barney in the morning and see if I can get him talking about the elusive village.'

'Be subtle.'

'Goes without saying.' And with a touch on her shoulder that sent goose pimples shooting all the way down her arm, he left her to it.

*

The next day Harvey went to see Barney and watched him pottering around the kitchen. 'You're moving a lot better. It's good to see you out of that chair.'

'That chair and I are good friends. I need my rest, remember.'

Harvey wished he hadn't mentioned it because Barney had already gone back to the chair in question. 'Remember to look out for Winnie. She has a habit of lying right in your path, I don't want her tripping you up.' She was currently settled on the floor between the table and the armchair, out of the way for now and within reach for Barney.'

'She's fine, stop fussing. It's good to have her around, I miss having a dog.'

'You could get another.'

Barney swooshed a hand through the air to get rid of the suggestion, his other hand still on Winnie's ear, tickling it the way she liked it. 'I'm too old. And it would live longer than me, it wouldn't be fair.'

'If you keep talking like that you'll make yourself old, whether you are or not.' Harvey made them both a cup of tea and delivered Barney's to the table by the armchair. 'It's a pity you're not up for a walk down to the cove.'

'I wish I was.'

'Soon, maybe.'

'Maybe. I'd love to get some sea air, it's the way I grew up.'

Harvey leapt in at the chance of delving more. 'Norfolk, wasn't it?'

'That's right, on the coast. Near the water. But the path down to the cove, wouldn't be a good idea. I know you're all for me pushing my recovery but even you must see that would be madness. The ground's uneven, the rail's not sturdy enough for me to use. It'll have to wait.'

'Fair enough.' He wasn't going to argue and he'd rather talk about where Barney grew up than the Cove. 'Where was it in Norfolk that you grew up, Barney?'

'I wonder if Melissa has been down to the cove yet.'

Talk about a change of subject. 'She has. She came with me to walk Winnie, and I saw her there a few days later too.'

'She used to do all her thinking down there,' Barney smiled. 'You both did from what I remember, and your canoodling.'

Their conversation gave way to friendly banter about the days of operating the apple press as kids, the playing in the barn and climbing up to those beams, the crazy summer days when they'd stay out until all hours, the short days in the winter when he'd miss each of them as they packed off to go home earlier and earlier.

'Growing up in Heritage Cove is what I want one day for my own family,' said Harvey.

'Kids? Got to find yourself a woman first.'

'Yeah, I'm working on it.' He winked and blew onto his tea.

'Casey not marriage material?'

'Never heard you use that phrase before.'

'Awful phrase, I agree, but can't think how else to put it. Maybe as well as my hip fracture, my brain is catching up with my age.'

'Never. And I'll get you some sudoku puzzles to do instead of all that television you've been watching, that'll keep you sharp for years yet.'

'So…Casey?'

'We're just friends.'

'And what about Melissa? Are you two friends now she's back?'

'She's hardly back. She's here temporarily, for you, and she'll be going back to her other half soon enough.'

'Shame. I think she's seeing what she's missing in Heritage Cove.'

'I think she's got it made doing all the travelling, seeing what's out there in the world. It's what she always wanted.' The tea finished, Harvey took his empty mug and Barney's, rinsed them beneath the tap and popped them into the dishwasher. 'Did you travel much when you were younger?'

'Not really. I got a full-time job and worked hard. Too hard.'

'That's life, I guess.'

'Sometimes you need to look up from the path you're tramping down to see there's more to life than work, than money.'

'That sounds very philosophical.'

'Just advice, Harvey. Give Melissa a chance.'

'She had her chance, we both did.'

217

'I disagree. I've seen the way you two still look at each other. Don't be so adamant about a situation that you fail to see what's in front of you. And never give up on someone, even if they caused you pain. Fight for them, don't give up.'

'You sound like you're talking from experience.'

'I'm rambling, I apologise.' He pushed himself to standing. 'And now I need to lie down.'

The way Barney was talking, it seemed Melissa was spot on about something holding him back – he seemed to have regrets he'd never shared and perhaps if they could find out more, they might be able to help.

But Harvey also wondered whether perhaps he and Melissa should be listening to Barney and taking his advice, talking about whatever happened between them so they could finally lay the past to rest and move on with their lives.

Chapter Eleven

Melissa had been sitting on the back doorstep at Tumbleweed House waiting for Harvey for almost an hour. She wanted to see him the moment he got home, find out if he'd wheedled the name of the village out of Barney.

'I tried,' he told her as he stepped out of his truck, predicting why she was here and what she was about to ask. 'He changed the subject and I couldn't get him back on course.' He let Winnie out of the house to join them and Melissa didn't waste a second fussing over the dog.

'That man is far too stubborn,' she complained.

'Don't I know it.'

Winnie seemed about to settle down in the sunshine when Gracie showed up and instead she trotted over to her trusted walker. 'Hey you two, hey Winnie.'

Melissa thought that made them sound like a couple and when she surreptitiously looked at Harvey he didn't appear to mind – but, more worrying, neither did she. She watched Winnie settle down again although close to Gracie this time for maximum fuss.

'I think maybe you're too tired for a walk,' Gracie said to the dog, but as if to prove her wrong, Winnie got up, stretched and shook her body.

'I'll grab her lead,' Harvey chuckled.

'And some more poo bags,' Gracie called after him, brown eyes dancing in amusement, and she told Melissa, 'I got caught out yesterday when I took her for her walk.

I had three bags, she did four poos. I had to leave the last one and I felt terrible, then later on I stepped in another batch of dog poo on my way down to the cove. I guess that's what they call karma.'

Melissa grinned. 'I suppose it is.'

'I'll be making sure I have lots of extras from now on.'

'Do you have your own dog?'

'No, I can't afford the expense right now, but one day for sure. You?'

'My job takes me away too often so it's not possible. And I live in a flat, it wouldn't be fair.' She stroked Winnie, head to tail. 'This one loves the outdoors and all this space, the patches of sunshine she can curl up in.' She caught herself, she was talking with such familiarity, as though Winnie and this place were a part of her own life.

'You're a flight attendant, aren't you? It must be glamorous,' said Gracie, ruffling her chestnut curls, using both hands to shake them out before unhooking a hair bobble from around her wrist to tie it all back into a low ponytail out of the way.

'People tend to think so, but the reality is a little different. I do love it though. I've been to a lot of places I wouldn't otherwise have seen.'

'I'd love to travel one day, but it's the money for me.'

'Where would you like to go?'

'Aspen is top of my list, always wanted to go there, but for now I have to make do with holidays in the UK.'

'They can be just as special.'

'Some friends and I rented lodges in Center Parcs last year, that was awesome. This year I've booked a cabin with a friend up the coast in a really pretty village called Leafbourne. We've got a whole week, a good pub nearby, access to beach walks, a barbecue and a spa. I can't wait.'

'I'll bet,' Melissa smiled as Harvey returned with Winnie's lead and handed it to Gracie, who waved them goodbye and set off with an enthusiastic canine.

'That's it,' said Harvey from where he was standing next to Melissa, who still sat on the step of Tumbleweed House.

'What is?' She covered her eyes with her hand to avoid the sun and looked up to find him grinning like a loony.

'Leafbourne. That's the village where Barney grew up.'

'No way, too much of a coincidence. And why didn't we find it on the maps when we looked?'

He took out his phone and began searching for it. 'Because it's not actually in North Norfolk, not officially. It's right on the cusp so it didn't come up when we looked.'

'I don't remember the name,' she said. 'I mean, I remember him talking about what was there – a duck pond, a fish and chip shop he went to every Friday, the local school with its huge playing field. I remember him recounting the time he and his best friend had taken a small boat out without permission and the rollicking they got for doing it,' she laughed. 'That story always amused me. Check if there's a marina there.' Maybe they were onto something after all.

Harvey searched again on his phone. 'Yes, there's a marina. It has to be the place.' He turned the screen so Melissa could see it too.

'It's been a long time though, years since he was there.'

'You never know, a lot of these places are family-owned, there might be someone at the marina who knows of Barney and anything that may have happened.'

Her hopes faded. 'I'll bet there are a few marinas in Norfolk. I promise you, I'm not trying my best to be pessimistic, just realistic.'

'You wait here, I'm going to Barney's to find out whether we're right about this village.'

'You're just going to come out with it and ask him?'

'Trust me, I'll handle it just fine. Then if it's the right place, we'll take it from there.'

'Good luck!' she called after him and although neither of them said anything, they both knew she'd be waiting for him right in this very spot, relaxing in the sunshine, until he came back.

*

Melissa climbed into the front of the truck next to Harvey. 'How did you get Barney to confirm the name of the village without him asking why you wanted to know?'

'Easy, as soon as I got there I spotted a chew toy Winnie had left behind so I picked it up, pretending I'd come to the house for that. I said Winnie was with Gracie for a few hours because she'd be off on her holidays soon, and when I said she was going to Leafbourne, I saw him flinch. So I added, "Isn't that where you grew up?".'

'And he answered, just like that?'

'No reason not to, he has no reason to think we might charge up there in search of scraps of information about him. The words "wild goose chase" spring to mind but before I talk myself out of this, put your seat belt on and we'll get going.'

'Can we make a stop at White Clover first?' She clicked her belt into place. 'I'm wondering whether they might know something. Barney's donated to them for years, ever since the Wedding Dress Ball began – they must have some answers. I never thought to ask before. It's worth a try,' she added when he looked doubtful.

Driven on by the prospect of finding something, they detoured to White Clover before they did anything else. 'Don't tell me they've no idea either,' Harvey said when she climbed back into the truck fifteen minutes later. 'Or are they keeping schtum?'

'The latter. I got a feeling when I spoke to Ashley that she knows more, she just won't say. She launched into a whole speech about how they had donors who have been supporting them for decades – once they start they don't stop – then she was on to telling me they had international donors, so I got out while I could.'

'She's a talker,' Harvey smiled.

'For sure, no wonder Barney gets on well with her. And I do understand confidentiality rules so I didn't press her too much. Come on, let's get going. I only hope we have more luck in Leafbourne.'

He pulled out of the small car park so they could follow the road that would soon spit them out onto the dual carriageway. As they travelled they talked mostly about the village and the memories Barney had dredged up over the years. They both agreed it was odd that not once, to their recollection, had he ever slipped up and said the name Lois.

Melissa gave directions when necessary and mid-week, away from the busiest times of the day, the estimated one-and-a-half-hour trip went by quickly.

'Take a left here,' she instructed as they came to the first roundabout off the dual carriageway. 'You really

223

need to get a satnav, I'm almost out of charge on my phone from using maps so much.'

'We're managing to find our way, aren't we? And there's a charger in the flap behind your seat if you need it.'

'Not the point. If I wasn't here, you wouldn't be able to have your nose in your own phone. How would you manage then?'

'Oh, I don't know, possibly use a real-life map?'

'Very funny.'

'Not everything has to be new and shiny to be right.'

'Technology was invented to make life easier,' she threw back.

'Don't let Barney hear you talk like that.'

She let out a laugh as the truck slowed on the narrow country road that linked to another roundabout and another after that. 'Oh, please, he's the worst for it – have you seen how much he uses his iPad, paying bills or doing those mind games to keep his brain active? At least he did before he started watching so much television.'

They drove on further, roads lined either side with tall trees, countryside spreading out on the left as they drew closer to their destination.

'This is a real long shot you know,' said Harvey.

'I know.'

'I don't want you to be disappointed.' He harrumphed. 'Hell, I don't want to be disappointed. Now you've got me thinking, I want to know more.'

She watched the scenery rush past the window. Was this totally crazy? At least they were in this together; no matter what happened and what they did or didn't find out, having Harvey here would stop any disappointment from being so crushing. She was well aware her time in

Heritage Cove wouldn't go on forever and she hated the thought of leaving Barney like he was now, a shadow of the man who'd been so present in her life until she left. He had little moments where she thought she saw a spark of his former self, but it soon faded away as quickly as it came.

The sky grew ominous as the first sign to Leafbourne came into view and as they drove into the village itself Harvey slowed to match the speed limit. He reached out and put his hand on her knee, briefly, with a reassuring squeeze. 'Stop worrying.'

It was enough to jolt her into feeling guilty at her reaction to a man who wasn't Jay. Her mouth was dry and a warm feeling spread through her belly. 'I'm not.'

'You are, you're frowning.'

All she could do was make a joke and beam an over-the-top smile back at him that was nothing like a frown.

'I'm hungry,' he confessed as both of them spotted the fish and chip shop. 'What about you?'

'Hungry enough to stop there,' she said.

Harvey pulled into the lay-by outside. 'Do you think this is the very same fish and chip shop Barney used to come to years ago?'

'Who knows, but as long as they do a decent portion of chips with a pickled onion on the side, I'm happy.'

'You and your pickled onions,' he whispered as they went inside, earning himself a good dig in the ribs.

They had a half-an-hour time limit in the lay-by and so took the parcels of chips with the added meat pie for Harvey over to a bench at the side of a green space. 'Can't see any marina,' he concluded, his mouth half open to let the steam billow out.

'You'll burn your mouth if you're not careful.' She finished the last of the cool pickled onion.

'Blame my stomach, it couldn't wait for the food to cool down.'

She'd do her best not to think about his stomach. The day she'd held the ladder for him in the barn she'd caught sight of his toned tummy and the teasing line of hair as he stretched up to the beams above, and when he mentioned it now, that was all she could see. 'These are good, lashings of vinegar, a sprinkling of salt, can't go wrong.' If in doubt, talk about the food or the weather, it usually worked as a distraction.

She blew out to let the steam escape from her own mouth and earned a laugh from Harvey when it seemed she couldn't wait any longer for the chips to cool down either.

Side by side, they finished their portions. 'I'm too full now,' Harvey announced as he balled up the rubbish and took it over to the nearby litter bin.

'Let's go and see if we can find this marina.' Now they were in Leafbourne she wanted to find out what they could and if that was nothing, perhaps she'd have no choice but to come out with it and ask Barney about his past before she headed back to Windsor. She was beginning to get desperate.

Back in the truck they'd only driven around two more bends in the road before they found the marina. Harvey pulled the truck onto the concrete alongside so other cars could pass. They could just about see that the river stretched out from behind the marina and went on to snake through the landscape beyond. A boat sailed out on the river beyond, its cream sail flapping in the wind, a power boat chugged back in the opposite direction.

Melissa nodded hello to a boy perched against a white sign dragging on a cigarette. 'I can imagine Barney coming here,' she told Harvey. 'The whole village is so pretty.' She wound her window down to get a better look at the marina and the grassy surrounds and buildings on the other side of the road, a thatched property as well as a row of cute cottages, all with little house names she couldn't quite read from this distance. She could hear the water lapping, the chug of the motor boat fading as it came in to dock at the marina.

With nowhere for them to park up, Harvey pulled out and drove further on until the road wound round to a village green, opposite which was a pub with bright bloom-filled hanging baskets, its sign gently swaying in the wind, low-lit windows that even on a summer's day told of a cosy inside. It was only a couple of hundred metres on and with the rain holding off for now they pulled into the car park and set off on foot back to the marina.

The same boy was still perched on the sign, he must be on a second cigarette, doing what he could to prolong a return to work.

Inside the office at the marina they waited to be noticed.

'We'd be waiting another hour if you weren't wearing those shorts,' Harvey whispered when at last a worker who looked to be in his early twenties spotted them and came over, his gaze firmly fixed on her.

'Can I help you?' The lad wiped his hands on an already-greasy rag. 'Small rowboat hire is around the other side, or there's one electric day boat left, or canoes if you like,' he said, not bothering to hide how impressed he was with Melissa's legs.

Ignoring the admiration, Melissa told him, 'We're not here to hire a boat. We're trying to find out about someone we know used to live here in Leafbourne, someone who spent a lot of time here at the marina.'

'Right. Well, I've been here seven years so I should be able to help you.'

'The person we're asking after is kind of a little older,' she said.

'How old?'

'He's in his seventies now.'

The young lad let out a whistle. 'Then you'll need to talk to someone else. Hey, Grandad!' he called without moving away and Melissa winced at the possibility of a burst eardrum.

'They have to yell,' Harvey laughed when the lad went off in a different direction. 'These places aren't quiet.' Indeed there was a cacophony of banging in the background. 'And out on the sea they'll be yelling back and forth, they probably only have one volume level.'

The lad came over again and told them, 'You'll have to come back.' He had a wrench in his hand ready to get on with another job although he still had enough time to run his eyes up and down Melissa's torso. 'You'll want to talk to Bill, he's been here the longest.'

Harvey lifted a hand in thanks. 'Pub?' he said to Melissa.

'You're on, although I'm still full from those chips.'

'It's somewhere to go,' Harvey suggested, holding the door open for her. 'And we can't hang around here, you're going to feature in that boy's dreams tonight. They obviously don't get many hot females in their boatyard all that often.'

She ignored the "hot" reference as they made their way back to the pub. It was comments like that one that had Melissa confusing her past with her present.

They grabbed a couple of drinks before settling into the booth at one side of the pub.

'Shame I'm only on the orange juice, I think I could do with something a little stronger,' said Harvey. 'Tell me, what's your boyfriend up to while you're away?'

She could do with a glass of wine right now too, especially with a direct question like that, but she wanted to stay sharp if they did get to talk to someone at the yard who may know something. And besides, with their own personal history constantly hovering between them, she needed to stay focused when Harvey was around. She wondered if they'd ever talk properly or whether she'd leave Heritage Cove before either of them braved it.

She set down her glass of Coke without taking a second sip. 'He's working.' She'd been trying to get hold of him on the phone yesterday evening after she'd left the pub, with an overwhelming urge to hear his voice, perhaps to allay her guilty conscience about spending time with Harvey, but had settled on text messages instead.

'Do you live together?'

'On and off but I have my own place.'

'Do you like living near London?'

'It's good for work, nice and easy to get to the airport.' She hoped their entire conversation wouldn't be like this with him firing questions at her like missiles from a tennis-ball machine that had her whacking back her answers the best she could. 'What about you, how's your work?' She got in quick before he could ask anything else.

'Nice and busy, the way I like it. More people are going up with another storey or converting existing loft space rather than moving house.'

'Are you still hoping to set up on your own one day?'

'You've got a good memory.' He smiled across at her, his arm resting on the table so close his hand was in danger of touching hers if she put her glass down. 'Right now it's easy to be on someone else's payroll while I learn the trade. I want to make sure I know what I'm doing before I start my own business, if I ever take the leap.'

She wasn't sure whether to probe too much but braved asking, 'Did you ever think about leaving Tumbleweed House? I wondered if you'd want a change.'

'Because of the memories, you mean.'

'I just thought…'

'That starting over is easier, that it would make me forget everything that went on? No, not so easy. And my dad took enough from our family. He was the one who put an end to the elderberry business, he sold off land, he took a lot personally from Mum, me, my brother Daniel. It was time to take back, I wanted to stay.'

'Good for you.' He was strong, not just to look at, but emotionally too. 'How is Daniel?'

'He left and never looked back. I don't hear from him.' He was watching her. 'You want to say something, I can tell.'

'A lot of kids would give anything to have a sibling you know.'

'Yeah, well sometimes it's better to be an only child.'

'Maybe he has regrets too, it's never too late to put it all behind you.'

'Not that simple.'

She didn't want to wind him up and talking about Daniel had always done that, so she let it drop. 'Your mum must've been pleased you took over the house.'

'Yeah,' he smiled, seemingly grateful she'd dropped the subject of his brother. 'And now she's able to visit and remember the better times, those with her own parents when it was theirs, with us as little kids when Dad was away. I worked a lot of overtime to pay for the house and keep the remaining land, and I'm glad I did.'

They were getting dangerously close to talking about their relationship and the way it ended so suddenly and Melissa didn't want to do that, so she turned the focus back to the reason they were even here. 'I expect the marina today is our last shot. And it's a very long shot, but thank you for humouring me and coming here.'

'It's my pleasure.' And something in his voice told her it really was.

She sipped her drink, down to the end with the lemon slice and ice cubes rattling around. 'If we don't get anywhere, I'm going to have to ask Barney outright.'

'Jeez, you're brave.'

'Time's marching on and I don't want to leave without talking properly to him, I want him to know he can share anything with us, that we'll help in whatever way we can. Honestly, the way he talks to everyone, it surprises me he's been able to keep anything secret.'

With a laugh, Harvey agreed. They finished their drinks and talked some more about other locals in the Cove, those who had moved on since Melissa was last there, others who had moved in, the local school around the corner that had such a good rating it brought newcomers to the village. And by the time they realised the man, Bill, should be back at the marina, even darker clouds were ganging up overhead and the rain had started.

They made a run for it, all the way from the pub to the marina. Laughing away, they piled into the office out of the inclement weather and must have looked like a pair of loonies. These men didn't look like a bit of rain changed anything for them, they were working inside and outside as usual, Melissa could see them. One man was sanding the side of a boat, another appeared to be fixing up a sail, someone else was hammering the side of a tiny boat. None of them cared about the rain or the wind.

'I understand you're looking for me.' Bill came over. He was a jolly-looking chap and he put down a spanner before extending a hand to shake Melissa's and then Harvey's. His skin spoke of the practical side of his job, the dryness from working with materials and tools all day combined with time out on the water.

'We're trying to find out about a friend of ours who lived in this village. Barney Walters,' said Harvey.

Bill shrugged. His clothing – jeans and a big fisherman jumper with enough holes that it could be worn in warmer temperatures – was weathered like many of the boats beyond the shed, the one inside that was being worked on and spruced up, the smell of varnish filling the air. 'Sorry, not heard of him.'

'He spent a lot of time hanging around this marina, we just thought someone might remember him,' Melissa tried. Please don't let this be a wasted journey. Even if the people round here didn't know what had happened with Barney and Lois, they might shed some light on Barney back then and perhaps lead them to someone who did. As they'd sat in the pub Melissa realised the village was very much like Heritage Cove, locals chatting in groups, anyone who came in shaking hands and greeting others like they were part of a tight-knit community.

'What year are we talking about?' Bill asked. 'I've been here donkeys.'

'It would've been around fifty years ago, maybe a little less,' Melissa told him.

He whistled. 'That's a long time, even for an old goat like me. This yard changed hands some forty-five years ago. I've been on board for all of those plus five or six years before.'

'Is it family-owned?'

'It is. But it's a different family to the original owners when I first started here. The Roystons own it now. They love it as much as I do. It's as much a hobby for me as a job. It's like they say, isn't it? Do what you love and you'll never work a day in your life.'

'That's right,' Melissa smiled.

'You say this Barney character was local?'

'He grew up here,' Harvey replied.

'I didn't come to Leafbourne until I started this job, I'm afraid. Excuse me a minute…' He'd spotted a couple coming into the shed.

Melissa looked out of the shed, across the concrete area in front to the sign that faced the traffic as it came in around the bend. It was just visible now; it hadn't been earlier, with the lad in front of it enjoying a smoke, or a couple of smokes. But now, he'd finally gone back to his job and the sign was there for all to see. On a white background was a navy blue anchor with intricate rope weaved through it with the name Leafbourne Marina split into two, one word arching over the top of the anchor, the other curving upwards beneath.

She put an arm out and her hand rested on Harvey's skin. 'Look at the sign.'

'I'm looking.'

'Don't you recognise it?'

'Can't say that I do.'

'Oh, God, what am I talking about? Of course you don't, you didn't see the letter in the wedding bag.'

His face showed he was as bewildered now as at the start of this conversation. 'Enlighten me.'

'The same anchor and wording was at the top of the letter. Well, the wording had faded, which is why I didn't put two and two together, the anchor symbol was faint but not so much that I can't match the two now I think about it. The letter from Lois must have been on a fancy piece of letterhead paper some people use, especially if they have a –'

'Family business,' he said at the same time as her.

Bill was busy taking the visitors outside to point them in the right direction of the village hall when it turned out they didn't need the marina after all and as they waited for him, Melissa began to wonder. 'Have you ever thought that perhaps we're asking about the wrong person?'

Harvey leaned against the desk nearby, strong arms folded in front of his body. 'You think Lois might be the connection to this place rather than Barney?'

'It's possible, isn't it?'

When Bill came in again, unbothered by the rain, Melissa asked, 'Have you ever heard of a woman called Lois? She'd probably be around the same age as our friend, although I can't be sure.'

'The name doesn't ring a bell, I'm afraid.'

'Who was the family that owned the yard before it was sold on?' Harvey asked.

Bill thought hard. 'The Charlestons, that was their name, and they were as high and mighty as they sound, let me tell you,' he added in a low chuckle. 'Mr Charleston, well, he was in this for the business ownership, he had a couple of boats himself, but there was no love for the craft. That's what he lacked. Although his wife was so serious all the time I'm not sure he had much love for anything. To be honest with you, I was glad when they sold the place on. The Roystons took over the business and have a clear love for boats. The whole family has a passion and it made a difference, let me tell you. Mr Royston wasn't all about the money whereas the Charlestons…well, let's just say we could've been making and selling tin cans and if it drew the same profits they wouldn't have given a toss. Pardon my language,' he directed at Melissa.

'Not a problem,' she smiled, realising Bill liked to talk as much as Barney once had. 'I don't suppose they had kids, did they? The Charlestons?'

One hand on the hip of his beige dungarees, he thought hard to remember. 'They had a son, he did the accounts…always late with the wages he was.' He rolled his eyes heavenward. 'Would've got the sack anywhere else but you know what it's like, Daddy's company and he had a job for as long as he wanted.'

'Just a son?' Harvey asked.

'Just the one kid, wouldn't wish that father on anyone else.'

Melissa and Harvey exchanged a look. She knew what Harvey had put up with better than anyone else.

Deflated at the dead end they'd just hit, they thanked Bill for his time. 'We really appreciate it,' Harvey told him.

'I wish I could be more help. I'm sorry.'

'Don't be,' said Melissa. 'It was a long time ago.'

Harvey opened the door and a woman came bustling in past them with what smelled like a parcel of fish and chips.

'You spoil me,' Bill smiled at the woman, who must've been his wife. 'It's a long day when you don't see the one you love,' he told Harvey and Melissa when they turned to venture out into the rain. 'These kids are asking about the Charlestons,' he explained.

The woman, a lot shorter than Bill, with a pea-green headscarf that would've protected her from the wet outside, pulled a face that suggested she had the same opinions of the family as her husband. 'That name takes me way back.' She hadn't moved from Bill's side and Melissa envied how in love they clearly still were. 'They were a strange family, very serious, not at all like the new owners. Are you related?' the wife asked Melissa.

'No, we're just trying to find out some information about a friend of ours, Barney Walters.'

'I'm afraid the name doesn't ring a bell.'

'Not to worry,' Melissa smiled. They said their goodbyes and uttered their thanks again before leaving Bill to unwrap the parcel of steaming-hot potato and battered fish. But Bill's voice stopped them before they could make a run for it and not get soaked from the rain that had become heavier as they sheltered inside.

'Come to think of it,' Bill began, 'the Charlestons did kind of have another kid, not theirs, but they took in a teenager.'

'Male or female?' Harvey asked quickly.

'Oh, I remember her,' the wife replied with what appeared to be a bit of a look to her husband. 'She was beautiful all right, turned heads she did.'

'Can you remember her name?' Melissa's hopes rose.

Bill shook his head but his wife spoke up again. 'Lois.'

'I'm not sure that was her name,' Bill countered.

The wife clearly had a better memory. 'Yes it was. I remember because one of you lot used to call her Lois Lane.'

'Ah, you're right,' Bill smiled. 'We did.'

The wife bristled. 'She was a looker, I admit.'

'I only had eyes for you back then, you know that.' Bill hugged his wife to him and planted a kiss on her cheek, making her blush.

'I didn't really know the girl,' Bill's wife carried on, 'but I did know that she'd lost her parents at a very young age. I think the Charlestons were her aunt and uncle. They took her in and raised her. I dread to think how strict they were given the way they acted around their workers. We didn't see much of her in here, but there was some hoo-ha involving a boy and that was when the Charlestons sold up and moved away.'

'Hoo-ha?' Melissa asked.

'Lois married the boy, there was a baby from what I remember. But then nothing. I stopped seeing them around the village.'

'That's right,' said Bill, his memory triggered by his wife's recollection. 'The trio became a taboo subject around here. Mr Charleston wouldn't speak about them if anyone asked and then they were gone.'

'I don't suppose you know where to, do you?'

'Not a clue, love,' said the wife, her voice softening at the look of disappointment on Melissa's face.

Harvey and Melissa thanked Bill and his wife again, they'd helped by at least placing Lois here. It had to be the same woman – what with the stationery letterhead, the name and the fact this was the village Barney had grown up in and left. And Melissa wouldn't mind betting that Harvey was the boy involved in the so-called hoo-ha.

They ran back to the pub and dived into the truck. 'It's teaming down,' Melissa shivered, her hair stuck to her face. 'That'll serve me right for thinking it was OK to come out in tiny shorts and not bring anything else.'

Harvey reached into the back of the truck and pulled out a jumper. 'Here, put this on.'

'Don't you need it?'

He flexed his biceps. 'No chance, I'm not soft.'

Smiling, she pulled the jumper over her head. It couldn't live in the truck as a spare, it smelled too good for that. The wool neck scratched at her face but not in a bad way and with the engine running and the heater on, she warmed up quickly. 'Where to from here?' She looked across at Harvey.

'No idea. I mean, at least now we know Lois was here, there was some trouble, and you can bet money that trouble involved Barney.'

'My thoughts exactly.'

He looked across at her when she picked up her phone again. 'What are you up to?'

Her hair kept niggling at her face so she hooked it behind her ears as she investigated any connection she could think of. 'I'm searching Charleston combinations – with the name Lois, with the words charity or philanthropic, with Barney's name too. Just a feeling I've got.'

Harvey put the truck into reverse and negotiated his way between a couple of shabbily parked cars before pulling out onto the road to take them out of Leafbourne.

Harvey didn't need directions as it was much easier to head for Heritage Cove than it had been to come up here, and as he drove Melissa kept on searching on her phone. The rain hammered down, the windscreen wipers swished away at the highest speed they could go, and her neck began to ache from looking down at the screen.

'Take a break, it can wait,' said Harvey as they enjoyed a journey with practically no traffic.

Frustrated, she leaned back against the seat, shutting her eyes to try to imagine the Barney in the photograph and Lois, his beautiful bride, and what trouble could possibly have been brewing for them to split up and have one half of a very happy-looking couple never speak about it again. She thought about Lois, the strict upbringing she'd faced with relatives, the loss of parents at such a young age. Melissa knew how angry she was that her own parents had been snatched away but at least she'd been an adult when it happened. It didn't make it less painful of course but she'd had extra years that Lois would never have experienced. Then you had Harvey, whose home life hadn't been happy at all with a father who tormented him, a mother who needed to get out but couldn't, a brother who'd gone off the rails and was no longer in touch with his own family. She sneaked a glance across at Harvey as he concentrated on the road and realised she'd been lucky to have such wonderful parents in her life for so many years. They'd been a happy family too. And for that she was grateful.

As Harvey drove she got back to her internet search, it was hard not to. But there were only so many combinations of Barney and Lois's names, the surname Bill had given them, the marina, Leafbourne, before she drew another blank. She tried a different approach when she thought again of White Clover. It sounded as though Lois's guardians were at the marina to make money so she tried to find more about the family but it was only after she exhausted all business- and marina-related search terms that she entered Philanthropic and the family name, combined with the name Lois, and she had what she considered a breakthrough.

She sat up straighter in her seat, heart beating fast. 'I've found an article about Lois.' She skimmed over it. 'It's about a woman called Lois…part of the Charleston family…the entire family is big in philanthropic circles…Lois is heavily involved with a children's hospital, in fact, it says here that she was a volunteer ambassador for a while. She's been involved in countless fundraising activities, this article really sings her praises.'

'So you think she might support children's charities and that's why Barney does?'

'Possibly. Maybe they both supported charities when they were together and it's part of the relationship that carried on, keeps him connected.'

She picked up her phone again, found the number of White Clover.

'Who are you calling?' Harvey asked although he had to focus on the twerp who'd cut in front of him, weaved over to the left to undertake someone else, then zipped across two lanes yet again. Harvey had slowed down in the hope of letting whoever the lunatic driver was get some distance from them.

'May I speak with Ashley please?' she asked when the call connected through. 'It's Melissa.'

'I thought you said she pleaded confidentiality,' Harvey reminded her.

Melissa put a finger in her ear so she could hear properly when Ashley came on the phone. The rain was lashing against the windscreen by now and she had to listen carefully. 'I've got a bit of a question, remember what I asked you earlier today? Don't worry, I'm not going to ask you to say anything or give out any information. But can you do me a favour?' When Ashley indicated she was listening, Melissa continued talking. 'I know you keep up with your list of donors, you're very efficient that way...' Flattery had to help, didn't it? 'So, when I say a name, I want you to simply hang up on me if that person is on your list of supporters. Then you aren't strictly telling me anything, are you, and this won't go any further.' Melissa closed her eyes, glad Ashley was on board. 'Lois Charleston.'

And when the call disconnected she knew they were a little bit closer to finding out whatever it was that Barney had never shared with them.

Chapter Twelve

Harvey pulled in at the end of the lane, outside Tumbleweed House. 'I've got some wine, if you're interested.' He fully expected Melissa to turn him down. 'I really need a drink after the day we've had.'

'I'd like that.'

Surprised and glad she accepted the offer, he added, 'Maybe it'll help us know where to go from here.'

The rain had teemed down as they'd driven back to Heritage Cove. Melissa had taken a call from Jay and as much as he hadn't enjoyed listening to the one-way conversation, Harvey had decided it was perhaps a good thing. It was a reminder that he'd been living in a bit of a dreamworld since she'd been back in the village, wondering whether they could once be as close as before. Usually his love life was something he might think about in the evenings if he was home alone, sitting out on the porch, the hazy evenings and a beer for company, wondering if he was ever destined to settle down. But lately it had been an obsession with Melissa back in town, plaguing his thoughts every single day. Perhaps the phone call was the dose of reality that he needed. She was with this pilot guy now, and how could he possibly live up to that? She had the jet-set lifestyle, she didn't stand still, she was seeing the world like she'd wanted. He'd only seen more of the surrounding villages and countryside by being up in someone's loft space when the roof came off.

Winnie was already waiting at the door like always and when Harvey opened up to let them inside the dog's tail thwacked against the walls as she tried to get a fuss from whoever would pay her the most attention.

Despite lower temperatures outside, Tumbleweed House had been shut up all day and clung on to its heat, so Harvey opened up the window in the kitchen before taking a bottle from the wine rack built in at the end cupboard. He poured them each a glass and took them over to the table. Winnie was so used to Melissa by now that she'd already settled by her feet as she sat on one of the chairs, using her foot to stroke the dog's tummy. 'Put your phone down,' he urged when he saw her pick it up again. 'Time to switch off.'

'You're right. I do need to step back.' She put it face down on the table and tugged the clip from her hair to let the wavy auburn locks cascade around her shoulders.

He had to look away, it was an image that played over and over in his mind when he let it, because he'd pulled that clip out enough times himself. He almost suggested they went through to the lounge where they'd be more comfortable but it might be the start of him making a total fool of himself. Maybe the kitchen was the safer option.

'I've been thinking about White Clover.' He needed to start talking, if only so he stopped staring at her.

'Now who's not switching off?' she grinned.

'I was wondering whether there's a reason why Barney and Lois both support White Clover in particular. The charity supports families after the death of a child. Think about it, it's not local to Leafbourne, there are far bigger and better-known charities that raise funds for the same purpose, so why that one?' He scraped a hand across his chin, the stubble beginning to come through and graze his palm.

She frowned. 'Is your mind going where I think it is?'

'Do you think it's possible that Barney and Lois had a baby who died?'

'I suppose it is possible – but to never talk of it, even when we'd pass comments about us being the kids he'd never had! We thought it was a nice thing to say, when maybe it was the most painful thing he could've heard. He never once let on.'

'We might be wrong.' When she looked at him, her eyes glistening as though she felt some of Barney's pain, he added, 'We're not, are we?'

'I don't think so.' She shook her head. 'It's heartbreaking. He's been alone all this time and kept something so painful from everyone he's close to. I don't know how he did it all these years.'

'I think Barney did the same as you did. He ran away, he left his pain behind.' When she said nothing he asked, 'Does your boyfriend know much about your life here in the Cove?'

'He knows enough.'

'Does he know your parents died?'

'Of course.'

'Does he know you lost them at the same time, on a road you saw every day, in the village you'd spent most of your life in?'

She jutted out her jaw. 'He doesn't need to know the nitty-gritty. And why are you asking me all this anyway?'

'Because you and Barney did the same thing. You took your problems with you and didn't deal with them.'

They stared at each other until she spoke first. 'I can't speak for Barney, but from my own experience, it was

244

easier to go and be a new person, without baggage, without people constantly asking about it or referring to it, never mind the physical reminders around the Cove.'

'Was I a part of that baggage?'

'Of course not.'

'But you just left.'

'And you didn't come with me!' Her shouting took them both by surprise. She leaned over, grabbed the wine bottle and topped up her glass.

He didn't miss the fact she hadn't refilled his, so he did it himself. 'I had my reasons. Did you ever stop to consider what they might be?'

'I knew you never wanted it as much as me, but I wish you'd told me.'

'Why? You wanted to go, there was an immediacy to it, you knew it and so did I. And you'd already booked the hotel room in London, you had a part-time job to tide you over and your savings behind you. You were never going to stop and look back.' He gently twiddled the stem of his wine glass between his fingers. 'I came after you, you know. Not the night you left, not even close. It was almost a year after you went to London. Things had settled down for me and one day I just snapped. I hated how I'd let you go. I persuaded Tracy to give me your address and I got the train into London. I waited across the road from your flat and I saw you. You were on the top step holding hands with a man and that was when I knew. You'd moved on. And I was too late.'

Her face paled, even Winnie couldn't get her attention. 'I thought you and I were over. You never called. I wanted to beg you to reconsider, but your silence told me what I needed to know.'

'Except that it didn't.' He stood, glass of wine in hand, and over at the window looked out across the elderflower bushes and the land that belonged to the property. Seeing it all bathed in the sun's golden glow, he couldn't imagine not waking up to this every day.

'I came back here too you know.' Her voice floated across the kitchen with the admission.

He turned to face her, she was still sitting at the table, running a finger around the rim of her wine glass.

'A few weeks after I left. I spotted you,' she said, 'on the street outside the bakery.'

'But you didn't say hello. And you didn't see Barney, as far as I know, unless he's kept that quiet too.'

'I didn't see Barney, but I did see you and I was angry at first that you looked as though life for you had carried on as normal, as though what happened between us had only happened to me and not to you. It was then I realised that leaving was my dream, it had never been yours.' She looked down at the table. 'I cried when I drove away but I knew I had to let you go. I wanted you to be happy, it's all I ever really wanted for you.'

'And I for you.'

Tears formed but she didn't let them spill over. 'I'm still dealing with my feelings even after all this time because I never understood why you didn't come with me. Is there something I don't know?'

He tugged a hand through his hair and knocked back some more wine. 'I can't believe nobody filled you in. I mean, I asked Tracy not to, I didn't want you to feel sorry for me. But I assumed with you two friends again, she might have told you.'

'All she's said is that I should talk to you. So I'm asking you now. Why, Harvey?'

He sat down opposite her again. 'My dad turned up, out of the blue, the night you and I were set to leave the Cove, that's why I couldn't come with you.'

'What happened?'

'He went ballistic, that's what happened. He acted as though he'd only nipped out for a pint of milk and expected us to be there and waiting for him when he returned, dinner on the table. But Mum and I were talking over a glass of wine each, she was wishing you and me luck for the year, telling me she'd get the train to London and visit or come to wherever else we were. She said she was happy I was spreading my wings even if it wasn't for ever. She told me she'd never been lucky enough to do the same.'

'I'm guessing your dad didn't see it that way?'

'We'd long ago stopped thinking he'd come back. He must've purposely come through the side door we often left open to let the air circulate in the warmer months, and then all of a sudden he was there in the kitchen with us and had heard every word. He accused Mum of being ungrateful – won't tell you the adjectives he used to describe her – he said I was worse, he asked what kind of man still lived at home when he was a grown adult. I told him perhaps the kind of man who had to protect his mother from her bastard of a husband.'

Melissa's face fell. She would've seen enough of Donnie Luddington to know how that remark would've gone down. As a kid she'd kept her distance whenever Donnie was around, they hadn't hung out much at Tumbleweed House.

'I was stupid to say it – talk about waving a red flag at him! And, boy, did he charge. He went for me first, Mum was screaming, he punched me in the face, I fought back and pushed him so hard I put him through the glass floor-to-ceiling window.'

She covered her mouth, something he'd forgotten she did. He'd always teased her before, asking whether she thought that by covering her mouth it would stop the worst happening, prevent things from being true. They both looked at the window in question, intact as though it had never been broken at all. It was at the side of the house and at one time his mum had kept a big stone pot on the paving slab outside, filled with seasonal colours. The space was empty these days except for the ivy that had taken over the fence opposite, the tangled weeds along the bottom of the wood.

'He went to the police,' said Harvey. 'I didn't come with you because how could I possibly leave?' He watched her expression change as she realised he'd had real reasons, it hadn't been him losing his nerve or simply changing his mind. He'd been stuck. 'I couldn't abandon Mum even though she told me it wasn't my mess to clear up. I couldn't be sure he wouldn't come back, and I was terrified the police would press charges, he was cut up pretty bad from the glass. I couldn't have a criminal record following me around and expect you to be all right with that.'

'You underestimate me, Harvey.' The soft voice that had comforted him many a time over the years fell on him like velvet. He'd missed her and he wondered, had he told her the truth at the start, would they be in a completely different place right now?

'I didn't want that for you, Melissa. I knew how much you needed to go and so I set you free. A couple of months after dragging us through all the angst and the fear, Dad did the first decent thing in his life and told the police he wasn't pressing charges, that it was an accident, and he upped and left for the second and final time.'

'How do you know he won't come back?'

'At first I fully expected him to, but then Mum got news from his sister that he'd died suddenly of a ruptured brain aneurysm, it was quick and he didn't suffer she told us in her letter. I wished he had, I wished he'd been as scared as I'd been some days when he bellowed at me, when he chased after me and Daniel, bullied us, took his belt to each of us if we played up. But he'd gone for good, and the relief I saw on Mum's face, even though she never expressed it in words, was all I needed to know it was a good thing and I shouldn't feel guilty.'

'Why didn't you come to find me when you knew your dad was out of your life for good?'

'I did.' The day he'd gone down to London on the train was the day after his dad was buried. He hadn't gone to the funeral but they'd been told the date and he and his mum had sat on the step of Tumbleweed House, holding hands together and watching the bumblebees zipping about the elderberry bushes trying to find what they came for. Neither of them shed a tear but she told him to go and find Melissa.

Realisation dawned for Melissa. 'That was the day you saw me with Jay.'

He nodded.

'And you thought I'd never given you a second thought.' When he shrugged she said, 'And I thought *you'd* never once regretted not coming with me.'

He reached a hand across the table and took hers in his. 'I don't regret it, because you were doing everything you'd planned to do, you'd gone away and found something to numb your pain. I was just getting sorted with my own, saying goodbye to a childhood that would've been a whole lot worse without you and Barney in it. I figured I needed to do what you did, I needed to find myself and that you'd come back one day if that was what you really wanted. As the years went on I assumed that was never going to happen and I did my best to make peace with it.'

Her phone ringing interrupted them. 'It's Barney, I'd better get it.'

A sudden panic shot through him that Barney might have needed them and they'd been off gallivanting around the country to play detective and delve into his personal business. It was then he realised he must've left his own phone in his pickup.

'He's right here,' Melissa said into the handset. 'Yes…we're together.' Her cheeks flushed a pale pink as she passed the phone over to Harvey.

'What's up, Barney? Yes, Melissa is here at the house.' He rolled his eyes. 'Do you need me?' He listened to Barney's explanation and finished up the call. 'I need to go.'

'He's all right though?' She finished the end of her wine when he did the same.

'He's got a leaky roof. It might have been like that for a while but given the rain today, it's only just become apparent. I've got some plastic sheeting in my shed, I'll take it over, see if that does the trick temporarily.'

'Be careful,' she said, 'it'll be dark soon.'

Maybe it was the wine or the air that had cleared between them, but he reached out a hand to cup her chin. 'Don't you worry about me, Melissa Drew.'

She stayed there looking into his eyes before she seemed to remember he wasn't her boyfriend anymore. 'I'd better get back to the inn.'

Moment over, he picked up his keys, fussed Winnie, who opened one eye sleepily at her master, and he locked up behind them before grabbing his phone from his pickup and going over to the shed. He'd have to bundle up the plastic sheeting and walk over with it, he'd had too much wine to drive, and he hoped Barney would be able to hold the ladder for him too.

'I've got another idea about pulling together information about Barney and what happened,' Melissa announced as she walked next to him down the lane towards The Street. 'I'm going to write to the newspaper that ran the article about Lois.'

'Was it a recent article?' He adjusted the plastic sheeting in his arms, it wasn't the easiest stuff to carry when it wasn't folded properly.

'It was published less than twelve months ago.'

'Won't they have the same confidentiality arrangements as White Clover?'

'Most likely, but I've got the journalist's name from his byline, I found an email contact, so I'll attach a letter to Lois and ask him to pass it on.'

'And what are you going to say in this letter?'

'I'm not sure yet.'

'Need some help?'

She smiled and seemed about to step forwards closer to him but thought better of it. 'I'll manage. Now you'd better go, sort Barney's leaky roof, and for goodness' sake, be careful – I don't need two invalids to look after.'

He watched her go thinking actually he wouldn't mind her playing nurse maid. And as he turned to walk in the opposite direction over to Barney's, he couldn't ignore the jolt of pleasure zipping through him at her company all day and this evening.

He only wondered whether she was feeling the same way right now.

Chapter Thirteen

The next day, glad the rain had passed, Melissa put on a light blue sundress with white edging and headed over to Barney's place. The caterers were due there so that they could taste everything and confirm their choices for the event. Melissa was thrilled Barney had sounded in good spirits when he called earlier, reiterating the time to come by. She had to remind him that she and Harvey had booked the session, of course she knew when it was. But perhaps this was a sign of the tides turning and this event was beginning to work the magic they'd hoped it would. Perhaps their interference and trip to Leafbourne to find out more hadn't been needed at all, which wouldn't be a bad thing given she'd had no response to her email to the journalist.

'How's the roof?' she asked the second she joined Harvey at Barney's place.

'A few months ago and I would've climbed up onto that roof myself,' Barney interrupted. Another sign he was improving, plying his way into any conversation he could, and Melissa knew by the nod of approval Harvey directed her way that he was thinking the same. But Barney ruined it by picking up the brochure for Aubrey House and flipping through it.

'You should throw that out,' Harvey told him.

'Why? It's my decision if I want to go there.'

'But you're a part of Heritage Cove,' Melissa urged.

Barney picked up the brochure and held it to face both of them. 'Look at the postcode, that makes it in Heritage Cove. What with the fall and the leaky roof, my time has come.'

Melissa didn't have the energy to argue. 'So, the roof?' she reiterated to Harvey.

'It was a dislodged tile,' Harvey explained. 'The rain was seeping in near the chimney, probably been doing that for a while at a guess. I've checked it again already and the roofer will be out later today to fix it properly.'

They exchanged a smile until Melissa realised Barney was staring at them both. 'I'm looking forward to trying all this food,' she said, shifting uncomfortably. She was all too aware herself of the change in her and Harvey's demeanour now they'd talked properly. She'd felt it last night as they talked over wine, again as they walked down the lane away from his house, and overnight Melissa knew she'd slept more heavily than usual as though a weight on her mind had finally moved away.

But her plan to divert Barney's focus by talking about food didn't work. 'You never told me what you were you doing at Tumbleweed House last night, Melissa,' he said.

'Just finalising a few things for the ball.'

'Like what?'

But his inquisition was cut short by the arrival of the food and to escape any more questions Melissa let the caterers in.

Harvey, Barney and Melissa made their way through Welsh rarebit tartlets, miniature Yorkshire puddings with beef in a creamy sauce, vegetables contained in a tiny filo pastry basket, chocolate tart with Chantilly cream, and white chocolate and Cointreau tiramisu. They tried tuna and cucumber sandwiches cut into triangles, creamy dips with tortilla chips or julienned cucumber and carrot pieces to scoop up the flavour.

'I don't think I'll ever eat again,' Melissa announced when the caterers packed up their Tupperware containers and left.

'You two did good, finding them,' Barney complimented. 'They're better than the last lot, there's more variation. Maybe that's why the last lot went under.'

'You can thank Tracy,' said Melissa. 'She put me onto them. And now we've got their details for next year.'

Harvey winked at her, knowing exactly what she was up to with her remark, and when he prolonged the eye contact she made her excuses to leave, telling them she had to rescue her laundry from the inn washing machine and hang it up before she ran out of clothes.

What she really needed to do was put some distance between herself and Harvey. Ever since he'd held her face in his hands last night at Tumbleweed House, her feelings had skyrocketed and had her torn, not knowing where to go from here. She had a life elsewhere, but she had something in Heritage Cove too, and what had all been so clear before Barney's fall was now anything but.

*

Melissa spent the next few days timing her visits to Barney as best she could to coincide with when Harvey was working. She'd texted Harvey to say she'd heard nothing in response to her letter via the journalist and they'd agreed that this would have to be the end of their detective work. They would just have to accept that, for whatever reason, Barney wanted to keep things to himself and run his life the way he saw fit. Both of them were even starting to see that if Barney wanted to move into that home, stop running the Wedding Dress Ball, then they may have no choice but to accept it.

After an afternoon of playing cards with Barney, Melissa was happy to be at the pub with Tracy this evening. The sun was still high in the sky and a fresh breeze flapped at the sleeves of the lilac top she'd teamed with jeans as they talked about the upcoming ball.

Tracy tore open three packets of crisps for them to share. 'How's Jay coping with your extended stay here?'

'He's busy working,' Melissa shrugged. 'Makes it easier I guess.' They hadn't spoken for a few days but she'd emailed him and told him how close she was to pulling off the event of the year. She knew she'd probably rambled on about a band, catering, the barn decoration, but she didn't really know what else to talk about when it came to Heritage Cove.

'Has anyone asked Lucy along to the ball?' Tracy asked when the local blacksmith came out to the beer garden clutching a bottle of beer.

Melissa picked up a few broken pieces of prawn cocktail crisps from the foil insides of the packets glinting in the sunshine. 'I assume she got an invitation, she certainly would've got a flyer as a reminder when Harvey and I handed them out. She must know about it.'

'She looks like she's here on her own,' Tracy frowned. 'That's not right.'

'We could ask her to join us but I don't want her to feel she has to.'

Tracy called out to her and when they invited Lucy to join them, she was only too happy to. 'We were just talking about the Wedding Dress Ball,' said Tracy. 'Are you going?'

'I do have a ticket.'

'But…' Tracy prompted.

'What I don't have is a date,' she admitted awkwardly.

'Neither do half the people who go,' said Melissa. 'It's not that kind of ball.'

'Really? It's not couples only? I mean I understood from the invite that there'll be plenty of married men and women in the same outfits they once wore when they got married. I figured…'

'Not at all,' said Tracy.

'My first Wedding Dress Ball was in a debutante gown,' Melissa told her. 'It was beautiful, and I felt lucky to finally be a guest. I'd been watching the event from afar for too long.'

'What she means is she watched it from high up in the roof balancing on the beams,' Tracy grinned. 'Yup, she and Harvey used to climb right up to the rafters and onto the beams – they weren't even that sturdy back then – and they'd linger up there watching the proceedings. They weren't hidden at all but nobody ever said anything.'

'I did hear a rumour you and Harvey were once a thing,' Lucy said to Melissa.

Tracy smiled. 'She has a fancy pilot boyfriend now.'

Melissa didn't let on that he was her fiancé. He'd asked her, she'd given him the answer she thought she meant, they'd planned to shop for a ring together, but now…well, now she had no idea. She wasn't proud of how her feelings had changed, Jay didn't deserve her indecision, and although she didn't want her time in Heritage Cove to come to an end too soon, she knew she needed to get back to Windsor and find out where she went from here. If she saw him, maybe she'd know.

'So, Lucy, you'll come to the ball?' The best way to handle this, Melissa decided, was to change the subject.

'I don't have anything to wear. And I promise you that's not an excuse. In my line of work there's not much call for white anything, let alone a gorgeous dress fit for an event.'

'I don't have anything to wear yet either,' Melissa admitted.

Tracy's face fell. 'Melissa, that's crazy!'

'Well, I didn't know I was going until recently and I've been busy.'

'Right, that's decided.' Tracy plonked her half-empty pint glass down on the wooden table. 'We need to go shopping. All three of us. Tomorrow. Leave it any later and you might not find anything at all.' Tracy was punching a text message into her phone. 'Sorted, got cover at the inn, I can be free at 10 a.m. You?' she directed to the both of them.

'I can take a couple of hours in the morning,' said Lucy before they both looked to Melissa.

'I'm having lunch with Barney but nothing before that, so I'm in.'

'Right, we'll head to the boutique I told you about near Ipswich. I know they've got some lovely white summer dresses in the sale – I was almost tempted to get one myself.'

'There's an incentive not to get married,' Lucy joked to Melissa, 'you're stuck with the same dress every year for this ball. We're lucky, we get to choose something new.'

And as they laughed together Melissa wondered whether she'd be in the exact same position as Tracy come next year. Was her future really with Jay still, or had coming back to the Cove changed all that?

Melissa had gone to bed last night looking forward to a girlie shopping trip with Tracy and Lucy. But right now, after cancelling on the both of them, she was driving over to White Clover after a strange phone call from Ashley. Melissa hoped she wasn't about to be hauled in front of an ethics committee for probing at confidential information.

When she parked up and went inside Ashley greeted her with a smile and asked, 'You weren't busy, were you?'

'I was meant to be dress shopping for the ball.'

'I do apologise, but I needed to speak with you and it had to be here.' But instead of keeping her inside she ushered her back out of the front door and pulled it closed behind them.

'Am I in trouble?'

Ashley's laughter, the jovial personality that was perfectly suited to the not-for-profit sector, boomed across the paved area out front. 'Of course not. But I do have a visitor. It's Lois.'

Melissa's jaw dropped. 'Are you serious? She's here? Now?'

'It must be the same Lois as the woman you're looking for. We only have one Lois on our books. What's going on, Melissa?'

'I'm not sure I know yet myself.' Melissa at best had expected an email from the newspaper in return to her own. She never thought Lois would show up here; she'd been caught well and truly off guard.

'The Lois I've got waiting inside got in touch with us a few months ago about running a wedding dress ball where she lives in Ireland. I didn't hear from her again until now, when she showed up introducing herself as one of our supporters and reminding me of her enquiry.'

'I suspect she may be here because of me rather than the ball or the charity.'

'I thought as much after your questions lately. I don't know what the story is, and I'm not asking, but do you want to go and see her and take it from here? No point me being the go-between.'

She leaned against the door. 'She's really in there right now?' The journalist must have forwarded her email and attachment, but not let Melissa know.

'I excused myself and said I'd get the organiser of the ball here in Heritage Cove to come and talk to her. Which isn't strictly a lie, because you have been helping out.'

All Melissa had said in the letter to Lois was that she was close to Barney Walters, that he'd had a spell in hospital and hadn't been the same since. Melissa had also added that since Barney had come to Heritage Cove he'd been running a wedding dress ball every year to raise money for the White Clover charity, and that following his hospital stay he was talking about stopping the event altogether. Melissa had left it at that, it was enough information to find out whether Lois was concerned, whether she cared enough to get in touch.

And now, here she was. Inside, waiting.

Ashley put a hand to Melissa's arm. 'Stay out here for a few minutes, think about how you're going to play this.'

'Will do.' Melissa shut her eyes, shook her head. She didn't have long and there was only one person she needed right now. Harvey.

But his phone rang out so she had no choice but to face this on her own.

Back inside Melissa followed Ashley down a thin corridor and into the kitchen, where a filter jug filled with coffee left a pleasant aroma. Melissa might not drink the stuff but she did love the smell and right now it kept her alert and ready in a room that was almost on the too warm side. There was only a thin window, high up on one wall, and having already been opened it wasn't doing much to bring in a stream of fresh air.

She introduced herself and shook hands with Lois. Slender wrists, pale skin with a delicate bracelet falling from the sleeve of her sky-blue cotton blouse – this was, without a doubt, the woman from the photograph Melissa had found.

'Melissa…you're the young lady who wrote to me, aren't you?'

'I am.'

Lois rambled on as though chatter could help her reach an equilibrium. 'This is such a wonderful charity. I've been supporting them for many years, right from when they were based near Colchester. But these are much nicer surrounds, not too dissimilar from where I settled in Ireland, out in the countryside, so much greenery.'

'I thought I detected a bit of an accent.'

'When you've moved around a lot like I have, your accent gets mixed up. You pick a bit up here, a bit up there, and in the end nobody really knows where you come from.' Thin, pale-glossed lips revealed straight if not white teeth, she had laughter lines that were so embedded they spoke of a contented life, at least in the end.

'I wasn't sure you'd even acknowledge my letter,' said Melissa.

'I started to write a reply, I tried a few times, and then I thought, why not go and see this girl. I decided I'd come here to Heritage Cove, visit the charity, and then I'd decide whether I was going to make my presence known. I wasn't sure I'd be able to do it.'

'Believe me, I totally understand.'

'Over the years I'd seen numerous reports on White Clover receiving funds every year from a wedding dress ball. I was thinking of starting a similar event where I live, or at least having someone else at the helm and I'd be in the background funding it, making suggestions. It's such a beautiful idea, I was really taken with it and had already made enquiries.' She paused, met Melissa's gaze. 'I would never have guessed Barney was behind it all.'

'It's quite the event. He's been running it for over forty years.'

'And you say after his accident he hasn't been interested?' Her voice wobbled.

'He's better now, not as on board with the event as we would like, still refusing to do all the exercises recommended to him for a better recovery. He's pretty headstrong and when he makes up his mind to do something it's hard to change it.'

Lois's focus was on her fingers, rested in her lap. She was smiling, as though she needed her thoughts to be inward-looking but was having trouble preventing them from leaping out into the present. 'He always was stubborn. Never one to be bossed about and told what to do, unless he really wanted to do it anyway.' She looked up at Melissa. 'Are you Barney's daughter?'

She smiled. 'No, but he's been like a father to me for a long time.'

261

'Did he ever marry? Is he married now?' Before Melissa could answer, Lois apologised. 'I'm sorry, too many questions.'

'I'm very happy to answer them. I can tell you all I know about Barney if you would like.'

Lois had taken a tissue from her bag and dabbed at her eyes. 'I'm sorry, dear, forgive me. I never thought I'd face a moment like this, it's quite something. After all this time.'

'I'm sure it is.' She waited for Lois to recover and then told her, 'I tried to ask Barney questions over the years, but he never really gave clear answers about his life before he came to the Cove, unless it was talking about sailing.'

'That man loved his boats. It was a real passion for him. He'd take me sailing down the river.'

'It sounds romantic.'

Lois smiled back at her. 'I have some special memories.'

Melissa carried on. 'Barney isn't married, he never had kids of his own. But you should know that he looked out for me and a close friend, Harvey, like we were his. And for Harvey it was especially important, he had a rotten childhood. Barney was always there for us when we needed him.'

'I don't know whether that makes me sad or happy,' Lois admitted.

Melissa reached out and took Lois's hand in hers. 'Let it make you happy, it really should, he's a wonderful man.' She gave Lois a moment to gather herself. She filled the kettle and made them both a cup of camomile tea, the steam from the liquid curling into the air.

Lois took a couple of sips even though it was almost too hot to do so. 'May I ask how you knew about me, Melissa? You say Barney didn't tell you much when you asked, so I'm wondering how you knew anything at all.'

Melissa felt guilty admitting they'd been snooping. 'There's a dress,' she began, 'a wedding dress. Harvey found it hanging in the wardrobe recently and when he asked Barney about it, he bit his head off. It got me thinking though. I'd seen it once before, years ago, and forgotten about it but I started to think about the way Barney reacted then, and now, and I wondered what he was keeping from Harvey, me, and everyone else who cares so much about him. I began to wonder why he ran the Wedding Dress Ball every year, why he supported that particular charity, why the dress with a chunk cut out at the bottom was still in the wardrobe and why he'd never mentioned that he'd once been married.'

Lois's hand covered her mouth, tears prickling her eyes.

'I'm upsetting you,' Melissa panicked. 'It wasn't my intention, I'm sorry.'

'The dress is mine,' said Lois.

Softly, Melissa told her, 'I guessed it was. There was a letter with it too, a goodbye letter, from you.'

When Lois gasped Melissa wasn't even sure whether Lois realised she'd made a sound. 'I hurt him badly.' She spoke as though she was at last admitting it to herself. 'For him to keep the dress and the letter all these years…'

Melissa waited patiently, she wasn't going to rush this, although she did check the time to make sure she wasn't yet late for Barney and lunch. If she was late, he'd call, and she didn't want to be sitting here with Lois when he did.

Tissue now sodden and disintegrating between Lois's fingers, she looked at Melissa. 'Harry was our baby boy. He was ten months old when we lost him.'

A lump caught in Melissa's throat. She and Harvey had already worked it out but it was still a shock to hear they were right. Her own grief welled up inside, reminding her she wasn't the only person to ever have loved and lost and all this time Barney had been in his own private pain, not sharing it with a soul. 'He never said a word,' she told Lois, her voice steady even though she wanted to burst into tears.

Lois's hand shook as she lifted her cup of tea but then changed her mind and set it down again. 'I'm afraid I didn't cope too well when Harry died. And I didn't let Barney step in and help either, I turned to my aunt and uncle because I couldn't cope with Barney's pain as well as my own. The dress, with the chunk cut out of it? I used the material to make a burial dress for Harry. I wanted to make an outfit with my own hands, the wedding dress was material for my little angel, it was a part of Barney and a part of me. Harry was conceived on our wedding night.' She let out a laugh, half in relief Melissa suspected. 'Sorry, is that too much information?'

'It's fine, I don't mind.'

'Barney and I didn't have much money back then. Joan and Roger, my aunt and uncle, they were my guardians after my parents died and they were always there trying to contribute but Barney was adamant they kept their distance from us, particularly after Harry died. He was so proud, he never liked them much and the feeling was mutual, they thought I could do better – it wasn't about who I loved, it was about my future and stability. All three of them clashed in a way I'd not seen coming. I'd thought it would be better once we were married, that Joan and Roger would accept Barney, but they didn't. Things were bad before I had Harry, and afterwards they just got worse. They argued all the time, I was stuck in the middle. My aunt and uncle didn't see the hard-working man who adored me, they saw a lad who was too young to marry and have a child, they saw a boy who had more of an interest in messing around with boats than anything else. He took a boat without permission one day, which I think was the last straw.

'I'm ashamed to say I distanced myself from Barney when we lost Harry. I loved him, but loving him was a reminder of what we'd lost. My aunt and uncle made the decision to sell the business, they said it would be good for all of us to leave Leafbourne, and I saw the light at the end of a very dark tunnel, because it was my escape, a way to run from the pain. Barney and I divorced without ever seeing one another again and I moved on. It was the only way I could function without falling apart. And if ever I thought about Barney I tried to tell myself we were better off apart, that we would be bad for each other, that being together would stop either of us getting past our pain.'

'I understand that more than you know, Lois,' said Melissa. 'Thank you for telling me, I know it can't be easy.' She watched Lois, hurting all over again, her hand shaking as this time she drank some of her tea when she lifted the cup. 'I must admit we were wondering about the dress. Harvey was speculating that Barney had done away with his bride and kept the dress as a souvenir.'

Lois laughed as though talking about all this had been a form of catharsis as well as being intolerably painful. 'Barney must've had his hands full with you two in his life.'

'We kept him on his toes,' Melissa admitted.

'There's something else too.'

'You can tell me anything,' Melissa encouraged, 'honestly, I won't judge.'

'The final thing that convinced me that leaving Barney and Leafbourne was the right thing was when Roger came home from the marina and told me Barney had been hanging around there again – it wasn't unusual, a whole group of them were regular customers, who mostly paid good money apart from the time Barney had indulged in the joyriding. But Roger told me he'd seen Barney with another woman, he made out that Barney was having an affair.'

'And was he?'

'I'm ashamed to say I didn't even bother asking Barney about it. I doubt it was true, but it was the final excuse I needed to walk away. Every time I looked into Barney's eyes I saw Harry. I saw our beautiful baby, and I couldn't stand it. I couldn't escape the pain and I couldn't face up to it either. I felt trapped. I had to run. And so I left Barney the letter, with my wedding dress. Up until then I hadn't thrown out the gown even though it was effectively ruined because it hadn't felt like the right thing to do after using the material in such a significant way. And so I left it for him to deal with.'

'I don't think he ever did,' said Melissa. And now she knew that the dress had been the least of the worries he'd had to deal with on his own. 'I think his way of coping was to eventually leave Leafbourne and come down here, settle somewhere nobody knew him. Not long after, he must have thrown himself into the organising of the Wedding Dress Ball and raising money for White Clover.' She smiled across at Lois. 'I understand why now, and maybe without anyone knowing what had happened, that was what saved him.'

'Barney had always wanted a family,' said Lois. 'Perhaps it was you and your friend Harvey who saved him.'

'I really hope so. And until this fall of his I'd say he's been happy. He's a well-loved, respected pillar of the community. Oh dear, I sound like I'm trying to sell him to you.'

'Oh no, please…' Lois reached out and squeezed Melissa's hand to urge her to continue. 'I want to hear all about him, please tell me. I want to know so much more.'

Now this, Melissa could do. She talked all about her days as a kid from the moment she befriended the man in the house with the big barn by taking over a basket of eggs. She told Lois all about the apple trees she and Harvey had climbed, how they'd played in the barn after school, and about the times they'd watched the Wedding Dress Ball from the high-up beams until they were told to get down. She rambled on about Barney's need to get everyone who lived in the Cove involved, how he spent most of his days cruising The Street and talking to people, how he'd supported her decision to leave the village when she so desperately needed to. And she told Lois more about the fall, how Barney wasn't himself, his talk of a retirement home and giving up running the event he loved every year.

'Thank you, Melissa, thank you for telling me Barney has had a good life. I always feared he'd never find himself after what happened.'

'Did you find yourself when you left Leafbourne and Barney behind?' She knew deep down that the question was partly about Lois and Barney, but also about herself.

267

'You don't get over the loss of a child but you learn a way of coping and moving forwards. I remarried, had two more children, I've been happy, I found a kind of peace. Sadly my husband passed away a while ago but my kids and grandkids are my joy.'

'Wow, grandkids.'

'They're hard work but a lot of fun when I have the energy.'

When Melissa's phone pinged with a message from Barney reminding her of the time for lunch, she quickly messaged him back to ensure him she'd be there. Some days she wondered if he panicked that she'd run again without telling him. She wouldn't, and she hated the thought that he might be worried she would.

With her phone still in her hand she asked, 'Would you like to see a picture of Barney?'

Smiling, Lois replied that she would, and she tentatively took the phone once Melissa had settled on one of the photographs she had on there. A couple of days ago, when Melissa was at Barney's, they'd been mid card game and he was in the kitchen cutting slices of the chocolate and orange upside-down cake Celeste had delivered from the bakery. Melissa had managed to capture the Barney of old with a huge smile and laughter in his eyes as he teased her about the next game he was going to beat her at.

Eyes misted, unable to fully suppress the surge of emotions, Lois said, 'I'd really like to go and see him in person.'

Melissa's heart soared. 'I was hoping you'd say that. Would you like me to talk to him first?'

'I think I've stayed away long enough, it's time. Although I do realise he may well tell me to bugger off.'

Melissa laughed. 'I guess we won't know until we try. Come on.'

And with a nervous Lois, it was time to find out whether her appearance could be the missing ingredient to bring back the man Barney had been before the fall, to make him see he wasn't all that different, to get him to face his own pain so he too could move forwards.

Chapter Fourteen

Harvey parked his pickup in the courtyard at Barney's. He was early for lunch but when he wandered inside and found no sign of Barney he went back through the gap in the trees and over to the barn. The door was ajar, he hadn't noticed before, but he pulled the wooden panel open to find Barney inside, sitting on a hay bale, head leaning back against the wall behind.

'What are you up to?' Harvey asked.

'I wanted to see the place, that's all.' He got up and shuffled slowly over to the walking frame and without another word made his way out of the barn. Harvey followed on after but it was a slow journey across to the house.

'You sit in the chair, let me get you some water,' said Harvey once they were inside. Barney didn't argue. At least going outside and over to the barn that was still done up ready for the ball suggested a vague interest in the upcoming event. 'Are you still happy with the way we've done the inside?' Harvey asked him.

'You've done a wonderful job, the both of you.'

'Melissa has been bossing everyone around, we're almost ready.' Although she'd been keeping a low profile the last few days, avoiding him since they'd begun to get closer again. She'd called earlier but he'd hesitated to answer, he wasn't sure whether he wouldn't end up telling her exactly how he felt.

'Glad to hear it, she won't let anyone make a mess of it.'

'Neither would I, Barney, neither would I.'

'Talking of Melissa…' Barney glanced at the clock. Sitting back in the chair, at least he had a bit more colour to his cheeks. 'Where is she? Not like her to be late.'

Harvey wondered whether that was why she'd called him, was she making her excuses not to come? He looked around. 'I thought we were having lunch.'

'We are,' Barney grinned. 'Benjamin is bringing it over. I thought as it might be my last summer here in the house, I'd entertain properly, look after my two favourite people.'

'Stop talking about it being your last summer, honestly, I've never heard anything so ridiculous.'

'I'm getting old, no denying it.'

'What's Benjamin bringing?' Best to change the subject, but he didn't get far in his line of questioning because Melissa's voice carried through from the back of the house.

'Barney, it's me,' she trilled, coming into the lounge, her beaming smile raising Barney's suspicions immediately.

'What are you up to?' was Barney's first question.

'I'm glad you're sitting down.' Melissa's smile had faded a little as she went over to him and crouched down, putting her hand over his as he sat in his favourite chair. 'I have someone here to see you.'

'It's not that blessed reporter from the gazette is it, fussing about photo shots on the night of the ball? I told him he could take as many as he wanted.'

'It's not the photographer, no.' Melissa looked to Harvey and then back at Barney, and they all turned

271

when another voice floated through the back door, calling out a hello.

Harvey looked up to see a woman about Barney's age with bobbed pewter hair. She had a bag looped over her wrist, her hands clasped together in a way that suggested she was extremely nervous. And it was within seconds he realised who it was. He looked at Melissa, he looked at Barney. And he looked at Lois.

'Come in,' Melissa urged Lois, who was hovering, unsure what to do. Barney, uncharacteristically silent, didn't move a muscle.

Lois took a few steps closer to Barney. How had Melissa managed this? And was Barney going to thank them for their interference or kill them with his bare hands?

When Barney still couldn't find his voice Harvey found his own instead and introduced himself to their overwhelmed visitor. 'It's lovely to meet you, Lois.'

'Likewise.' But she was focused on Barney, nobody else, and he was still in his chair staring at her in disbelief, blinking now and again as though this apparition may vanish if he wasn't careful.

Barney looked across at Lois. 'You're here,' was all he said.

'I'm here,' she smiled, bravely sitting on the sofa opposite.

Harvey heard Melissa's sharp intake of air and he cocked his head to indicate they go outside and leave Barney and Lois to talk.

'Did you know she was coming?' he asked the second they were out in the fresh air.

Melissa briefly explained Ashley's summons to White Clover, meeting Lois for the first time, the story

Lois had shared with her. 'I tried calling you earlier, I wasn't sure how to handle it.'

He sat next to her on the big tree stump that was wide enough for two. 'Barney and Lois went through hell,' he said with a shake of his head. 'No wonder they both buckled under the strain.'

'It would've been a dreadful time.' She swished a persistent fly away from her arm. 'I still can't quite believe she's here. I wonder if Barney's found his tongue yet.'

'Never seen him so quiet,' Harvey grinned.

Barney and Lois's situation might be very different to his and Melissa's, it may have spanned decades rather than five years, but even he could see the similarities. Lois had left Barney, Melissa had left him; Lois and Barney had shared pain and dealt with it alone, he and Melissa weren't so different.

They stayed outside enjoying the sunshine as they talked more about what Lois had told Melissa. And just when they were contemplating going to the convenience store for a cold drink and some food because they could hardly wander inside, Barney and Lois appeared in the courtyard.

'The food is heating up in the oven,' Barney said as though this were a day like any other.

Harvey went straight over because Barney wasn't using his walking frame. He was linking Lois's arm but she was slight-framed, everything about her was delicate, and Harvey didn't want Barney to lean his weight on the woman and send her flying.

'You're fussing again.' But at least Barney was smiling when he delivered the remark. 'I can move just fine.'

'But you've needed your frame up until now,' Melissa pointed out, 'and you've barely moved since you got out of hospital. You'll put yourself right back there if you're not careful.'

Barney and Lois looked at one another, the decades seemingly falling away. Barney kept his eyes on Lois when he said, 'I'm fine, it'll take a lot to break me. I wanted to show Lois the barn and then we'll eat the pasta bake Benjamin made. He even delivered a container of fresh salad when he came by a moment ago.'

Harvey realised he and Melissa must've been so heavily engrossed in one another that they hadn't heard anyone else arrive at the house.

'I'm surprised he's managing so well,' Harvey whispered to Melissa as they followed Barney and Lois towards the barn. Harvey pulled both doors fully open, fixing them back with the hooks, and sunlight flooded into the interior, casting a glow on the stage, the golden hay bales, the barrels they'd brought in, the photograph display wall.

'Nothing like love in the air to make you stronger,' Melissa whispered to him when Barney and Lois went inside, their bodies close, hands joined.

It almost felt as though they were intruding. 'At least now we don't have to venture out for a drink. I'll go and grab us something.' While Melissa waited outside in the courtyard he fetched two glasses of apple juice. His didn't last the journey outside, he was so thirsty.

Melissa followed suit by drinking hers in long gulps. 'That's good.'

'It's really sad they went so long without being in touch,' he said, nodding towards the open doors of the barn.

'Harvey…'

'I'm not having a dig, honest.'

'I'm glad I'm here,' she admitted and when their eyes met he was desperate to know whether she meant glad to be in the Cove for Barney or happy to be opposite him right now.

But he didn't get a chance to ask before music drifted to them. It was coming from the barn and with grins on their faces he and Melissa tiptoed over to the open doors. Peeking in, they saw that Barney had put the iPad out and the classic 'At Last' by Etta James echoed around the barn. And even if he and Melissa weren't hiding, Harvey suspected neither Barney nor Lois would even notice them watching. They both had their eyes closed, they moved slowly to the music. Barney was managing to be not only upright but to move as well as Lois.

'Would you look at that,' Harvey whispered to Melissa.

'I don't think he ever stopped loving her.'

'No, I don't suppose he ever did.'

They stayed there, watching, Harvey doing his best to ignore the fresh scent from Melissa's hair assaulting his senses, making him want to take her into the barn and dance with her, never let her go again. Was he going to be like Barney in years to come? Would Melissa go off and start over, have a family with Mr Pilot, and he'd be the one left in the village, his life stagnating in the same place?

The delicate tune washed over them as Melissa leaned closer. 'We should get the lunch ready.'

He shuddered at the feel of her breath against his ear before leading the way inside and pulling himself together at the same time.

Melissa fussed with finding the plates, taking out only those that had no chips on them, the surfaces undamaged. She pulled out cutlery and gave it a polish, even found some napkins from the Welsh dresser and laid them out.

'Bit fancy,' said Harvey. 'I don't think he'll notice now Lois is in his sights.'

'It's so romantic,' she beamed at him as she pulled the dish from the oven and set it onto a mat in the centre of the table. She added a serving spoon beside it. 'He seems a lot happier already.'

'About that…'

'Do I smell lunch?' came Barney's voice.

'You certainly do,' Melissa called back. 'The pasta bake is ready, the salad is dressed. Lois, can I get you something to drink?'

Melissa continued playing the hostess, she fussed over Lois and Barney and for once Barney didn't protest, in fact he seemed to enjoy it.

Lois was excellent company. She was shy at first when all four of them sat down but it didn't take her long to come out of her shell and she was soon producing anecdotes about Barney's younger years, his mischief at the marina, the way he'd always seemed to be the troublemaker even when he wasn't, how much fun they both had over the long lazy summers they'd shared. They stopped before it got to the crux of the moments that broke them, shared a knowing glance, and moved the conversation on.

As Harvey cleared the plates, talk turned to the Wedding Dress Ball, its history, how Lois wanted to organise one where she lived. Barney was full of advice, Harvey hadn't seen him this animated in a long while.

'The barn does look wonderful,' Lois complimented. 'And you have music all sorted?'

'We certainly do,' Barney chimed. 'I have the same band every year, they work the crowd, they do a mixture of songs from different eras, some to get you moving, others more sedate and romantic.'

'And the food?' she asked.

Barney took the lead again as though he couldn't stop talking now he'd started and explained their choices, how the catering would be served. Harvey and Melissa shared a look of amusement. Barney was well into his stride.

'And do you have your outfit?' Lois asked Barney.

'If there's one good thing about hospital it's the revolting food.' He patted his stomach. 'I'll definitely fit into my suit.'

'And what about you, Lois?' Melissa asked. 'Will you come?'

Lois didn't reply until she'd looked at Barney. 'I think I'd like to, very much. I could extend my stay.'

'Well that's settled.' Neither Harvey nor Melissa missed the wobble in Barney's voice. 'You'll need a dress.'

'Don't get any ideas, I won't fit into the one I know is still in your wardrobe. A little birdie told me,' she said, both of them looking Melissa's way. 'I was a slip of a thing back then and although I'm not much bigger now, I wouldn't fancy my chances.'

'You know,' Melissa began, 'a lot of people have their dresses altered to fit. I'm sure there's something we could do.'

'I'd rather not,' Lois admitted. 'The dress holds a lot of memories as it is. But it seems a shame for it to go to

277

waste.' Barney seemed to intuit her meaning straight away as they both looked at Melissa.

'Me?' Melissa asked. 'You want me to wear it?'

'Do you have a dress?' Barney asked.

'Well…no –'

'Then that's another thing settled. Let me get it.' He went off to his bedroom.

Melissa moved across to his vacated place, next to Lois. 'I know what the dress means to you, I don't want to ruin it or bring either of you any pain by wearing it.'

'It won't – in fact, it may well help. It's about time it did something other than hang in a wardrobe.'

When Lois received the dress from Barney, each of them touching the material at the same time, it was a moment of peace, an acceptance of the pain they would share forever.

Lois sniffed gently. 'Barney, do you have any pins?'

He bellowed a laugh that was just like their Barney of old. 'Of course I don't.'

'Don't look at me,' Harvey chuckled. 'I'll give Mum a call, she'll have some.'

As he did the honours he pretended to only be taking notice of his conversation on the phone when really his attention was fixed on Melissa. Lois was holding the dress up against her, talking about her measurements, how much they'd cut off the length to avoid the material with the chunk already cut out, discussing taking it up to above the knee, how they'd pull it in at the waist, the way it would flatter her figure.

When his mum began to talk about his brother having sent another letter, passing on his regards, Harvey bristled and finished the call he was only half focused on anyway. 'I'm going to head to Mum's, pick up pins and her sewing machine. She said she'd be happy to come over and help with adjustments if you need it.'

'The more the merrier,' Lois declared as though she was a part of the household already. And Barney didn't seem to mind at all. 'I may take her up on that over the next day or so.'

'I'll pass the message on,' said Harvey.

Harvey was glad to get out of there even for only half an hour, and he returned a lot calmer – at least until he walked into the lounge and found Melissa standing in the dress. Despite the section cut out at the bottom, the waist that needed pulling in a little, she looked drop-dead gorgeous and he had to pick his jaw up from the ground before she caught him staring.

Lois soon got busy with pins and a tape measure and Melissa was chatting away, being herself. Barney had taken a seat and was taking all of this in, his eyes brighter than they'd been since before his fall that day in the barn.

When the women began talking hemlines and beading patterns Harvey checked on how Barney was really feeling.

'It's been one hell of a day,' said Barney.

'You've got that right.'

'I never thought I'd see her again.' He reached out and patted Harvey's arm. 'Thank you, both of you, for meddling.'

'You sure about that?'

'I'm more than sure. Take it from me, life's too short to let your past take over the rest of your life.'

Harvey didn't let the words sink in for long. 'Talking of life being too short, I meant to ask, since when have you been able to dance?' His question piqued Melissa and Lois's attention too. 'Last I knew, you were barely out of that chair, certainly not without the aid of the walking frame to go any distance, and then I find you in the barn dancing with Lois.'

Barney shrugged. 'What can I say?' But Melissa didn't miss the look of mischief – or was it guilt? – either.

'Wait a minute…' Melissa came over, holding the dress against her chest so it didn't fall down. It was all Harvey could do not to reach out and touch her delicate skin, hook his hand around the back of her neck and pull her close. 'Barney, truth time,' she said. 'Have you been faking it all this time?'

'Faking it?' Harvey asked and looked Barney's way too.

'I really fell, I was in hospital,' he said, eyes innocently wide.

Melissa readjusted the dress but not before Harvey got another glimpse of cleavage. He was standing in just the right spot. 'I don't mean that part, I mean the part about this being the beginning of the end, you not being interested in anything other than sitting in that chair you're in now, not wanting to put on the ball. Was it all make-believe?'

One look at Lois's stern expression and Barney confessed. 'You got me.' He held up a hand before anyone could say anything else. 'When I first came out of hospital I wasn't myself. That fall scared me witless. I thought, what am I doing trying to live on my own as though I'm in my forties and not my seventies? I thought, this is it, a reminder I'm getting old, I'm past it. When you first came back to Heritage Cove, Melissa, I promise you I was not pretending.'

'When did your little performance start?' Harvey stood at Melissa's side, arms folded across his chest.

Barney had the grace to look sheepish. 'I heard a nurse talking to Harvey at the hospital and didn't think much of it at the time, but then once I was home I began to really consider what she'd said. She told him how some elderly patients – I had to bite my tongue when I heard that – withdrew from usual activities after a fall like mine. As soon as Melissa turned up and I saw the way you two acted around each other, I decided to use that to my advantage. I could tell there was a lot of history to be dealt with and I didn't want you to end up doing what I'd done, Harvey, letting her go without putting up a fight.' He looked over at Lois, whose stern look gave way to understanding. 'Five years is a long time, I didn't want that to turn into decades like it was for me. And I didn't think either of you would either.'

'But surely that was for us to decide, Barney,' Melissa protested, the dress fitting temporarily forgotten, shoulders bare as she waited for answers.

'I thought, if you were to join forces and put on the Wedding Dress Ball, knowing what it meant to me and this village, then you'd be forced to spend time together.'

'You thought you'd get us back together?' Harvey wondered.

'I had no idea whether it would come to that. I thought at the very least you'd see one another, you'd end up talking, and then if you still went your separate ways, so be it.'

There was an uncomfortable silence until Melissa snatched up the brochure for Aubrey House. 'And what about this? Was this part of the act?'

He nodded. 'It was. No way was I ever going to that place. My home is here, I'm not leaving until I'm dead.'

Harvey shook his head. 'Do you have any idea how worried we've both been?'

'He's right,' Lois admonished, albeit with a small smile, 'it was a cruel trick.'

'I was desperate. Please, it was with the best intentions.'

'So you haven't been slumped in that chair in front of the TV the whole time?' Melissa demanded.

Barney shook his head. 'Whenever you two left me alone I used every opportunity I could to move with the aid of the walking frame until I was able to get about without it. There was no way I wasn't going to dance with Melissa at the ball, it's what I did every year until she left.'

He knew how to placate her. She shook her head. 'Barney…'

'I was exhausted with all the physical effort but happy too. I tackled the balance exercises, carefully.' He hesitated before telling them, 'The health visitor was in on it too, she knew I'd been doing exercises, I told her everything. She loved the conspiracy said it was one of her most fun visits in a long time.'

'Who else was in on it?' Harvey asked.

'Lottie from the little shop on The Street. She brought round a basket of mini muffins as a get-well-soon gift, she told me she'd been taking dance lessons ready for the ball, and I asked her to help me practise. We moved very slowly at first, but I didn't want to be sitting in the corner at the ball like some invalid, not when you were back in the Cove, Melissa.'

'You had us fooled good and proper,' said Harvey.

'My intentions were all good, I swear. With Melissa back in Heritage Cove the thought of not having the ball and not dancing with her became unbearable.' Eyes glistening, he looked her way. 'After we lost Harry I wasn't lucky enough to become a father again, but having the both of you in my life stopped me getting washed away with my grief in the moments when I could've easily let it happen. You two gave me a reason to carry on.' He looked at each of them.

Now he focused on Melissa. 'I hadn't told a soul about Lois and me, or about Harry, but one day I told your mum.'

'Mum knew?' Melissa gasped.

'I think it's why she sent you round here so often, she knew the pain I was in. She never breathed a word and for that I was grateful. I never talked about it with her again, I didn't want to, you were the therapy I needed. The both of you.'

'Even when you were angry at us?' Harvey asked.

'I was never angry.'

'I beg to differ. Remember that stinking-hot summer when Melissa and I had a water fight using your garden hose?'

Barney's laughter had him clutching his side. 'They were so naughty,' he told Lois. 'There was a hosepipe ban that year and I came back to find them soaking one another and the entire courtyard. Lord knows how many litres of water they wasted.'

'You know what,' said Harvey, 'you saved me too. You were a father figure in my life when I needed it the most, so I guess I can forgive you for your little games now.'

Barney looked too emotional to talk, he just nodded. Lois dabbed her eyes discreetly with a tissue. Nobody said anything for a moment, Barney looked scared they'd throttle him, and it was Melissa who finally broke the silence.

'You're a kind man, Barney. Thank you for being you, even though you played us good and proper.'

'I'd never make you stay after all of this,' Barney told her, 'not unless you wanted to be here. I let you go once when you needed to, because I'd done the same thing.' Clasping Lois's hand, he told them, 'I moved away from Leafbourne, came to a village where nobody knew me, to lick my wounds if you like. On the anniversary of Harry's death I walked past White Clover and it was a sign. I know that kind of thing sounds ridiculous, but I stood there staring at the building, asking myself, why today? And I found myself going in. It wasn't Ashley running it all then, of course, it was another woman, Lesley I think her name was. But we talked for hours, it was almost a kind of counselling. I ended up helping out with odd jobs around the premises and while I was there I soon got to realise that Lois and I weren't the only ones to go through the horrific pain of losing a child.' His voice caught for a moment. 'It was then that something clicked. I wanted to do something, I wanted to move forwards in whatever way I could. I'd done a terrible job of doing so up until then. A couple of weeks later I saw a feature on the evening news about a family who ran a wedding dress ball every year to raise money for some charity or other. I took one look over at my barn and thought, I can do that. I imagined a band, people dancing, guests chatting away, the company, the social life I'd shied away from. It was all there for the taking.'

'And you made it happen,' said Harvey. 'Without anybody ever knowing why.'

'They didn't need to know,' said Barney. Throughout his recount he and Lois had never let go of each other's hand.

284

Melissa shuffled the dress a little as the weighty material became harder to hold on to. 'I'm glad you confessed, Barney, but right now, can we put any more tales of your antics on hold and get on with pinning this dress? I'm well aware that I'm standing here half naked.'

Harvey was well aware too.

Lois did the honours and finished pinning the section she needed to. 'There, I think we're done. Let's get the dress off and I'll set to work.'

'Are you sure you don't mind?' Melissa asked.

'It won't take me long. I'm a whizz with a sewing machine, and Harvey, if your mum wouldn't mind helping me out I'd really appreciate it.'

'Of course, how does tomorrow sound?'

'Tomorrow sounds perfect.'

Lois seemed on the surface to have slotted in with the man she hadn't seen for such a long time. They referred to the years they'd been together, not dwelling on the painful times. But when he'd glanced at her on occasion he'd detected a vulnerability, most likely the same feeling that had made her run in the first place.

Now, with Melissa in the bedroom and Lois helping her, Harvey told Barney, 'I could get very angry, you know.'

'I know, son.'

Barney knew how to get him in his weak spot, addressing him that way. 'But I won't.' He sat down, arms outstretched along his thighs. 'Melissa is at least here and we're talking.'

They shared a brief look before Melissa rejoined them. 'You're both so kind to let me wear the dress,' she told Barney and Lois, who followed behind her with the garment and laid it on the table next to the sewing machine. Barney had already fussed over the table and made sure there wasn't a single crumb from lunch, or drop from a drink.

'I'm looking forward to seeing you in it for the ball,' said Barney. 'Now, would you two mind if Lois and I had some alone time? You don't need to worry about me now you know I'm doing just fine and I have company.'

'Right.' Harvey picked up his keys and, in his other hand, the brochure for Aubrey House. 'I'll throw this away, shall I?'

Lois covered her mouth to stifle a giggle.

Harvey didn't wait for an answer, he slung the brochure in the recycling on his way out the door with Melissa, rolling his eyes in the process.

Outside beneath the sunshine Melissa smiled. 'Ten days to go until the ball. Do you still have your tux?'

'I've upgraded, I have another I bought for a workmate's wedding a couple of years ago.'

'What happened to the old one?'

'Time for a change – that one was second-hand and never fitted as well as it could. I got this one tailored, I figured I'd be wearing it for plenty of years to come.'

They were loitering by the trees that led through to the courtyard. 'I'm going this way.' Melissa indicated the little gate at the front of the path that led out to the pavement and the bend that wound around to The Street.

'I can give you a lift.'

'I think I'll walk, clear my head a bit – it's been a crazy few hours.'

'You're not wrong there.'

'I'm just pleased they're talking, even more pleased we didn't give Barney the shock of his life.'

'I've a good mind to after what he's been up to.'

'He had the best intentions.'

'Yes, I suppose he did.' He pushed his hands into his jeans pockets. It was probably too warm to be wearing them but he'd needed them this morning when he walked Winnie along the beach down at the cove with the wind whipping unforgivingly. It had died down now to a gentle breeze. 'Even Barney has a date for the ball this year,' he grinned.

'Lucky Barney.'

'You could be my date, like old times.'

'Harvey…'

'I'm kidding.' He wasn't.

And with a smile she went out of the gate and on her way.

Harvey had a quick peek in the window of the house before he left and saw Barney and Lois smiling, laughing about something. The way that pair had danced in the barn must have pulled back the years for them, it was probably as though time had stood still in some ways.

He only wished he and Melissa had the same chance to make things right. Barney was happy enough, he was on the mend well and truly, but that meant Melissa would soon be leaving the Cove.

And there wouldn't be anything he could do or say to stop her.

Chapter Fifteen

Melissa answered the door to her room at the inn and was surprised to see Lois on the other side. 'I didn't expect door-to-door service,' she smiled, standing back for Lois to come in. The ball was tonight and she was already nervous, not about the event itself but about spending more time with Harvey. Because now she knew it was time to be honest with both of the men in her life.

Melissa had spent the last ten days keeping busy. She'd taken the final deliveries at the barn so the venue was totally ready for the ball, she'd confirmed bookings in her paranoia that something would go wrong, she'd helped Lucy choose an outfit for the event, and she'd spent days in the cove amongst friends. Jay had been busy with work and their contact had been emails and messages with time zone clashes, but rather than find it difficult she'd found that the space it afforded her helped to clarify things in her mind.

'It's no bother,' Lois smiled. 'I thought I'd leave Barney to it for a bit, he can introduce me to more people later.'

'That sounds about right. I take it he's getting back into his stride?' She hung the dress over the open-doored wardrobe.

'I'll say.'

'It must be overwhelming for you, I do sympathise, because now he isn't pulling the wool over our eyes and pretending to be on his last legs, he'll be making up for lost time.'

'He told me it's been hard for him to stay home so much.'

'Hmm…I'm sure it's been a nightmare for him.'

'He always had the best intentions.'

'I know,' Melissa sighed. 'I'm not angry, I don't think I ever could be with Barney.'

Lois gestured for Melissa to open up the zipped plastic cover and when she did, the excitement built.

'What do you think?' Lois asked, fingers steepled together against her chin.

'It's stunning, the beading is beautiful.' She lightly ran her fingers across the intricate detail. 'Did you add more?'

'Harvey's mum brought around some extra beads and sequins and I've added those on. Now don't make me wait any longer.'

'You want me to try it on now?'

'I need to check the alterations are good.'

'Are you sure you have the time?'

'Honestly, I left Barney at the bakery and they'd brought him out a chair to sit on. I think he's in for a long visit so I said I'd meet him back there in half an hour.'

With butterflies zipping around in her stomach Melissa took the dress and behind the open wardrobe door, which acted as a mini separation and therefore changing room, she pulled it on. 'It feels snug.'

'Not too snug?'

'I hope not.' When she stepped out she wasn't so sure.

'Melissa, it's perfect. Wedding dresses should fit the body like a glove, and this one does. Turn around, let me do the buttons.'

With a bit of wiggling and breathing in, she was in the dress for real. Her eyes misted up when she saw her reflection. The bodice shone beneath the light Lois had switched on to get a better look and Melissa could almost imagine a veil drifting down towards the ground, a bouquet clutched in front of her.

'Oh dear, why the tears?' Lois was quick to grab a tissue from the table beside the bed and hand it to her.

'I'm a bit emotional.'

'You're thinking of your boyfriend.'

'Am I that obvious?'

'He's a fine man, and what is it you all say these days? Hot.'

Melissa burst out laughing, Lois must've got her wires crossed, because she was surely referring to Harvey, the guy Lois had met, but Melissa wasn't. She was crying because after all this time, all these years, her path had suddenly become clear. And the first person she needed to tell was the man she was supposed to be engaged to.

Lois pushed another tissue at her. 'You'll be seeing him in a couple of hours, stop crying or your eyes will be all puffy. He won't like that.'

'No, I don't suppose he would.'

When they'd admired the dress some more Lois undid the buttons and they talked hair and make-up as Melissa put on the fawn shift dress she'd had on before. 'And what about your outfit?' she asked Lois. 'Did you find anything?'

'Barney and I went shopping yesterday and I found something suitable. It was quite the day out for us, we taxied both ways, we had lunch at a glorious country pub. It felt like a date,' she confided.

'You both deserve it.'

'I want to thank you, Melissa.'

'The dress is a big thank you, you don't need to say any more.'

'I do, and I will. Thank you, from the bottom of my heart. When you get to our age, you know that most of your years are behind you and second chances don't come along for many. You getting in touch was a gift, I'll be forever grateful.'

'You'll have me blubbering again in a minute, and those puffy eyes will need a lot of make-up to disguise them.'

Lois dabbed at her own eyes with a tissue. 'I don't want them either so I'll stop rabbiting on and go and rescue the staff at the bakery.'

'Good idea,' Melissa laughed. 'I'll see you tonight.'

After Lois left Melissa went out onto the tiny balcony. On some evenings during her stay she'd come out here with a glass of wine and watch Heritage Cove drift from its sun-filled day to dusk, and finally to night, when a star-studded sky blanketed the homes and the village she knew so well. Now, she watched the odd car pass below, noticed cows on a field in the distance, sheep on another, rolled golden hay bales on the farthest field her eye could see. A tractor trundled its way down the road before disappearing behind the trees, its rumble fading away gradually.

When a cloud passed across the sun she shivered and went inside. It was only a matter of hours before her first Wedding Dress Ball in five years, and she was so excited she felt just like the same girl who'd watched the event from high up on the beams and longed to be one of the party down below.

*

'Mum, I'm not fifteen anymore.' Harvey undid his bow-tie for the fourth time and pushed away any attempts from his mum to fix it. They were in the courtyard at Barney's place and people were starting to arrive for the ball. Harvey had only come out here because he'd given up trying to perfect the bow-tie inside and he didn't want to miss Melissa's arrival.

'You're all fingers and thumbs. Why so nervous?' Carol's grey hair curled in large waves, skimming the back of her neck. She had a small white gardenia in her hair, a floaty white dress to show her slight figure. Given what Harvey's dad had been like, wearing a wedding dress to this ball had never been an option for Carol because of the memories it would evoke, but she'd gone out and spent over a hundred pounds on a three-quarter-sleeved dress with delicate beading that made her feel like a new woman – her exact words when she'd returned from the shops with it one day. Harvey had known from that moment that his mum had her life back.

'I'm not nervous,' he lied unconvincingly, and with a bit more fiddling he was done. 'There, sorted. Just a bit out of practice at tying them, that's all.'

Carol smiled. 'What a beautiful evening for it, thank goodness you talked Barney out of cancelling.'

Since he'd talked more to Barney it seemed plenty of others had been in on this little game of his. The bakery knew full well they were doing the cake but had pretended to Melissa it wouldn't be easy, the band had never been cancelled but had been told to go along with the pretence, even Ashley from White Clover had known about this from the start. Harvey swung between wanting

292

to throttle Barney one minute and wanting to thank him the next, because if he hadn't lied to them then Melissa would already be back in Windsor. And he wouldn't miss seeing her tonight, here at the ball once again, for anything.

The sun held the summer warmth that bathed the barn and courtyard in a soft glow as guests continued to arrive and mingle. The wooden doors of the barn had been folded back, hay bales graced the entrance for anyone who wanted to step outside for some air when the ball began. The food tables lined one wall and caterers would bring everything in at the agreed times. Barney and Lois were standing inside the barn doors greeting guests as though they were a couple who hadn't missed out on decades together, and the band was playing a classical melody Harvey didn't recognise but one that sat perfectly as a calm, country-wedding-type tune.

Harvey fiddled with the cuffs of his shirt to straighten them beneath the sleeves of his tux and nodded a hello to Ashley, who was next to arrive. She had on an ivory dress with a bustle – he only knew what it was called because she'd pointed it out last year when someone else asked her about it – and she was soon gossiping with his mum and discussing dressmaking, a topic that was always covered given the theme of the event.

Harvey was glad people weren't wasting time in getting inside the barn, he didn't want an audience to see how he reacted when Melissa arrived.

Casey turned up and came over to give him an enormous hug. 'Your girl here yet?'

He was about to deny what she was implying, but how could he? It was all true. She knew it, he knew it, everyone else probably knew it too. 'You look beautiful tonight.' But their conversation ended swiftly when a girlfriend of hers whisked her into the barn. He'd heard her mention eligible men so he figured they'd be flirting it up a storm very soon.

Tilly was next to arrive with a couple of girlfriends he didn't recognise, all chatting at a rate of knots, then came Gracie.

She did a twirl in a dress that only revealed itself to be pink when she stood next to someone in white. Her curly chestnut hair was pinned into an up-do that made her look sophisticated and totally different from the girl who bummed around the Cove in denim cut-offs and walked his dog for him.

'How's Winnie?' she wanted to know.

'Trust you to ask…most girls here probably want to check whether their lipstick is on their teeth or if their hair is perfect.'

'You know me and dogs, Harvey.'

'I do, and Winnie's fine, made a real fuss of her before I came out.'

'Save a dance for me later?'

'Of course I will.'

And when she went inside he didn't miss the admiring looks from Declan, a local lad about her age. He probably hadn't recognised her when she first turned up but he'd certainly noticed her now.

Locals flocked, people from nearby villages and towns who'd bought a ticket returned for another year or to give it a go for the first time. And when Tracy arrived she confided in Harvey that she felt like a newlywed all over again. Her comment was bordering on too much information but he chatted with Tracy and Giles before they both went inside. He didn't have to tell either of them why he was waiting there.

Jade and Celeste looked stunning when they arrived with the cake and set it safely in place on a table well out of the way. No sign of an apron for either of them, it was perfectly applied make-up against porcelain skin, and white dresses that were totally different and beautiful on the sisters who were the close siblings Harvey had always envied. They not only worked together, they lived in the same home, they got on apart from the odd cross word at the bakery making you steer clear until the dust settled, and it made Harvey wonder whether he might have had that same bond with Daniel had their father not been so terrible.

Harvey shook away thoughts of family problems and smiled, welcoming Patricia from the tea rooms, who was excited to be here and more than proud to be in her wedding dress for another year. She was instantly chatting away to anyone who'd listen about the laced-up back of the gown that was a godsend if your weight fluctuated year on year. Her husband looked at her as though their wedding day had been last week not years ago; his hands told the same story. Lottie was next, the tan she'd built over the summer even though she worked inside the convenience store striking against a white gown. Like everyone else here, she was transformed from the usual attire of jeans and a top or shorts and T-shirt, and it was all part of the fun of this event – seeing the same people you spoke to day in day out look different, act different and feel different.

The atmosphere here in the courtyard and beyond the doors of the barn was one of togetherness, excitement, heady summer love. Some arrived hopeful with a date on their arm, others were relishing an evening as a couple after the demands of family life and jobs, an evening where they could remind themselves of how they'd fallen in love. Some came here with friends and no intention of anything romantic, some would be surprised tonight, he wouldn't mind betting – there was usually an unpredicted hook-up in the air. Last year it had been Jules, his boss's sister, who'd got together with another of Harvey's work buddies, both a little regretful the morning after apparently.

Lucy arrived next and on her arm was Fred Gilbertson, back in town for the event. 'Fred, great to see you.' Harvey shook his hand. 'And Lucy, you're looking beautiful.'

She did a quick twirl in an off-the-shoulder ivory dress that finished almost at the ground. 'Why thank you. I found this beauty in a charity shop and it fits perfectly.'

'If only all brides were this easy,' Fred joked before winking at Lucy. 'You never know, your future Mr Right could be in this very barn right now.'

'I doubt it,' she laughed. 'And I'm not even looking.'

'Come on, this place is synonymous with romance,' Fred insisted.

'Not always,' Harvey meddled. 'Remember Clara and Michael?'

Fred's brow furrowed. 'The couple who met bellringing at the chapel and had their wedding there?'

'The very same. They had a huge row right in this very barn, ended things once and for all when she admitted she was seeing someone else.'

Lucy laughed. 'Come on, Fred, you can look out for me,' she said. 'I'm not after meeting anyone just yet, friendship is all I need.'

'You're on,' he said, leading the way.

When they went inside and more people flocked the same way Harvey began to get restless. He was starting to wonder if Melissa would ever turn up when a voice behind him had him turning around. Melissa had come through the front gate when he'd been expecting her to arrive via the lane and the courtyard.

He couldn't stop a smile from forming. 'You took your time.' But you were worth the wait, he almost added out loud.

She passed between the juniper trees and came over to him. The gown looked completely different from when it was being fitted against her body in the lounge, his focus torn between her, and Barney's revelations. Now, it fit her like a glove, finishing just above the knees. A pair of white heels added more shape to her legs than he thought possible and when she turned to show him the full effect his eyes couldn't help following her silhouette up and down. Her auburn hair fanned across her shoulders, left loose, curling into big waves.

He'd need a cold shower at this rate. 'You look beautiful,' he stammered.

'You look pretty good yourself.' Hazel eyes sparkled across at him. 'Nice tux.'

'Bet you say that to all the boys.' His gaze fell to lips covered in a glossy pink he knew he could kiss away in seconds.

A couple of guys from work chose that moment to turn up. Harvey introduced each of them to Melissa and with one look he conveyed that she was out of bounds.

When the catering van pulled up Melissa's focus altered and she leapt into action. She took them inside where they could get organised and prepare to run the service from there. Harvey knew Melissa's instructions would ensure the event was seamless.

Harvey was soon swallowed up by the next crowd to arrive. They'd come by minibus from a town twenty miles away after reading about the ball in the newspaper last year, and after he'd directed a couple of them to the portaloos around the back of the barn, he got talking to a patron of a similar charity to White Clover who wanted to know the intricacies of organising a wedding dress ball. Harvey filled him in the best he could with his limited knowledge and introduced him to Barney. The band had everyone moving already. Harvey swore it was busier than any other year, a sea of white, cream, ivory and pale colours mixed with the darkness of tuxedos and suits filling the barn. Some guests danced, others sat on hay bales, a few huddled at the edges gossiping, some had already snagged places at the chairs and tables. A couple of teenagers were kissing in the corner until their parents pulled them apart and it reminded Harvey of all the times he'd wanted to kiss Melissa and couldn't.

He grabbed himself a beer and watched Barney dance with Lois. The odd word passed between them, a tender glance whenever they could, and the special night that had been on Barney's social calendar for a long time had suddenly found its way onto hers too.

Ashley came to stand with him as she fanned her face with her hand. 'It's hot in here, but what a wonderful turn-out.'

'Indeed it is. Best yet, I suspect.' He knew she'd caught him looking over at Melissa, who'd finally come inside.

'Go and ask her.'

'Ask her what?'

'To dance, of course.'

He couldn't, because if he held her he wasn't sure he'd ever want to let her go.

Lois came over next in search of a glass of water and Harvey found a jug and filled one for her, handing it

over, welcoming a distraction. And by the time he turned
back he saw that Barney hadn't sat down or come for a
refreshment like Lois, instead, he was dancing with
Melissa.

'Missed your chance,' Ashley whispered.

'Yeah, story of my life.' He hung back to let the
women talk, but was soon commandeered by Celeste to
join her on the dancefloor.

'If you're sure you can keep up with me,' he laughed.

'I'm fuelled by baked goods, course I can keep up.'
And she did, even when the band switched to a faster
number. She had hold of the bottom of her dress, she
gave it her all and beckoned the youngsters to join her,
and as she mingled with them, loving every minute of it,
he saw Melissa looking over.

Barney was back with Lois and suddenly it was as
though everyone else had fallen away, leaving just the
two of them in the room.

His mouth dry, he walked over to her. Without a word
he held out his hand and when she smiled and took it he
pulled her closer. Their bodies almost met. But someone
else cut in.

'May I have this dance?' the voice asked.

And judging by Melissa's reaction, Harvey didn't
even have to ask who the mysterious stranger was.

*

'Not interrupting, am I?' Jay, standing before her, took
her hand once Harvey took a step back. 'I've missed my
fiancée, I'm sure he won't mind letting me cut in,' Jay
told her, a brief glance over at Harvey before he turned
his attentions back to her.

Melissa watched Harvey's reaction to the instant
engagement announcement she hadn't shared with
anyone yet. He looked defeated as he turned to leave and

as Jay pulled her closer. She looked past Jay's shoulder and saw Barney try to stop Harvey walking out, but he just kept going.

'Am I pleased to see you at last,' Jay breathed into her hair as he had them moving in time with the music.

She let herself be swept up with the flow, the slow strains of an Elvis Presley tune sounding out as couples came to the dancefloor and the mood mellowed for the song. The smell of food drifted towards them as caterers lined the tables at the side and those who had already worked up an appetite finally stopped paying so much attention to her or the newcomer to the ball.

Something inside her shifted. She pulled back and took Jay's hand in hers. 'Come with me,' she urged.

She led him outside and into the courtyard, across to the other side where she knew they wouldn't be disturbed. She couldn't see Harvey anywhere.

Jay bent his head to kiss her. He thought she was bringing him out here to be alone and now she had to break his heart. She touched a hand to his chest to keep him from getting too close.

'It's all right,' he smiled, the handsome pilot she'd thought she'd fallen for when all along she'd never really stopped loving Harvey. 'Nobody will notice we've gone.' He hooked a hand beneath her hair and held the back of her neck, edging her back towards him.

She pulled back out of his reach.

'What's wrong?'

Shaking her head, tears in her eyes, she didn't want to hurt him any more than she was already going to. She hated that it had taken her until now to finally realise what she'd given up all those years ago but had never truly let go of. 'You didn't do anything, I promise.'

'It's not you, it's me?' he laughed. But the laughter faded. 'You're not messing about.'

'No, Jay. I'm really not.'

'What's going on? I thought you'd be pleased I turned up as a surprise, you've been on about this event for the last couple of weeks.'

She had, hadn't she? He'd listened to her talking about the reason she had to stay in the Cove, the event for the village that she couldn't give up on. Unwittingly, in her ramblings to make conversation and avoid talking about their engagement or anything wedding-related, she'd encouraged him to come here. She looked up at him, no longer worried that her tears might make her mascara run. Because this was over and she should've realised a long time ago. They were so busy in their day-to-day lives that she'd been swept up with the excitement of it all, going from dating to almost living together to being engaged. She'd said yes to his proposal but had never dreamed about a wedding, she had her own flat and had resisted moving in with him and now she realised why. He wasn't the man that she really loved. Over the last couple of days she'd imagined saying goodbye to Harvey, then she'd imagined saying goodbye to Jay, and each time the farewell that upset her the most had been the one to the man who'd held her heart ever since he kissed her on those beams in the barn and then properly in the loft of Tumbleweed House. She hadn't known it then, but she knew it now. She'd been living in a bubble since she left the Cove five years ago, a bubble where Harvey didn't exist, where she couldn't be hurt and think about what she'd lost. Coming home to Heritage Cove had made everything clear for the first time in years.

'Your friend Barney is going to be OK, isn't he?' Jay thought this was about Barney, not about him.

'Barney's going to be fine.'

'I'm glad.' Grinning, and before she could add anything else, he pulled out a small box from his pocket, and even in the dim light now the sun had started to set, the shine of the diamond was unmissable against black velvet. 'I want us to set a date, Melissa. The sooner the better.'

She knew that if she started at the beginning, that if she told him how she'd not only fallen back in love with Heritage Cove but also with the man she'd once promised her heart to right over there in the barn where people were mingling and dancing, then she'd hurt him even more than she had already. And he didn't deserve that. But he didn't deserve dishonesty either. She'd got together with him because it was new, it was exciting, there was no pain attached, only adventure. And she'd been swept away, all the while hiding a part of herself she couldn't face up to, the part that let in the memories and embraced all that she'd lost.

'Jay, I…'

The ring lay there in the open box, still in his hand, still waiting for her, but then the fingers of his same hand flipped the lid shut. 'Why do I get the feeling I'm not going to need this?'

'I'm really sorry.'

'What happened, Melissa? When you came here only weeks ago we were engaged, and what, now you've simply changed your mind?'

All along she'd thought she wasn't ready to tell anyone because she didn't have a ring yet. But, deep down, maybe it was because she knew it wasn't right. 'It's complicated.'

'You either love me or you don't.' He gave her a chance to speak but what could she possibly say? 'You never told me much about this village, but I always knew there was someone or something holding you back.'

'I left here and started over and if I hadn't come back this time, I never would've realised that a part of me is still here.'

They smiled at the caterers, who were coming back from the house to the barn with more containers of food. Sensing it wasn't a moment to interrupt, they didn't even acknowledge Melissa apart from with quick nods of their heads.

'You've got a whole life in Windsor, Melissa.' He leaned back against the wall, their gazes drifting over to the barn where music played out as though nobody else had a care in the world.

'I know I have. But it seems I still have one here.'

'Does this have anything to do with the guy you were dancing with when I arrived?' Before she could answer he held up a hand to stop her. 'You know what, I don't need to know. And I won't beg you to reconsider. That would be a waste of time for both of us.'

She didn't dare look at him to see whether he meant it kindly or whether he was seething more than his voice let on. 'I'm really am very sorry, Jay. I didn't mean to hurt you.'

And without another word or a backwards glance he put the ring box in his pocket and strode over to where his car was parked at the end of the lane leading into the courtyard. There wasn't anything she could say to lessen the hurt for him. And if she hadn't ended it tonight she'd have hurt him even more in the long run, he didn't deserve that.

She waited for Jay to leave. She looked over at the barn, people milling around with plates of food. Lois was laughing as she danced with Fred, Barney was having a rest at one of the tables flocked by people wanting to talk to him. But Harvey wasn't anywhere to be seen. Melissa checked around the back of the barn, she looked down the lane that led the back way to Barney's, she looked inside the house, but he was gone.

And there was only one place he could be.

She ran, from the house, out the front gate, which predictably took an effort to undo, along the pavement and around the bend onto The Street. It was a nightmare doing this in heels and it was more of a trot than a run, so she kicked off her shoes, picked them up in her fingers and instead carried on in bare feet, hoping she wouldn't stand on anything untoward.

She reached the end of the lane that would lead down to the cove. In the dark it would be terrifying if the last vestiges of sunlight weren't still visible over the water ahead and the bushes that concealed the way down. The dirt track became part sand and she kept going until eventually she was at the end. She took the steps down to the beach, her hand finding the barrier every now and then before she remembered how wobbly it was. And when she reached the bottom, her bare feet moulding around the rocky formation before the last jump onto the sands, she saw him. In the fading light she made out the lone figure, his arm hooked in the telltale way that said he was holding a collection of stones, skimming each and every one of them in an effort to get it to skip over the water's surface better than the last.

As she walked her feet sank into the damp sand that in a couple of hours' time would be completely covered by the tide. The foam had already crept up, they wouldn't have long before they'd have to get back up the steps to avoid the sea. The bodice of her dress restricted the movement of her chest that she needed to recover from the exertion of charging down here but in silence she stood beside Harvey as her breathing returned to normal and he skimmed the last few stones in his palm.

When he ran out he turned to her, eyes full of sadness. The bow-tie his mum had told Melissa he'd spent forever nervously perfecting had been yanked undone and hung loose around his neck, his dark brown hair was more dishevelled than usual and she could picture him raking a hand through it when he first came down here to think, the spray from the water leaving its salty remnants behind.

He looked away, out to sea instead. 'Tide will be in soon, you don't want to get caught down here.'

'I could say the same to you.'

'Why aren't you at the ball, dancing?'

'Because I wanted to find you.'

'Relax, I'll be back by the end of the event, you know I wouldn't let Barney down.'

'I know.'

'So what's the problem?'

'The problem is, you owe me a dance.'

He harrumphed. 'And you think your fiancé would be happy with that?'

'Of course not.'

'Then stop playing games, Melissa.'

She moved in front of him so he was forced to look at her. Her feet were submerged in the water and it was freezing, but she scared away her chattering teeth the best she could. 'I'm not playing games.' She threw her shoes back onto the sand in case she dropped them. 'Stop being so stubborn and talk to me.'

305

'Said all there is to say.'

'Well I haven't.' The noise of the crashing waves behind her made it impossible to talk quietly. 'I'm sorry for running away from you five years ago, I'm sorry I never got in touch until now. But I don't regret going. I needed to see who I was without my parents, without this village, without you.' She saw his jaw twitch in frustration.

'Good for you, glad your head's all sorted.'

'It is, at last. And it's over with Jay.'

He stared at her as the skies darkened and the only light now came from the moon casting its silvery glow across the water.

'Aren't you going to say anything?' She almost lost her footing when a gentle wave lapped behind her.

'What could I possibly have to say?'

'Well, you could say sorry too, I wasn't the only one in the wrong. You could've told me why you didn't leave with me.'

'I had my reasons.'

'And so did I.' She watched his jaw twitch again. It happened whenever he knew she had a point.

'I still love you, Harvey.' Her feet were almost ice cubes in the temperature of the water than even for the bravest of souls would be a challenge. 'You could tell me that you still love me too.' Another wave crept up from behind. It wasn't big but it unsteadied her and she was falling, about to get very wet, until suddenly she was up in the air.

He'd scooped her up in his arms, his stare fixed on her. 'Now why on earth would I do that?'

And with a smile his lips found hers, her world went dizzy, and the salty tang of his kiss told her all she needed to know. Being with Harvey was like coming

306

home as much as it had been to set foot in Heritage Cove all over again.

He pulled back, his gaze moving from her eyes to her lips and back again. 'I love you, Melissa.'

She smiled at him, in his arms, safe, exactly where she wanted to be.

He kissed her once more. 'You do know that even though I love you, I'm not carrying you all the way back to the barn.'

She gasped. 'The speech!' Barney gave one every year at the end of the Wedding Dress Ball.

He set her down and they ran across the sand, as fast as they could up the slope and the uneven steps, down the track that was now only lit by the moonlight, just enough for them to find their way.

Laughing as they reached The Street, Harvey told her to jump on his back. 'I'll piggyback you there, you're too slow,' he insisted.

She didn't hesitate and with his strength he took her all the way there. When they finally reached the courtyard at Barney's, she put on her heels, they both took a deep breath and went inside where the crowds were gathered and ready as Barney took to the stage.

Barney's speech was a mixture of funny and serious. He spoke about his fall, the way he'd thought he was going downhill fast – his precise words – but that he knew everyone here was a friend, that he had so many in Heritage Cove, that he hoped he'd be able to live out his days in this very house. He paid homage to Harvey and Melissa for looking after him despite his attitude and then the game he had played, he asked Lois up to the stage and told everyone there that they'd been man and wife once upon a time. He shared their sadness, their pain, in a way that spoke of love and hope and had more than one member of the audience dabbing away the tears. He talked about White Clover and all the good work they continued to do for people like them, families hurting in the worst way possible.

A photographer had been snapping away throughout the event and with the help of a band member steadying a ladder, he climbed up to capture a final shot of all the guests as they crowded into a big group, everyone huddled up close – the village residents, visitors, friends and couples, the young and the old – representing this year's Wedding Dress Ball, the event that brought people together and raised money for a charity that meant so much. Melissa got her dance with Barney, who muttered more than one I-told-you-so when it came to Harvey, and she left that night exhausted from the emotions of it all, hand in hand with the man she'd never really stopped loving. It had just taken her a while to realise.

*

The photograph of the crowd who went to the Wedding Dress Ball that night was developed and came through the door at Tumbleweed House courtesy of Barney a few days later. He hadn't knocked, he hadn't wanted to disturb the happy couple who hadn't left the confines of Tumbleweed House much since the ball, except to pick up food or walk Winnie down at the cove.

Harvey climbed back into bed and pulled Melissa against him. Her head on his chest, he adjusted the sheet so her naked body didn't get cold. He held the photograph he'd pulled from the envelope that had landed on the mat moments earlier.

'It needs a frame,' said Melissa.

'Everyone looks really happy in this picture.' Harvey was still admiring the shot. 'This one will definitely go up on the wall of the barn.'

'For sure.'

'Do you think Barney meant it when he said he was thinking of doing two events a year?'

'Either that or someone spiked his drink,' she grinned.

'I hope he doesn't want me and you to organise them.'

'I don't know, it wasn't so bad, was it?' She looked up at him. They both knew that if Barney hadn't kept up a pretence, if they hadn't been thrown together to do the organising, she might well have returned to Windsor without ever sorting things through with Harvey. And she didn't want to even think about what life would be like without him now.

'He's thinking of doing the second at Christmas time,' said Harvey. 'Maybe not this year but the idea is there, brewing, and the great thing is that he's passionate about it. It's good to see.'

Melissa suddenly thought of the village in the festive season, the lights along The Street, cosying up in the pub, the frosty rooftops when the temperatures dipped. 'I love Christmas in Heritage Cove. Does the tree still get lit up on the little green behind the bus stop?'

'Sure does, you can see it the moment you drive into the village.'

'I'm looking forward to it already.'

'You might be working.'

'I worked the last three Christmases and last New Year's. I'm sure I can get time off – if I ever get back to work, that is.'

He held her tighter. 'Let's not think about that.'

309

She looked at the white, sequinned dress hanging on the front of Harvey's wardrobe. Harvey had almost torn it off the night of the ball when they got back here desperate to feel each other's touch again but she'd made him take pause and undo the buttons carefully. He'd struggled because they were so tiny, his lack of patience making her giggle and the harder she laughed the more difficult it was for him to get the dress off because she couldn't suck in her breath to make it any easier. She'd torn a button from his shirt when it was his turn, but he hadn't cared, and his tux was still draped over the chair in the corner of the room waiting for its trip to the dry cleaners.

Melissa had called Jay yesterday when Harvey ducked out to pick up takeaway. He'd not answered but texted minutes later to say he was in Shanghai. He wished her well and she did the same. He told her he'd already taken all of her things she'd left at his place over to her flat and posted her spare key through her door when he was done. She'd been a little shocked but knew it was for the best. She'd arranged two more weeks' unpaid leave before she really had to head back to her job, and for that time she fully intended to lose herself in Harvey, in Tumbleweed House and Heritage Cove. Because Heritage Cove was her true home. She knew that now. She could be miles away from it yet it would always be there for her, and rather than a place to run from it was an anchor to keep her grounded if she ever felt her emotions welling up and spilling over.

'Look how happy Barney is in the picture.' Harvey had propped the photograph up on the chest of drawers next to the bed so he could hug Melissa with both arms.

'That's the best thing of all. And look at us…we look happy too.' In the shot, Harvey stood behind her, she

310

was leaning back against his chest and laughing. She couldn't remember what about now, it hardly mattered. The important thing now was that she was here in Heritage Cove. She had no idea what this meant long-term, their discussions hadn't progressed that far, but she did know that she'd be spending a lot of time here from now on.

He planted a kiss on her forehead. 'Very happy. And you've no idea how good it feels to hear you say that.' He locked his fingers through the fingers on her hand that lay on his chest. 'I don't want you to leave, I don't want you to go back to Windsor.'

'I have a job, a flat.'

'How about I take some time off and come with you?'

She pushed herself up so that her hands lay on his chest and she could look at him. 'I thought you had a big conversion going on.'

'We're almost done, I could take a couple of weeks to explore a bit of London, travel in to the city while you're away working and see what I've been missing. I'll be there keeping the bed warm when you come home.'

'I'll be away a fair bit, but the good thing is the stretch of rest days I'll have.'

'I'm afraid you won't get much rest if I'm there, not if I have my way.' He deftly flipped her body over and moved on top of her before trailing kisses down her neck and along her collar bone. 'Are you sure you're ready for me to be there with you?'

'I've never been more ready.'

His lips hovering dangerously near hers, he breathed, 'Me too.'

And if it wasn't for Winnie racing into the room and barking to demand attention, they might have enjoyed another hour or so in bed.

But they had plenty more time to do that.

Melissa and Harvey had done their time apart. Now it was time to be together all over again.

THE END

For more books by Helen J Rolfe, visit
www.helenjrolfe.com/books

If you would like all of Helen's latest book news direct
to your inbox you can also sign up for her monthly
newsletter at www.helenjrolfe.com/newsletter

Christmas at the Little Waffle Shack

It's December in Heritage Cove and along with the village Christmas tree, frosty mornings and the promise of the most wonderful time of the year, the new Waffle Shack is about to open. And its owner isn't a stranger to the Cove, because after all this time, Daniel is back to make amends with his brother Harvey. And when he meets the local blacksmith, Lucy, could there be love in the air for both of them this Christmas?

OUT DECEMBER 2020!

A Letter from Helen

Thank you so much for reading Coming Home to Heritage Cove. Part of the adventure when I set out to write a new book is creating a new world and a cast of characters. I hope you all enjoyed your first visit to the beautiful village of Heritage Cove set on the east coast of England! I had so much fun dreaming up a fictitious place, conjuring up where locals would hang out, where they would mingle and best of all, fall in love.

I love hearing from readers on social media or via my website at any time, especially if my books brought a smile to your face, you loved the characters, or you revelled in the escapism of reading. I'd love it if you could leave a short review on amazon too. It doesn't have to be more than a few words but it makes such a difference and it could persuade new readers to try my books for the very first time.

A huge thank you to readers who have messaged me or left lovely supportive comments on my social media posts. I love chatting about anything and everything and hope to hear from you all again soon. Stay tuned for more book news, there's always something else on the horizon and I'm excited about bringing you your next read!

Love Helen x

Acknowledgements

A huge thank you to Berni Stevens for her patience and dedication during the cover design phase. She has produced a beautiful cover to introduce this new series to my readers!

My thanks to Katharine Walkden for being a whizz with grammar and punctuation, as well as spotting potential plot holes. Her care and precision are second to none and she is a pleasure to work with every time.

Thank you to my husband for encouraging me when I have doubts, for cooking delicious meals during the week, for managing my website and being there as my sounding board when I need to work out plot problems or issues with my characters. I love my job as an author and I know how incredibly lucky I am to have his unwavering support.

Although I work on my own at home in the corner of the spare room, my thanks also goes to all the writers I have met over the last few years. Social media keeps us close and the constant support and encouragement is something I could never imagine being without. I can't wait to catch up with you all at the next function!

And finally, to my readers … thank you for buying this book. I hope it was a pleasure to read.

Printed in Great Britain
by Amazon